# ALSO BY KRISTEN PROBY

# FALLING
## FOR *Jillian*

## KRISTEN PROBY

POCKET BOOKS
New York   London   Toronto   Sydney   New Delhi

Pocket Books
A Division of Simon & Schuster, Inc.
1230 Avenue of the Americas
New York, NY 10020

This book is a work of fiction. Any references to historical events, real people, or real places are used fictitiously. Other names, characters, places, and events are products of the author's imagination, and any resemblance to actual events or places or persons, living or dead, is entirely coincidental.

First Pocket Books paperback edition February 2015

POCKET and colophon are registered trademarks of Simon & Schuster, Inc.

For information about special discounts for bulk purchases, please contact Simon & Schuster Special Sales at 1-866-506-1949 or business@simonandschuster.com.

The Simon & Schuster Speakers Bureau can bring authors to your live event. For more information or to book an event, contact the Simon & Schuster Speakers Bureau at 1-866-248-3049 or visit our website at www.simonspeakers.com.

Cover illustration by Alan Ayers

Manufactured in the United States of America

10   9   8   7   6   5   4   3   2   1

ISBN 978-1-4767-5938-8
ISBN 978-1-4767-5940-1 (ebook)

For April

# Acknowledgments

As always, I need to thank my team. My editor, Abby Zidle, for being patient yet persistent. My agent, Kevan Lyon, for being simply the best there is. And my amazing publicist, K. P. Simmon, for all the things. Too many things to list.

I also need to thank Officer Karen Webster of the Kalispell, Montana, police department for all of her invaluable guidance on police matters and protocols. Any mistakes in this story are my own.

# FALLING
## FOR *Jillian*

# CHAPTER

*One*

## JILLIAN

*What is it with master bathrooms that makes people hem and haw?* I glance down at my watch and offer the couple from Ontario a wide smile as they browse through the multimillion-dollar home near the Whitetail Mountain ski resort. In real estate, it's always the master bathroom that people get hung up on. You'd think it would be the kitchen, and sometimes it is, but invariably, they want to take a second or even third look at the master suite.

"This home is beautiful," Mrs. Langton says with a smile. "I love it. What do you think, sweetheart?"

Her husband smiles and nuzzles his wife's ear, making my stomach turn. "You know I'll buy you any house you want, my love."

She laughs and takes another look around the

great room as we descend the staircase, our footfalls echoing through the empty space.

"Out of all of the homes we've seen, this is my favorite. The view is fantastic. And we're just down the road from the resort."

I glance out the wide picture windows that overlook Whitetail Lake, and wince. The snow is coming down harder than it was this morning, so getting off this mountain in my little Honda sedan isn't going to be easy.

"Does that mean you've finally decided?" Mr. Langton asks his wife.

"I think so." She claps her hands and bounces on the balls of her feet. "We'd like to make an offer on this house, Jillian."

"Fantastic," I reply and shake their hands. "I'll get the paperwork ready this evening and we can meet at my office tomorrow."

"The weather sure has decided to get nasty," Mrs. Langton comments as we make our way outside and I lock the door to the mansion behind us.

"They're calling for a storm," I reply. "We had a mild fall, but it looks like winter is going to be a doozy." I glance longingly at the sturdy 4×4 the Langtons are about to climb into.

*I really need to replace my car.*

"I'll be in touch tomorrow." I wave them off as they pull out of the circular driveway and up the mountain toward the cabin they've been renting at the resort while they house-hunt.

And now I get to make my way *down* this mountain in my two-wheel-drive Honda with no studded snow tires.

Fantastic.

I wasn't exaggerating when I told the Langtons that we'd had a mild fall. Until about two weeks ago, we hadn't had any snow that stuck around for more than a day or two—unusual for early December.

*I'll bet it's seventy and sunny in LA right now.*

I sigh and resign myself to struggling down the narrow road to the bottom of the mountain.

I adore my hometown, Cunningham Falls. I grew up here, along with my parents and their parents before them. It's a town that welcomes the hordes of tourists that flock in during both the ski and summer seasons to explore the wilds of Montana. But, despite the many newcomers each season, the "locals" pretty much all know each other, whether we like it or not.

And there have been many times over the years that I'd rather they not.

I bite my lip and turn left out of the driveway, taking it slow, mindful to pump my brakes rather than ride them. The snow is coming down so hard, it's like a thick blanket draped all around my car, making it hard to see the road before me, or the steep drop-off to my right.

If not for the dark trees, I'd be screwed.

I inch my way carefully down the hill, around two switchbacks, and breathe a huge sigh of relief

when I safely come out at the bottom and see the
stoplight through the large snowflakes, marking the
main road.

As I come to a stop at the light, I hear screeching
tires and the unmistakable sound of rubber sliding
on ice just before a Mercedes SUV comes to a stop
against my rear fender.

*Perfect.*

I open my door and step out, as does the driver of
the Mercedes, and we survey the damage.

"Well, it could be a lot worse," I mutter.

"I'm sorry," the tall stranger says, kneeling by the
wreckage. "I guess I took that corner too fast."

"I guess so," I agree with a nod. "You barely
touched me, though."

"Looks like you have a bit of a dent there," he
replies and stands, then grins down at me. "Jillian
Sullivan. You haven't changed a bit in all these years."

I feel my eyes widen and I cover my mouth with
mittened hands, then laugh and throw my arms
around the tall, broad man who just slammed into
my car.

"Max Hull!"

He hugs me tight and then pulls away, offering me
a wide grin. His blond hair is short and styled con-
servatively. His green eyes are happy, if somewhat
guarded, and he seems to be distracted.

*God, the Hull brothers are hot.*

"Are you visiting Brad and Jenna?" Brad Hull is
a cop here in Cunningham Falls, and their sister,

Jenna, runs a beautiful bed-and-breakfast called the Hideaway on Whitetail Mountain. I grew up with all three of the Hull siblings.

"I am." He nods, frowns, and then adds, "Thinking about moving home."

"Really? Is this good news?" I ask and then laugh, looking up into the snow that continues to fall around us. "Now that I think about it, maybe we should catch up when we aren't standing in a blizzard."

"Good plan." He grins and kisses my cold cheek chastely, and I pray with all my heart that I feel a tingle of awareness, but there is nothing.

*Damn.*

"Let's exchange numbers so I can at least have your car fixed." Max pulls his phone out of his jeans and begins typing away on the screen. I rattle off my number, then grin when I see a text come through from him and save his number to my contacts.

"My brother can probably just knock the dent out with a hammer, Max, but thanks. I'm more worried about your expensive Mercedes."

"Doesn't look like I got a scratch. We got lucky." He winks and backs toward his car. "How is Ty?"

"Good. He's engaged to Lauren Cunningham, you know."

"I had no idea. Speaking of brothers and dating, I heard you and Brad went out a couple months ago."

"Yeah, once. We decided we're better at being

friends." *Because I'm a dating failure and I have too much damn baggage.*

"Sounds like there's lots of news to catch up on."

"Be careful, they haven't sanded that road yet. I'll see you later!" We wave and I climb back into my car, soaked through from the quarter-size snowflakes. I shake my head and send snow spraying through my car, put it in drive, and make my way home.

I slide several times while turning corners, and curse myself for not replacing my tires before the snowy season.

Truth be told, I should just get a new car. A bigger one, with all-wheel drive. Especially since I show homes all over this valley, which means I drive through snow, mud, and the elements every day. It hasn't been a matter of not being able to afford a new vehicle, it's been a lack of time. Between the move home, starting the new job, and my soon-to-be sister-in-law's horrible attack at the hands of her ex-husband, there just hasn't been time to car-shop.

As I approach the little house that I rent from my best friend, Cara, I see that the snowplow, thankfully, has been down my street already, but then I see that they blocked in my driveway.

I hit my fist on the steering wheel and curse a blue streak as I pull my car to a stop at the side of the road, jerk my ballet flats off my feet and toss them in the passenger seat, then reach into the backseat for my boots.

I have to shovel the goddamn driveway.

I trudge through the knee-high snowbank that is currently blocking my driveway and grab my snow shovel, gazing over at Ty's old house, which now sits empty with a For Sale sign perched near the curb. I miss having my brother close by.

I dig in, tossing clumps of snow into my front yard, and when I've finished, I climb back into my still-running car.

It takes me three tries to get it into the driveway.

*I definitely need a new car.*

Finally, I stomp up to my front door, wet, sweaty from shoveling, and bone-tired. Pushing inside, I frown at the cold air that greets me. Did I turn the thermostat down that far?

I immediately cross to the thermostat and crank the heat, then rush into the bedroom and quickly replace my wet clothes with warm sweatpants, a T-shirt, and a heavy gray sweatshirt over that.

I wrap my favorite quilt around my shoulders and grab my laptop and settle on the couch, ready to type up the paperwork for the Langtons.

The Langtons, who can't keep their hands off each other.

I smirk and rub my cold nose on my sleeve, then sniffle. Damn, it's really cold in here.

Maybe I need something to help keep me warm, like a dog. Or a cat. Or a man.

*Not a man!*

"Why am I in Montana in the middle of winter in a cold-as-hell house?" I ask the room at large and stomp across the room to check the thermostat again.

Fifty-eight degrees.

No wonder I'm freezing my nipples off.

Maybe the pilot light thingy on the furnace blew out? I have no idea what to do. I dial Ty's number with numb fingers and curse when I get his voice mail. He's probably keeping warm with Lo.

Well, that leaves Cara.

"Hello?" she answers on the second ring.

"Hey, I think there's something wrong with the furnace. It's fifty-eight degrees in here, and I've cranked the heat and nothing is happening."

"It's way too cold outside for you to be sitting in a house with a broken furnace."

"You think?" I roll my eyes and burrow under my blanket again. "I can't reach Ty. I know the roads are horrible right now, but I'm just not sure who to call after five p.m. around here. Everyone has gone home for the day."

"I'm sure Josh can fix it," she replies, and I hear Josh laugh in the background.

"It's a long drive into town in the snow, Cara."

"Josh can handle the snow," she replies confidently. "He'll be there in about a half hour. Are you okay until then?"

"Yeah, I'm bundled up. If need be, I can shovel my driveway again and I'll be nice and sweaty in no time."

"Well, that sounds . . . gross," she replies with a giggle. "No sweating. Just stay warm."

"I'll try. Tell Josh thanks."

I hang up and fix myself some hot cocoa while I wait. Josh will fix the furnace, and everything will be back to normal in no time.

Just as I'm settling back into the cushions of the couch, surrounded by all of my throw pillows and blankets, there is a knock on the door.

Thank God, I thought I was going to suffocate under all that fabric.

With my trusty quilt held around me, I jog to the door and fling it open.

"I'm so happy to see you!"

The man on the other side of the door offers me a slow grin, allows his chocolate-brown eyes to roam from the top of my messy hair to the soles of my wool-covered feet, and then steps inside out of the snow and takes his army-green beanie off his head, uncovering rumpled brown hair. He stomps the snow off his boots and sets a tool chest on my floor.

My brain has locked up. I was ready for Josh.

I wasn't prepared for his twin brother, Zack, or the damn tingle of awareness that zings through me at just the sight of him. The man is a good twelve inches taller than my five foot two and he's just . . . *big*.

And the sexiest thing I've ever seen in my life.

"Hey, Jilly."

# CHAPTER

## ZACK

"Hello?" Cara answers her phone and giggles while my brother, Josh, nibbles at her neck. Seth and I are on the couch, controllers aimed at the TV mounted above the fireplace in Josh's living room. Seth's black Lab, Thor, is curled up by the fire, snoring. I hear Cara say, "It's way too cold outside for you to be sitting in a house with a broken furnace."

"Is that Jilly?" Josh asks softly. Cara nods, and now I'm completely focused on the conversation happening over the phone rather than on the virtual cars that Seth and I are racing. I crash and burn.

"I win!" Seth exclaims.

"I'm sure Josh can fix it," Cara says, and Josh laughs.

*Fuck that.* If Jill's furnace is broken, I'll go to town

to fix it. It's too cold and stormy outside for her to be alone in that house with no heat.

Cara wraps up the conversation, assuring Jill that Josh can drive competently in the snow and that he'll be there soon.

"I'll go," I announce when she hangs up. Cara and Josh both look at me in surprise.

"But Dad, we're racing," Seth protests.

"You can race with Uncle Josh," I reply and stand to grab my coat and boots.

"I can go in with you," Josh offers, but I shake my head no.

"We shouldn't both be gone in this weather." I shrug into my coat, step into my boots, and pull my beanie over my head. "I won't be long. Is it okay if Seth and Thor stay here until I get back?"

"Of course," Cara says and smiles at Seth.

"I'll kick Uncle Josh's butt at this game," Seth proclaims. I wave at them and jog through the heavy snow to my truck.

It's snowed at least another six inches since Seth and I came over for dinner a few hours ago. It'll be a busy morning on the ranch, plowing the snow and checking the livestock.

The road to town has recently been plowed. My four-wheel drive handles the weather with ease, and I'm soon pulling up to Jill's small house.

Now that her brother, Ty, has moved in with Lauren, the thought of Jill living here alone makes me uneasy, and for good reason.

Not that I have a damn say in the matter.

Her amazing blue eyes would flash in indignation at me and she'd have no problem reminding me that she's a grown-ass woman who can take care of herself. She's adorable when she's pissed.

I park behind her small Honda, taking note of the way it's parked diagonally in the driveway, and trek through the snow to her front door.

Her walkway needs to be cleared, so instead of knocking, I grab her shovel and quickly clear her sidewalk, along with a path to her car door.

At the rate this snow is falling, it'll need to be done again when I leave.

I brush as much of the snow off my shoulders as I can and knock on her door.

"I'm so happy to see you!" she exclaims as she flings the door open. She's bundled up in a worn, brightly colored quilt, her long chestnut hair pulled up into some sort of knot on her head, and those killer eyes of hers widen when she sees it's me and not Josh.

I smile slowly as I take her in: those small, strong hands clenching the quilt, her slender form hidden beneath about six inches of fabric from neck to feet.

Yet she's the prettiest thing God's ever put on this earth.

I step inside and pull my beanie off, set my tools by my feet, and resist the urge to pull her against me and kiss her senseless.

"Hey, Jilly."

"Zack. I thought Josh was coming." She shuts the door behind me and doesn't meet my eyes as she walks to the back of the house, which is where I assume the furnace is.

"I had him stay with Cara and Seth," I reply, and leave it at that. "How long has it been this cold in here?" I can see my breath, for God's sake.

"I don't know. It was like this when I got home. It was warm when I left, though, so it must've happened sometime during the day."

She gestures toward a natural-gas furnace in the utility room off the kitchen. I brush past her, gritting my teeth at the zing of awareness that comes from just the brief touch of my arm on her shoulder.

I can think of better ways to warm Jillian up than fixing her furnace.

I'd rather haul her into that bedroom, pull her under the blankets, cover her tiny body with mine, and sink inside her. Hear those whimpers and moans she makes when she's turned on, and hear my name screamed from her mouth when I make her see stars.

*Jesus, King, get a grip.*

Maybe I should have let Josh come in to town.

I wipe my hand over my mouth and squat next to the furnace.

"What's wrong with it?" Jill asks from behind me, hovering over my shoulder.

"I just opened the thing up, Jill."

"Oh."

She bounces from one foot to the other and braces her hand on my shoulder to lean over and watch what I'm doing.

"Must you hover over me like that?"

"I want to see," she replies stubbornly.

"You're blocking my light," I grumble. If she keeps touching me, I won't be responsible for my actions.

She suddenly shoves a flashlight in my face.

"Here."

"Point it down here," I direct her and resign myself to sporting a hard-on while Jill "helps" me fix the furnace.

"Is the pilot light out?" she asks.

"Yeah, but I'm not sure why." I'm not a mechanic— hell, neither is Josh—but I'm pretty handy. I tinker around but can't find anything obviously wrong; nor can I get the pilot light lit, no matter what I try. "Damn," I mutter.

"What?"

"I think your thermocouple needs to be replaced."

"Oh." She pats her hips where pockets would be and looks around. "I don't have a thermonuclear thingamabob on me right now."

"You have no idea what I'm talking about," I say with a laugh.

"You would be right."

"It means that it can't be fixed tonight."

Her shoulders sag in defeat, and I have to fight the desire to pull her into my arms and reassure her that it's all going to be okay.

"Go ahead and pack a bag," I murmur.

"Where am I going?" she asks with a frown.

"Jill, it's about fifty degrees in here. You can't stay here all night."

"I'm sure I can borrow an electric heater from someone," she replies.

"You'll be safer in a hotel. Just pack a bag and I'll follow you over there."

She shakes her head and looks like she's on the verge of tears, sending panic through me.

"I don't think my car will make it to the hotel," she replies softly.

"Why not?"

"I never had studded tires put on it." She shrugs with frustration. "I didn't have time, and then this storm hit. It took me almost an hour to make my way off the mountain this afternoon, then Max hit me at the bottom, and I slid most of my way home from there."

My heart stills at the mention of someone running into her. "Who hit you?"

"Max Hull is in town, and he took the corner too fast and clipped my back fender. It's a tiny dent. Ty can pull it out."

"I don't give a fuck about your car, Jilly. Are you okay?" Without thinking, I wrap my arms around her and hug her tight, her arms trapped between us. I can feel her trembling, and whether it's from the cold or being in my arms, I'm not sure. I press my lips to her head and breathe in her fresh lilac scent.

I rub my hands up and down the quilt covering her back, trying to soothe her.

"I'm fine. He barely hit me." She pulls away all too soon, and I'm left feeling . . . empty.

"We've been telling you for the last two months to replace those tires," I remind her.

"Yeah, well, now you can say 'I told you so.'" She rolls her eyes and marches away from me, grabbing her phone from off the couch.

"Who are you calling?"

"I'm going to see if I can borrow an electric heater."

"Just pack the bag, Jill. I'll take you to the ranch."

"You don't need to do that."

"Leaving you here in this house with no heat in this storm is not an option, Jillian. I'm taking you to the ranch. Grab your shit and let's go." I shove my hands into my pockets and glower at her, daring her to argue.

"Why are you so bossy? Just because you bossed people around in the army doesn't mean you can boss everyone else."

I pinch the bridge of my nose and sigh deeply. "Jesus, you are the most infuriating, obstinate woman I've ever met."

"I doubt that's true." She sniffs and tugs the quilt more tightly around her.

"Please," I begin again, as patiently as I can, "pack some clothes and let me take you to the ranch. Everyone would feel better if we know you're safe."

She bites her lip and finally nods. "Okay."

"Thank you," I say in exasperation and take my tools out to the truck. Sure enough, I can't even see the paths I shoveled earlier.

When I stomp back into the house, Jill has a duffel bag set by the door and is shoving her computer into a briefcase. She's wearing sweats and a big, warm hoodie. She's got her black-rimmed glasses on now. "I'm almost ready."

"That was quick."

"I won't need much." When she's gathered all her papers and pulled on her coat, she turns and looks expectantly at me, and all the breath leaves my body.

*God, she's gorgeous.*

She bites that pouty, pink lower lip, her blue eyes wide as she peers at me through her glasses. She looks vulnerable and small, and I want to scoop her up and protect her from everything.

"Are we just going to stand here and stare at each other all night? We'll die from hypothermia."

"Funny." I take her bags and follow her out to my crew-cab Ford, stow her things in the backseat, and start the engine.

"Could you have bought a taller truck?" she asks as she pulls herself up into the cab. "I need a step-ladder to get into this thing."

"I don't drive many short people around," I reply with a smile.

"Seth is short."

"Seth hops in without a problem."

"I'm not a twelve-year-old boy," she reminds me and rubs her hands together briskly to warm them up.

"No, you're definitely not that, Jilly."

"Damn, it's really coming down," she murmurs in awe. She's right—the snow is falling faster than crews can clear it from the streets. As we drive on the highway heading out of town toward the ranch, the snow is coming down so hard and thick, my headlights bounce off the white flakes, almost blinding us.

"Oh no! Someone's in the ditch!" Jill points to a small SUV with its hazard lights blinking, the front end in the ditch and the back tires spinning worthlessly in the snow. I slowly pull over to the shoulder, put the truck in park, and take Jill's hand in mine, demanding her attention.

"Stay in this truck, Jill. I'm gonna pull them out."

"I can help."

"If I need you, I'll let you know, but for now just stay here."

I don't need to worry about her out in this mess. She nods and I hop out of the truck and make my way down the brush- and snow-covered ditch to the driver's side of the SUV. A woman is inside, frantically talking on her phone. A baby is crying in the backseat.

I knock on the window, startling her.

"I'm Zack King," I yell through the glass. "I have a truck and chains. Just stay here, put it in neutral, and I'm going to pull you out!"

She sighs in relief and smiles as she cracks her window.

"Thank you so much!"

Pulling my gloves out of my coat pocket, I nod and climb up to the truck, then yank my tow chains out of the bed. Once I have the chains attached to both my truck and her SUV, I climb into the cab.

"What's happening?" Jill asks.

"I'm pulling her out," I reply, looking both ways on the highway for oncoming headlights. There are none.

As quickly as I can, I pull out onto the road, put the truck into the lowest gear possible, and pull the small SUV out of the ditch and onto the road. As soon as I see she's out, I throw the truck in park and get out to unhook the chains and wave at the woman as she drives slowly and carefully away.

After throwing the chains back in the bed of the truck, we're on our way to the ranch.

"You're soaked," Jill murmurs.

"I'll dry."

She turns up the heat and takes my right hand in hers, pulling my glove off and warming my fingers. "You're freezing."

I glance over in surprise as she continues to warm my hand, confused as all hell at the riot of emotions racing through me. One minute she's stubborn and impossible and the next she's soft and sweet.

"I'd do the other one, but it's kind of busy right now," she says with a grin.

"Yeah, not a good idea to drive with no hands," I agree and chuckle. She keeps my hand in hers, resting in her lap, until finally, I gently pull it away. "Thanks. That's better. That could have been you, you know."

"I know." She sighs deeply. "I need to replace my car. I drive a lot for my job, so I probably need an SUV with all-wheel drive."

"Sooner, rather than later."

She just nods and continues to watch the snow in the headlights. "So, are you still living with your mom and dad?"

I glance over at her, expecting to see a teasing smile on her lips, but she's just watching me with wide, quiet eyes.

"Well, you know how it is. I could do my own laundry, but Mom makes it so extra soft and it smells good."

"Don't be an ass." She laughs and smacks my biceps.

"Actually, Mom and Dad moved into the new cabin last week."

"Oh! It's done already?" she asks.

I nod. Mom and Dad decided this past summer that with me home and running the ranch with Josh, it was time for them to retire. But they would never leave the ranch, so Josh and I had a small single-story home built for them on the property.

"Does your mom like her new place?" Jill asks.

"Yeah. No more stairs to climb every day, less

house to clean, and Dad made sure her kitchen is badass, so she's been baking and cooking like crazy."

"Good for them." Jill grins. "Your parents have worked hard all their lives. I'm glad they're going to take it easy."

"Well, we'll see how long it lasts. Dad loves ranching too much to retire completely."

"How is Seth?" she asks as I pull into our driveway.

"He's doing so much better," I reply. "His grades are awesome, and he's got friends. I wish I'd moved him here years ago."

The guilt sets in as I think of what my son went through before coming home to Montana.

Jill lays her hand on my arm and squeezes gently. "I'm glad he's doing so much better. He's a great kid."

I grin and nod. "Thanks."

Pulling up to Josh and Cara's place, I park and turn to face Jill, who is frowning and biting her lip again. She looks almost . . . disappointed.

"What's wrong?" I ask.

She shakes her head and offers me a smile. "Nothing. Thank you for rescuing me."

"You don't need to be rescued, Jill," I reply and return her smile. "I'm just glad you know how to ask for help when you need it."

I step out of my truck and retrieve her bags from the backseat, then trudge through the snow to Josh's front door, which is now open as Cara has rushed out to hug Jill. Thor runs out of the house, lifts his leg on a snowbank, and then dashes right back in.

Smart dog.

"Dad! I creamed Uncle Josh in Need for Speed!"

"That's my boy," I reply and ruffle his hair when he runs over to me.

"He cheats." Josh glares at Seth, who laughs hysterically.

"Do not. You suck."

"I bet I can beat you," Jill announces and Seth stills, watches her with narrowed eyes, and then shoves his controller at her.

"You can try, but I'll beat your girl butt."

"We should go, Seth."

"Just one game? Please?" Seth asks, bouncing on his toes.

"Please?" Jill joins him, both of them about the same height, looking up at me with hopeful eyes, and I can't help but burst out laughing.

"Go ahead."

"Yes!" Jill cries and races Seth to the couch, where they settle in to race.

"Couldn't fix the furnace?" Josh asks.

"We're gonna have to send someone over there tomorrow," I tell him and watch the dark-haired woman with my son.

"Thanks for going in to help," Cara says and hugs me around my waist.

"Anytime," I reply.

Jill is laughing and when Seth beats her in their race, she smiles widely at him and offers her fist for him to bump, which he accepts happily.

*What the fuck am I going to do about her?*

# CHAPTER

## Three

### JILLIAN

"All right, Seth, it's time to head home. You have school tomorrow."

"Dumb school," Seth grumbles under his breath next to me. "Maybe we'll get a snow day."

"Doubtful," Cara replies with a frown. "This isn't Texas. We're used to snow around here."

"Dumb school," Seth grumbles again, making me laugh.

"Thanks for playing with me." I nudge him with my shoulder. "This was the best part of my day."

"It was?"

"Yeah, I had a crappy day. So thanks."

He shrugs like it's no big deal, but smiles and pets Thor before standing, putting the game away, covering his dark hair with his hat, and stuffing his feet into boots.

"Thanks again, Zack," I murmur and offer the tall, sexy man a grin. He just nods and shoos his son and their dog out to the truck, leaving me with Josh and Cara.

"Want to watch a movie?" Cara asks.

"I can go find something to do, give you some girl time," Josh offers, but I shake my head no.

"Honestly, I've had one of the worst days I've had in a long while, guys. I'd like to just go take a long, hot shower and go to bed."

"Okay, follow me." Cara leads me down the hall to a bedroom with a soft queen-size bed, and towels and washcloths stacked neatly at its foot. "The linens are clean. The bathroom is just across the hall. Let me know if you need anything."

"Thanks, friend." I hug her close. "I'll see you in the morning."

I gather my toiletries and towels, turn on the water in the shower as hot as it goes, and take my clothes off.

This has been one long day. I can't seem to get warm, despite sitting in front of the fire with Seth, playing the game. I step under the water and flinch as it bites my cold flesh, then sigh in relief when it begins to warm me up. I go through the motions of washing my hair and shaving, and then just stand in the blissfully hot water until the temperature starts to fall.

It's stupid to be disappointed that he brought

me here rather than taking me home with him. Of course he would bring me to Cara's. Why in the world would he take me to his house?

We're just friends.

He has a twelve-year-old son, for the love of Moses.

Yet, for just a few moments, the thought of staying with him for the night was a tempting fantasy.

When I'm dry and dressed in clean yoga pants and an old University of Montana T-shirt, I comb out my long dark hair and blow it dry, and as I watch my fingers comb through the strands, I can't help but remember that night months ago when Zack was inside me, surrounding me with his big, hard body. I was coming down from the best orgasm of my life as he pushed his fingers through my hair, whispering about how soft and beautiful it is. My legs go weak and my stomach tightens as I switch the dryer off and brace myself on the sink, staring at my own reflection.

"He has baggage," I tell myself. "And you do too. Jesus, between the two of you, you could fill the cargo hold of a 747. It doesn't matter that he's hot as fuck and makes you crazy. It'll never work."

I lean in and give myself the stink-eye. "And he doesn't want you anyway. Get over it."

I climb into the soft bed in Cara's spare bedroom and curl into a ball as exhaustion takes over and pulls me into sleep.

●   ●   ●

Someone is trying to bulldoze the house down.

I wake with a start as I push my hair out of my face and gaze about the still-dark room in confusion. Then I remember the cold house, Zack coming to help, and him bringing me here. I lie down and listen. Loud voices and a gurgling engine are coming from out front.

*What in the hell are they doing out there?*

I check the clock and wince when I see it's not quite six yet. After yanking the covers aside, I stand and walk out into the hallway, almost running smack into Cara.

"What are they doing?" I ask and rub my eyes.

"Plowing," she mutters, evil and bloodshed coming from her narrowed hazel eyes.

"Are you going to beat Josh up?" I ask hopefully.

"Oh, it's all three of them," she replies.

"What?"

"Put your eyes in and follow me." I hurry into the bathroom to put my contacts in and join Cara back in the hall. She leads me to the front door, we shove our feet into boots and throw scarves around our necks, and step out into the cold.

The snow stopped falling at some point during the night, but not before dropping at least two feet of fluffy white powder.

And right now, at the butt crack of dawn, Josh and Zack are plowing the driveway with a big green

John Deere tractor. They're bundled up in Carhartt jackets and boots, gloves, and hats. Thor is running about, jumping in the snow, chasing sticks that Seth throws for him while he helps direct his uncle and father.

"Hey!" I call out. They don't hear me. "How do you deal with this?" I ask Cara.

"They're not typically this loud in the morning." Cara props her hands on her hips and glares at her fiancé. "I usually just wake up alone."

We continue to glare at the boys until I decide that the best way to get their attention is to demand it. With a shot to the head.

I pack snow into a nice, hard ball, and throw it, hitting Josh in the shoulder.

"Good shot!" Cara announces and joins me, scooping balls of snow and throwing them at the guys.

Seth gets into the spirit, throwing snowballs back at us while Thor barks encouragement.

"They've declared war, Dad!" Seth exclaims when Zack cuts the engine to the tractor and watches us.

"No, you did!" I yell and throw another snowball, hitting Zack square in the chest. He looks down at the snow on his coat and then narrows his eyes at me. "You woke us up!"

"How is Cara supposed to drive to work if we don't plow?" Josh asks with a laugh and hops off the tractor.

"You didn't have to plow this early," she replies

and throws another snowball. We duck and weave, avoiding the snow being hurled at us by Seth.

"This is a big ranch," Zack says as he also jumps off the tractor and slowly advances toward us, ignoring the snow being flung at him. "We had to start early so we could get the other chores done too."

"You woke us up," I reply haughtily, but can't smother the giggle that comes out when I hit Zack in the right shoulder, sending snow spraying up onto his face. He wipes his eyes on his sleeve and then slowly kneels to scoop up a ball of snow. "Oh shit."

"We're dead," Cara agrees and giggles when Josh runs after her, tackling her before she can run into the house, tickling her and rubbing snow in her hair.

Zack stalks me slowly, his brown eyes pinned to mine, the dimple in his cheek winking at me as he tries to hold the laughter in.

"You don't scare me," I lie. I will not show fear. I clench my lips to keep from screaming as he advances. "I'm going inside."

"Oh no, you're not." He catches me and shoves snow down my shirt.

"Oh my God!" I scream and run away from him. I grab snow and throw it haphazardly over my shoulder, missing him by at least six feet, and he laughs loudly.

"Is that all you got?" he taunts me.

"You're a bully!" I laugh and try to get away, but

suddenly Seth and Thor are there too, tossing snow and laughing, and I can't take it anymore. I fall into the snow, on my back, heaving and laughing and wet. My eyes are closed for a moment, but when I open them, two brown-haired heads are staring down at me as Thor licks my cheek. "Uncle."

"We won, Dad!" Seth and Zack high-five each other and Zack holds out a hand to help me out of the snow, but I shake my head.

"I'm comfortable."

"Aren't you freezing?" he asks with a frown.

"Yeah, but it's not bad. I worked up a sweat kicking your ass."

"I'm not the one on the ground, sugar."

I giggle again and when he offers me his hand, I take it and pull him down onto the snow beside me.

"You were saying?"

He chuckles and looks over at me, flat on his back. "I never would have pegged you for someone to get dirty in the snow."

"I'm not *dirty*," I reply. "I'm wet."

I laugh at the implication and see his brown eyes spark with awareness.

"You know what I mean," I whisper.

"Yuck," Seth grumbles. "Uncle Josh is kissing Aunt Cara again."

We glance over to see that Josh has rolled them so he's under Cara, taking the brunt of the cold, and they're kissing like high school kids.

"Get a room!" I yell.

They laugh, then come over to help us out of the powder.

"That'll teach you," I say and toss my wet hair over my shoulder.

Cara mimics me and follows, stomping to the front door. As we step inside, I can hear the guys laughing. Cara shuts the door and we dissolve into giggles, high-five each other, and strip out of our boots and sopping-wet scarves.

Suddenly the door opens and Zack pokes his head in.

"Jilly, I'm taking you car-shopping today. I'll come get you at noon, after I wrap some things up."

"I have to work today."

"You can work here," Cara offers with a grin. "You brought your computer."

I look back and forth between them and then sigh in defeat.

"Fine."

Zack winks and shuts the door as Josh fires the beast back up.

"I'll get the coffee brewing," Cara offers. "We won't be going back to sleep now."

"You don't have to go with me," I insist as Zack and I drive back into town. "You've done enough. Josh called the guy to come fix the furnace and will meet him at my place in about an hour. I can take my old car to the dealer and trade it in."

"I don't mind," he replies without glancing at me.

"If you're worried that I'll be taken advantage of because I'm a single woman buying a car—"

"That's only part of it," he interrupts and parks his truck on the street in front of my house. The snowplow blocked my car in again this morning. "You're not driving that again." He points to my little Honda and I bristle.

"It's perfectly safe."

"Not during a Montana winter, it isn't. I'll drive you in it and we'll trade it in."

"You're very bossy," I accuse him.

"Your point?" He cocks a brow and stares at me, and I can't help but laugh and shake my head.

"Fine. Thanks. I have to shovel the driveway first. The car will never get through that mess."

"Just take your stuff inside, Jill. I'll shovel."

"You've been shoveling since very early this morning."

"It won't kill me."

He pushes out of the truck and I watch him walk around the hood to open my door for me.

The man moves effortlessly. The feel of his muscles and smooth skin under my hands will be forever branded on my brain.

I know what he looks like under those clothes, and it's enough to make my heart skip several beats.

"Coming?" he asks.

*Yes, please.*

I just nod and hop out of the tall truck. He follows

me inside with my bags, then leaves with my shovel to get to work on the driveway, but I refuse to be left out. I find another shovel and dig in, helping him. He scowls at me, but I shake my head.

"My driveway, my responsibility, Zack."

"You're the most stubborn woman I've ever met."

I smile widely and we continue to shovel in silence, working until it's all clear and my car will have a fighting chance of making it out of the driveway.

"Okay, let's go."

I pass him the keys when he holds his hand out, unwilling to fight the issue, and settle into the passenger seat as he maneuvers us out of my drive and onto the street.

"Jesus, you *drove* this yesterday?"

"I drive this every day."

He swears under his breath and carefully drives the fifteen miles or so to the next town over.

"What kind of car do you want?" he asks.

"I think a Ford."

"Okay." He nods and pulls into a Ford dealer, just off the highway.

Zack and I wander among the Ford SUVs until a salesman wanders out to ask us what we're looking for.

"She needs something with all-wheel drive," Zack begins before I can even open my mouth. "I'd rather she drive a V-8, but I know she's going to want something that gets better gas mileage than that, so a V-6 is fine."

The salesman nods and points to an Explorer.

"Wait," I interrupt. "I do want those things, but I also want heated seats and a moonroof."

Zack frowns down at me.

"And satellite radio," I add.

"Seriously?"

"Absolutely, I have to have my tunes."

"You don't *need* those things, Jill. You need an independent front and rear suspension."

"I *need* GPS."

"You *need* antilock brakes."

"They all have antilock brakes." I roll my eyes at him and his lips twitch but he keeps that stern look on his face.

*God, I want to kiss him.*

"How long have you two been together?" the salesman asks with a chuckle and Zack and I both freeze.

"Oh, we're not together," I rush to assure him. "We're just friends."

Zack doesn't say anything at all, his jaw just ticks when he clenches it shut, and the salesman just shrugs and chuckles.

"Okay then. Sounds like the Edge might be a good fit for you."

"Do you have red? That's one of my must-haves."

Zack mutters about women and their priorities as we're shown to a beautiful red Edge that has all of my wants and Zack's requirements.

I sit in the driver's seat and sigh in contentment.

"I'll take it."

Zack shoots me a scowl. "Can we have a moment, please?"

"Sure, take your time." The salesman leaves us be, sitting in the warm vehicle. I push the button for the seat warmer and grin when I feel my ass begin to warm up.

"My ass is warm."

"It's going to be when I put you over my knee and spank your ass."

I gape at him and then laugh, holding the steering wheel in a death grip.

Just the thought of it has me squirming.

"What did I do wrong now?"

"'I'll take it'?" He rubs his fingers over his mouth and I can't help but watch the motion.

"I want this car."

"He's a salesman, Jill. Jesus, play a little hard to get."

And just like that my heart freezes.

"Thanks for reminding me that that's not my strong suit." My voice is hard and I hate that I can feel heat on my cheeks from embarrassment. "*I'll take it* doesn't mean he'll get the price he's asking for. I'm also a salesperson."

"That's not what I meant."

"You know, I don't just jump into bed with men."
*Dear God, shut up! Stop talking!*

"Jilly, that's not what I meant at all, damn it."

I shake my head and move to open the door, but he grips my hand in his, stopping me.

"Of course I don't think that about you. Jill . . ."

He cups my cheek in his palm and forces me to meet his gaze.

"Look . . ."

Before he can say any more, my phone rings in my pocket.

"Hold on." I smile when I see Max's name on the caller ID. "Hey, Max."

Zack's eyes narrow on mine as he watches me, listening unabashedly.

"Hey, Jill. I wanted to check in with you to make sure that you're okay after our run-in yesterday."

"Oh, I'm fine. It was a tiny dent. I'm actually at the dealership now, trading it in anyway."

"Good, I'm glad to hear it. Hey, let me make it up to you. I'd like to take you out to dinner tonight."

"Really?" I bite my lip and watch Zack's face redden, his jaw clench. *Why is he so pissed?*

"Sure, it'll be fun to catch up. Sounds like there's a lot of gossip to fill me in on."

I smile. "There is. Sure, dinner sounds good."

"Awesome. I'll pick you up at seven."

"Actually, I'll just meet you at seven. Just text me and let me know where."

"No problem. See you later, Jill."

I click off and frown at Zack.

"What?"

"You know, Max always was a womanizer."

"So?"

"Are you sure you want to go out with someone

like that?" He crosses his arms over his chest and won't look me in the eye now. Our moment before Max's call is over.

"It's just dinner, Zack. There's no ring on my finger."

"It's your call."

"Damn right it is."

He turns his head and pins me in his brown stare. He looks angry and frustrated and *hurt*.

"Zack . . ."

"Let's go take care of the paperwork." He pushes out of the car, shutting it firmly behind him, and stalks off toward the office, leaving me to follow behind him.

What the hell is wrong with him?

When I join Zack and the salesman—Bob Larue—in the office, we all sit at the desk and get to business.

"Okay," Bob begins. "Here is the sticker price."

"I'm going to make this very easy for you," I reply before Zack can. I push the window sticker back to Bob, pull a pen and paper out of my handbag, write down a figure, push it to him, and smile. "That's what I'll pay, including tax and license, and my trade-in."

Bob scowls and looks at Zack, who just shrugs and sits back, letting me take control.

"I'll have to run it by my boss."

"Of course." I smile sweetly. When he's gone, I sigh. "I hate this part."

"You're doing just fine. Maybe you didn't need me after all."

I chuckle. "I'm glad you came."

Bob sits back behind his desk and passes the paper back to me with a much higher figure on it.

"Now, that's with a couple rebates that my boss was able to come up with for you."

"Okay." I turn to Zack. "Are you ready to go?"

"Where are you going?" Bob asks nervously.

"To a different dealership, Bob." I smile and lean over his desk. "I'm a woman, not a moron. I knew exactly what I wanted when I walked onto this lot, and I've done my research. I know you can match the fair price I wrote on that paper. I see that neither you nor your boss is taking this sale seriously, so I'll go to someone who will."

Zack smiles serenely as we turn to leave.

"Wait," Bob says. "Let me go talk to him again."

"I'll give you five more minutes of my time," I reply coldly.

"By the way, have you secured financing?" Bob asks.

"I'm paying with a check."

Bob nods and walks away and Zack cocks an eyebrow in question.

"I just received a decent commission from the last house I sold in LA."

"Good for you."

Bob returns a few minutes later with a smile. "Looks like you've got yourself a new car."

I smile widely and lean over to kiss Zack's cheek in excitement.

"I have a new car!"

"Looks that way," Zack agrees with a smile.

"Now I just need your autograph about five hundred times," Bob says with a wink.

# CHAPTER

## *Four*

"Hey, it's good to see you," Max says as he rises from his seat in the downtown restaurant and kisses me on the cheek.

"Thanks, you too." I grin and take in his dark blue sweater and black slacks, the way they cover his lean body and muscular arms. He pulls my seat out for me, then sits down again across from me. "I hope you haven't been waiting long."

"Nope, just got here." He grins. "You look great."

"Thank you." I wrinkle my nose and order a Diet Coke when the waitress stops by to take our drink order. "So, how are you, Max?"

"I'm good." He sits back in his seat and watches me with happy eyes. "You know, you haven't changed a bit since high school. It's crazy."

"Oh, looks are deceiving, my friend." I glance down at my menu, make my decision, and set it aside. "Where have you been living? Last I heard was Portland."

"I did live in Portland for a while." Max nods. "I'm based out of Seattle now, but like I said yesterday, I think I'll be moving back home soon."

"What do you do?" I ask and sip my soda.

"I'm a programmer."

"As in computers?" I ask and cock my head.

"Yes, but I work with software. I recently sold two programs to Google."

I feel my eyes go wide in surprise and then I smile and clap my hands. "That's awesome, Max! Good for you. What kind of programs?"

"They're ranching programs, actually. Bringing farming and ranching into the new millennium." He shrugs as if he's embarrassed and twists his glass of scotch on the table. "So I may be in the market for a new house."

"I happen to know someone who sells houses," I tease him. "What are you looking for?"

"Something newer, not in the heart of town. I'd like to be close to Jenna in case she needs me." He shrugs again and his cheeks heat. "Price isn't really an issue."

"I'll see what's available and email you a list if you'd like."

He nods. "Thanks, I'd appreciate it."

"How is your sister?" I ask after the waitress takes our order.

"Jenna's great. I worry about her being up on the mountain alone, though. Especially in winter."

"I've heard nothing but great things about her B and B," I say.

"She's done a great job with it." He turns bright green eyes to mine and offers me a half grin. "Tell me about you."

"I just moved back myself," I inform him. "Moved back this summer from LA."

"Why the move?"

I cringe inwardly. I've only told Cara about the fiasco that was my life in LA. I'm not baring my soul to Max.

"It was time to be closer to family," I tell him. "I missed Montana."

"Me too. Although snowstorms like yesterday make me wonder why."

"No kidding."

"Did you get a new car?"

"Yes, a new Ford. It's red and shiny and the seat keeps my ass warm. I love it."

Max laughs and leans toward me. He's so handsome, with his wide smile and gorgeous eyes. He's successful and intelligent and kind. Please, God, let there be some kind of awareness when he touches me.

"That was your laundry list of requirements?" he asks and covers my hand with his, and I'm disappointed that there is no spark, no sense of awareness.

Damn it! A nice, hot guy is interested in me, and I feel zilch.

Typical.

"Pretty much," I shrug and slowly pull my hand out from under his. He notices, but doesn't say anything and I sip my soda in relief. We spend the next hour chatting about our hometown and mutual friends, enjoying our meal.

"Wow, Ty and Lauren Cunningham," Max comments as he polishes off his chocolate soufflé.

"They're really great together." I sip my coffee. "I don't think I've ever seen Ty so happy."

"That's awesome. I'll call him while I'm in town." He reaches for my hand again, but I lean back out of his reach.

"Max, it's been so great to see you again . . ."

"But you're not interested in doing it again," he finishes correctly.

"I'm sorry," I sigh and hang my head. "You're great and I like you."

"It's cool. Friends can have dinner together." He smiles and I can see that there are no hard feelings.

Thank God!

"Thank you," I murmur. *Nice guy. Totally sweet. Hot as hell. Successful. And I can't even stand to hold his hand.*

I want to bury my face in my palm, but manage to smile as he settles the check and walks me outside. "I'm parked over there," I tell him, pointing to the right.

"I'm that way." He points in the other direction. "It's been great catching up, Jill. Drive safely home."

"I'll email you a list of houses in the next few days," I reply and tilt my head when he moves in to kiss my cheek.

"Perfect, thank you." He pats my shoulder, winks, and walks off toward his Mercedes.

I watch him walk away, then sigh and kick at the snow before walking toward my car.

When I get close, I see Zack sitting in his truck, parked right next to mine.

*Why is Zack here?*

As I approach, Zack gets out of his truck, his handsome face pulled tight.

"What's wrong?" I ask. "Has something happened to Cara? Or Josh?"

"No." He shakes his head and comes to a stop a few feet away from me. "Everyone's fine."

"Then why are you here?" I ask, confused.

He sighs and scrubs his fingers through his hair, then props his hands on his hips and hangs his head. "I just needed to make sure you're okay."

"Why wouldn't I be okay?"

He doesn't answer, and it all starts to make sense.

"Zack, why wouldn't I be okay?" I ask again and cross my arms over my chest.

"I told you, Max has a history of being a womanizer."

"Max has always been a friend of yours," I remind him. "He's a good guy."

He rubs his fingers over his mouth the way he does when he's agitated and shrugs again. "I'm just making sure you're okay."

"Let me get this straight. You drove all the way into town and sat in your truck, waiting for me to finish dinner, just to make sure I'm okay? Do you know how ridiculous you sound?"

"I'm ridiculous because I want to make sure you're safe?"

"Zack, what do you care who I date? You don't want me, remember?"

His mouth drops and his face pales before his eyes narrow. He steps forward and pushes his nose close to mine and I can smell the earthy, clean scent of him.

"I wasn't the one who got on a plane and left the fucking state the next day, Jillian. I never said I didn't want you."

"I woke up and you were gone!"

"I had to check on my son!" he yells back.

"Well, you should have woke me up or left me a note! I'm not a fucking mind reader." I shake my head and back away. I can't believe this. He wants me? "You've avoided me like the plague!"

"When a woman flees the fucking state after I've had the best sex of my life with her, I take that to mean she's not interested."

I'm struck dumb.

*Best sex of his life?*

"You wanted to see me again?" I ask in a small voice. "I thought it was a one-night stand."

He grips my shoulders in his hands and yanks me against his hard chest and covers my lips with his. This is no soft, seductive kiss. It's hard and possessive. Hungry. He growls as his arms loop around me and pulls me closer to him. I open up to him, allowing him inside my mouth to dance and plunder, to take control.

God, I missed the way this man kisses.

I lose all sense of place and time. I don't give a shit that every person in the restaurant is watching us right now. Or that we're out in the cold in the middle of winter. All I care about is having his arms around me, his mouth on me, and hearing the moans of pleasure coming from his throat.

Finally, he breaks the kiss and pulls away. We're both panting, our breath coming in clouds in the cool winter night, watching each other with hungry eyes.

He blinks and turns to open my car door for me, waits for me to climb inside, and then, without another word, walks around to his own truck. He follows me all the way to my driveway, and I'm sure he's going to come inside and finish what he started with that hot-as-hell kiss.

But when I climb out of my car, he doesn't make a move to follow. I walk back to his truck and wait for him to roll down his window.

"Are you coming in?" I ask.

His jaw ticks and his lips are pulled into a thin line. Finally, he shakes his head stiffly and mutters, "No. I just wanted to make sure you got home okay."

I frown and back away from his door, embarrassment coloring my cheeks.

"Well, I'm home. See you." Without another word, I turn my back on him and stomp up to my door, unlock it, and push inside, closing the door behind me.

*What in the name of all that's holy just happened?*

I would have invited him in without another thought to finish what he started in the parking lot. God, is this what I've been reduced to? Taking any scraps Zack decides to throw my way?

When did I become this woman?

I scrub the tears from my cheeks and march back to my bedroom to change, wash my face, and pull my hair back in a ponytail.

Who the hell does Zack King think he is anyway?

Just as I sit on the couch with my laptop to start researching houses for Max, my phone pings with a text from Zack.

I delete it without reading it.

Screw him and his hot kisses and his sexy body. I don't need a man who thinks it's fun to play with my emotions.

I don't need a man, period.

Oh God, I've become a man-hater.

No, I'm not. I love men. I love Ty and Josh. I'm even quite fond of Seth.

But Seth's dad can suck it.

Deciding that it's probably best if I'm not alone for the next few hours, and not wanting to drive out to the ranch to hang out with Cara, I text my brother.

Me: **Make sure you're dressed. I'm coming over.**

I grab my purse and hit the remote start on my new car—damn, I love that car—just as Ty texts back.

Ty: **We're dressed. Come on over.**

My car handles like a dream on the slick roads across town to the house Ty now shares with Lauren. Her great-grandfather was one of the founding fathers of Cunningham Falls, and the house they live in was passed down to her by her parents, who died a few years ago. The house is the biggest in town, a colonial-style white home with a circular driveway and beautiful gardens.

Cunningham Falls is gorgeous in winter. Not only because of the snow that covers everything, making it look clean and fresh, but also because of the lovely holiday decorations that have been hung every year the weekend after Thanksgiving for more than fifty years.

Big, red bells and fresh evergreen garlands are strung above the streets, along the streetlights. White lights twinkle through the branches. Snowflakes and snowmen made of white lights are hung on the telephone poles.

Thanks to the snowfall last night, everything is blanketed in the white powder, making our little town look like something out of a Dickens novel.

As I pull into the driveway, I see that white Christmas lights are hanging on the house.

I guess I should put mine up this week too.

"Nice car," Ty calls as he jogs down the front steps.

"Thanks." I grin proudly. "I bought it today."

"You went alone?" He frowns as he opens the passenger door and slips inside, checking it out.

"No, Zack went with me."

His head whips up and he stares at me in surprise.

"Something going on there, Jill?"

"No." I shake my head, turn my back on him, and climb the steps of the porch. "He's just a friend. The lights look nice."

"Are you sure?"

"Yeah, I like the plain white. I think I'll do white rather than multicolored on my house too."

"I'm not talking about the fucking lights, princess."

I chuckle and turn back around to face my brother. He's tall and tattooed and the best lawyer this city has ever seen.

He's also always been my protector, in every way, and I'd do anything for him.

"Zack is my friend, Ty. Where's Lo?"

"She's working. Have you eaten?"

"Yeah, I had dinner with Max Hull."

Ty ushers me inside and leads me past Lauren's closed office door to the family room off the kitchen. There's a fire in the gas fireplace.

"I didn't know Max was in town."

I explain to Ty about Max running into my car yesterday—was it just yesterday?—and how we came to have dinner tonight.

"Why didn't you call me?"

"It was nothing. Barely a dent. If I hadn't traded the car in today, I would have just had you knock the dent out. No biggie."

He nods and hands me a glass of white wine, then sits with me and braces one ankle on the opposite knee. "What's on your mind, Jill?"

"Do all men hurt women?" I blurt, then swiftly cover my mouth with my hand, mortified that the words escaped. "Forget that."

"Oh, hell no, I'm not forgetting that." He sits on the edge of the couch and sets his wine aside, watching me carefully. "What's going on?"

"Seriously, I don't know where that came from." *God, I'm so embarrassed.* I rub my hands up and down my denim-covered thighs nervously. "Of course not all men hurt women. You'd never hurt Lo."

"I think it's time we talked, Jilly." Ty sits back again, but every muscle is tight and I can see it's taking every ounce of patience he possesses to not shake me until I spill the beans.

"About?"

"What happened in LA. Why you moved home so quickly. Why in the name of God you'd ask me if all men hurt women." He stares at me with sad eyes. "Talk to me, princess."

I glance toward Lo's office uncertainly.

"She's in the zone. She won't be out for a while. I promise."

I take a deep breath and scrub my hands over my face and then decide *fuck it.* I need to talk.

"Dad hurt Mom, Ty, you know that."

He winces. "I'm sorry, Jill . . ."

"Stop that right now. It wasn't your fault. You and I both know this, and you need to stop with the guilt. It pisses me off." He glares at me but I continue. "He was a son of a bitch. He just had no respect at all for women. Not at all." I stand and pace the length of the family room. Now that the floodgates have opened, there's no reeling it in. "So, one would think, as an intelligent woman, I would be more careful about who I chose to marry."

"Are you telling me that Todd laid his hands on you?" Ty asks deceptively calmly.

"No." I wave him off. "I would have been out the door the second he raised his fist. No, Todd liked to fuck other women behind my back." I smirk and turn to look at my brother, who now has his mouth dropped in surprise. "I caught him red-handed. In my bed."

"Oh my God, Jill . . ."

"And of course," I interrupt, "it was all my fault. I couldn't get pregnant, so I only wanted to have sex when I was ovulating. I was moody from the drugs. I was a shitty wife."

Ty sputters and shoves to his feet, but I smirk. "No, he's probably right. But I'm not going to pretend that when I heard right before the Fourth of July that the new wife—the one he'd been banging in my bed—was pregnant that it didn't hurt me. 'Cause it fucking ripped my heart out."

Before I can say more, Ty's phone rings. He checks the caller ID, then mutes the sound and sets the phone aside. "That's Mom."

"Yeah, that's exactly what I need. More shit from my past brought up tonight."

"She's not calling you."

"She will. Eventually."

"She'd like to talk to you."

"It will be a cold day in hell before I'll sit down and have a nice chat with that woman. She allowed both of us to be terrorized and abused for years. It was *her job* to keep us safe. I don't respect her as a mother or as a woman." My chest is heaving now with anger and indignation. "And, you know, maybe it was a good thing that I couldn't get pregnant. I come from that. What kind of a mother could I possibly be? Todd reminded me of that as I stormed out of the house and told him to go fuck himself."

"I'd like to set this aside for now, because I'm going to find Todd and kill him with my bare hands." Ty clears his throat and swallows hard. "Why today? What happened?"

I take a deep breath and close my eyes, pulling my mind back to the reason I'm here.

"What is it about me that makes men think it's okay to walk all over me?"

"Did Zack . . ."

"Zack either likes to play mind games, or he doesn't know what the fuck he wants, but either way, I'm not interested in dealing with it."

Ty sighs and rubs his hands over his face.

"You're in love with him."

"Hell no. He's a hot piece of ass, Ty. He's never let me get close enough to him to see if he's someone I could fall in love with."

"My guess would be that you haven't let him get close either, Jill."

I stop pacing and turn to stare at my brother and think back on the past few months.

"I've seen you. You brush him off, laugh at him, or just avoid him altogether."

I shrug and look down at the floor. "So maybe neither of us knows what in the hell we're doing."

"You've both had a rough year."

I nod and cringe. "It doesn't matter anyway. It'll never work with Zack. He just hit a nerve tonight, and I needed to vent."

"Do I have to kick his ass?" Ty asks with a hopeful grin.

"He's taller than you and outweighs you by a good twenty-five pounds."

"I don't give a shit."

My spine tingles at the edge in his voice, but I laugh and shake my head. "No."

"Damn."

"Hey, Jill. I didn't know you were here," Lauren says as she comes into the room. She sits next to Ty, kisses his cheek, and grins over at me. "What are you up to?"

"Just thought I'd come over and raid your fridge,

watch some TV. Basically be a freeloader for the night."

Ty winks at me as Lo laughs.

"Good idea. Let's see if we have ice cream." Lo takes my hand in hers and leads me into the kitchen.

This is what I needed. A night with my family, where I don't have to guard my feelings and my heart.

My phone vibrates in my pocket, but I have a feeling it's Zack, so I ignore it and settle in to enjoy two of my favorite people in the world.

# CHAPTER

## Five

I always take Friday afternoons off, usually because I inevitably have to show houses on the weekends, so taking a few extra hours on a Friday afternoon for just me is important. So far, I don't even have any properties to show this weekend either. Though bad for business, it's not uncommon to be slow in the winter in Montana.

No one wants to move during a blizzard.

Looking forward to a relaxing weekend at home, I bundle up in my winter gear and carry a red plastic tote full of Christmas lights outside and set them on the porch, then trudge through the now-crunchy snow to the shed at the side of the house to dig out a ladder.

I could hire someone to come do this for me. I'm sure there's a high school kid around who could use an extra fifty bucks, but I like decorating and taking care of my little home. I'm thankful that Cara offered it to me when she moved in with Josh last summer. I'll eventually buy my own place, but in the meantime, this is home.

I take a deep breath in and out, and watch my breath float through the crisp December air as I lean the ladder against the eaves of the house, ensuring that it's planted solidly in the snow and won't slip.

Coming home was the best thing I ever did, even knowing that I'd run into Zack King on a regular basis. His brother is marrying my best friend, and we hang out as a gang often. At first I dreaded facing him after spending one amazing night with him over the Fourth of July weekend, and for good reason.

The man rocked my world and then cut out before I woke up. To say it was a hit to my ego is an understatement. Being in his company over the past months has been difficult. The man oozes raw sensuality, and keeping my hands off his tight, firm ass is a test of my self-control. He's always been perfectly polite, and before our fight the other night in the restaurant parking lot, we've never spoken of it.

And then I find out that he *didn't* mean for it to be a one-night fling? Is this not something he could have mentioned *months ago*?

Men.

I grab a strand of multicolored lights—I changed my mind about the color, again—and climb the ladder carefully. Because my arms are so short, I have to climb up and down repeatedly, repositioning the heavy metal ladder every few feet.

After the third climb, I pause at the top, already winded. Geez, I should buy a treadmill or something. If climbing up and down a ladder three times has me winded, I'm out of shape. I secure the lights to the gutter and then lean on the top rung and stare at a shoe on my roof. How did that shoe get up there? Cara just had this roof rebuilt, after a tree fell through it in a summer storm.

Must have been kids playing around.

I feel my phone vibrate in my pocket, but can't pull my gloves off and maintain my balance, so I ignore it and chew my lip as I stare at that wet, black shoe.

Zack has called or texted at least once every day this week. He probably wants to apologize for yelling at me, or come up with some lame excuse for not coming in with me that night, and frankly, I don't want to hear it.

Rejection doesn't taste good twice.

But, God, it felt divine to have his lips pressed to mine, his tongue exploring my mouth, and those large, strong hands braced on my hips, pulling me into him. Zack King can kiss.

And I mean *kiss*.

But he's stellar at the rest of it too. The touching.

The whispering. What that man can do with his mouth should be illegal.

And it just might be.

"What in the bloody hell are you doing up there?"

I gasp and clench my hands around the ladder, knowing exactly who is standing below me, as if I conjured him from my thoughts.

How did I not hear him approach?

"You scared me!"

"If you'd answer your damn phone once in a while, I wouldn't have startled you." I look down into deep brown eyes that have dark circles under them. His hair is stuffed under that beanie and his hands are braced on my ladder.

He's scowling.

"What are you doing?" he asks again.

"I'm curing cancer, Zack." I roll my eyes and secure another plastic clip to the gutter. "What does it look like?"

"You shouldn't be on a ladder in this weather."

"It's not snowing or raining."

"It's still slippery."

"I'm careful." I shrug and grin to myself. I love getting him riled up, and I can't explain why. It's just fun.

"Let me do this for you."

"My house, my lights, my problem."

"Come on, Jilly, get down."

I shake my head no, and suddenly, strong hands

circle my hips and I'm pulled off the ladder like a five-year-old.

"What the hell!" I cry out as he sets me effortlessly on the ground.

"I won't have you on that fucking ladder in the middle of winter, Jillian." He scowls down at me and I get a clear look at his face.

He looks tired, and maybe a little sad.

"I was doing fine," I insist.

"Hand me the lights," he replies and moves the ladder. As he climbs it, I have a prime view of his spectacular denim-covered ass.

"What are you here for?" I call up to him as I feed him the lights.

"We'll talk about it after we finish this. Do you just want these on the gutters, or do you want some up on the other eaves too?"

"I was just going to do the gutters, but I have more lights. I don't want to walk on the roof."

"That's the smartest thing you've said all day," he grumbles, making me grin again. "I'll put them up there for you, if you bought enough. Just grab my staple gun out of my truck."

"I have a staple gun in the Christmas box." I rummage around and hand it up to him.

He nods and goes about the task, not saying much. I can't help but admit that he does the job at least three times faster than I could have, and before I know it, he's climbed up onto the roof.

My heart is in my throat and I watch with wide

eyes as he carefully steps around the eaves, stapling lights as he goes. My hands are clenched tightly under my chin and I'm whispering prayers that he doesn't fall.

"You can go inside, Jilly," Zack calls down as he staples lights around a window. "I have this covered."

"Hell no, I'm not going inside!"

"It's cold out here."

I'm not even aware of it. It occurs to me that I can't feel my nose or my feet anymore, and I don't care. My eyes are pinned to the tall, handsome man on my roof.

"I'm fine," I reply.

"Have I mentioned that you're stubborn?"

"Once or twice."

He laughs and shakes his head and secures the last staple.

"Okay, plug them in."

I run to the porch and plug in the lights, then run back into the front yard to see them.

"Oh, they're so pretty!"

"Thank God they all work," he says as he tosses the black shoe down to the ground and then moves carefully down to the ladder. "It would be a bitch to have to take them back down."

"I checked them," I assure him, and when his foot finally lands safely on the snow and he turns to me, I hit him on the arm. "You shouldn't have done that! You took ten years off my life!"

I throw my arms around his torso and squeeze him tightly, then back away.

"No, *you* shouldn't have been on that ladder. If I catch you on one again, I'll spank your ass until it glows."

My jaw drops as I gaze up into his frustrated face. For once in my life, I'm speechless. I scowl as I pull myself together and clench my fists. "You wouldn't dare . . ."

"Put yourself in danger again and see if I don't," he replies calmly and crosses his arms over his chest.

"Did you come here to bully me?"

He sighs and pulls his beanie off his head, pushing his fingers through the messy brown strands. I want to sink my fingers in that thick, dark hair.

"No. I came because you won't answer your fucking phone so I can apologize for the other night."

"I don't want your apology," I reply and throw the extra lights and staple gun back into the tote and turn away, but he catches my arm and turns me back to him, takes the tote, and sets it down.

"I'm going to give it anyway." His jaw is firm. "I had no right to kiss you like that in the parking lot for everyone to see."

I jerk back, mortified. "You're apologizing for *kissing me*?"

He shakes his head and starts to speak, but I interrupt.

"So let me get this straight. You're not apologizing for yelling at me, or for walking out on me that morning without a note or a word, or even for turning me on and then leaving me. You're apologizing for fucking *kissing me.*"

I'm so mortified, I don't know what to do with myself. Before I can turn and run away from him, he catches my arm again and turns me to face him, his hands holding my shoulders firmly.

"What do you want from me?" he growls.

"I want you to be honest," I reply. "I want you to look me in the eye and just tell me you don't want me. Stop playing with me. We had sex months ago, and I was afraid it was going to make us all uncomfortable, and for a little while it did. But then it got better, and now we're back to awkward. Zack, our families are entwined, and we're going to see a lot of each other. I don't want to always be on edge around you."

"Jilly," he whispers, his eyes pinned to my lips. "I'm trying to apologize for hurting you. For not talking to you."

"You could just stay away from me," I say and try to back out of his hold, but his fingers tighten. "We'll be civil at get-togethers and just ignore each other the rest of the time."

"That's not possible." He steps closer and tips my chin up with his cold glove-covered finger. "That's just it, Jill. I can't stay away. I've tried for months. I know I'm fucking this up because when I'm around

you, I turn into a tongue-tied idiot. I wanted to apologize for hurting your feelings and ask you to come
out to the ranch tonight for dinner."

He's panting like saying that was the hardest
thing he's ever pushed past his lips. He looks uncertain and vulnerable and suddenly, something in
me . . . shifts.

"You want to do dinner with Josh and Cara?" I
ask uncertainly.

"No." He shakes his head and chuckles humorlessly. "I'm asking you out on a fucking date."

"And eloquently at that," I reply dryly. He swears
under his breath and backs away, and I gasp at the
loss of his heat on my cold shoulders.

"You know what? Never mind."

We're still standing in my yard. This is insane.

"Wait." He stops with his back to me. I walk to him
and stare up at him. "What about Seth?"

"He's staying with a friend in town tonight," he
replies.

"I'm not sleeping with you," I tell him defiantly. He
lets out the breath he's been holding and laughs, and
when he sobers, he pulls his gloves off and tosses
them to the ground, then cups my face in his hands
gently.

"I'm not asking you to my home to fuck you,
Jillian. I want to make you a meal, maybe watch a
movie or bad TV, and spend some time with you."

"Why now?" I whisper.

"Because I can't get you out of my head. I haven't

slept in days because I couldn't stand the thought that I'd hurt you. I just want to be with you."

"Okay."

He pulls back in surprise and studies me carefully. "Okay?"

I nod and offer him a soft smile. "I'd enjoy having dinner with you. And I get to pick what we watch."

"It's a deal."

His thumbs are rubbing the apples of my cheeks and when he leans in, I'm sure he's going to kiss me, but instead he plants his lips on my forehead and rests there for a few long seconds before pulling back and smiling at me, that dimple in his cheek on full blast.

That dimple alone is going to be my undoing.

"Six o'clock?" he asks.

"Sure. What can I bring?"

"Just you." He stows my ladder away in the shed and carries the tote inside, setting it next to the rest of the decorations I'd dug from the attic.

"Thank you for helping. And for the invitation." I pull my boots and gloves off, and just when I reach for the scarf, he tugs the ends, pulling me to him.

"I'm looking forward to it." He kisses my forehead again, my nose, and then lays those lips on mine in a quick, chaste kiss. "I'll see you soon."

He pulls the door closed behind him and I sigh, watching him climb into his truck and pull out of my driveway.

Why do I suddenly feel like everything is about to change?

❀ ❀ ❀

It's raining. I swear, Montana Mother Nature is on her period. She's all over the damn place this winter. It started to rain about a half hour ago, so the roads are just wet, but if the temperature drops, it will be emergency travel only by this evening.

I shouldn't go to Zack's. I should stay home.

So why am I pulling into his driveway?

I park and stare at the front of the large white house that sits nestled in tall evergreen trees, draped in snow. There is smoke swirling out of a chimney. Chickens are clucking and scratching the dirt in their pen, drifting in and out of their coop in the side yard.

Mrs. King always liked having the coop close by so she could gather eggs early in the morning.

I grin and climb out of my car, carrying my famous angel food cake and strawberry topping, along with whipped cream, for dessert.

Of course, I'd rather lick the whipped cream off Zack's body than this cake, but I'll take what I can get.

Before I can knock, the door swings open and Zack grins widely, wiping his hands off on a green kitchen towel. He's in his usual faded jeans and a T-shirt that says *Army Strong* across the chest. The sleeves are tight on his biceps as they flex with the movement of his hands, and just like that, my mouth has gone dry.

*Pull it together!*

"Hey," I say lamely and offer him a smile.

"Hey, come on in." He closes the door behind me and tosses the towel over his shoulder so he can take the cake from my hands as I remove my coat, scarf, and boots and then leads me into his house. Thor comes running out of the kitchen to greet me, his tail wagging furiously, his whole body shaking with excitement.

"Well, hello, sweet puppy. I'm happy to see you too." I pet his ears and kiss his head. "Wow, the house is different," I comment. I haven't been in the Kings' home in years; when I was a teenager Mrs. King had it furnished in feminine, soft fabrics and furniture, with handmade quilts thrown here and there.

Now the space is more masculine, full of leather and darker tones. Zack grins as he leads me into the kitchen, which hasn't changed much.

"Mom and Dad took their furniture to the new place. Dad offered to buy her all new stuff, but Mom said she likes hers." He shrugs and begins to stir something in a pot. "I needed new things anyway, so Seth and I went shopping about a month ago and picked out some furniture."

"I like it," I tell him honestly as I watch him move competently about the kitchen. Thor sits next to me and settles his head on my lap. He sighs contentedly as I rub his soft ears. "It smells great."

"I hope you eat meat."

"I'm from Montana. Of course I eat meat."

"You never know." He adds some garlic to a sauté pan. "You spent a lot of years in California."

"You know what they say. You can take the girl out of Montana . . ."

"But not Montana out of the girl," he finishes and leans his hands on the Formica countertop, watching me. "I know I haven't said it before, but I'm glad you're home, Jill."

I blush and look down at the sweet dog's face. I'm not used to this side of Zack. This relaxed, honest side of him. He's always been so intense, and I know that he doesn't reveal his emotions easily.

"I'm happy I'm home too."

"What made you decide to move back, anyway?" he asks, slipping some bread into the oven.

My hands still for a moment and I bite my lip. I'm not going to admit that I'm here because of my cheating ex-husband.

Not a chance.

"It was time to come back," I answer instead. "I missed home."

He nods thoughtfully, pours us each a glass of red wine, and hands me mine. "I hope you like spaghetti. It's the only thing I make really well."

"I love it."

"You're just saying that."

"No." I laugh and take a sip of my wine. "I love Italian food. I brought dessert."

His eyes warm and narrow and a smile tickles his lips, showing me that dimple. "You've already said that I'm not allowed to have what I really want for dessert tonight, so strawberry shortcake will have to do."

"You'll live," I reply dryly.

He drains the pasta and plates our meals before throwing the crusty garlic bread in a basket, and motions for me to grab our wine and follow him to the kitchen table.

"Thor, bed," he commands and snaps his fingers, and Thor immediately curls up on the dog bed in the corner of the room.

"He's already trained really well."

"Seth has done most of the work." He joins me at the table and grins proudly. "He loves that dog. And Thor's smart."

"Mmm, so good," I mutter with a mouth full of pasta drenched in red sauce. "I didn't realize how hungry I was."

He nods and eats, watching me. "How's business?"

"Slow this time of year." I shrug and take a bite of bread. "Typical. How about you?"

"The same. We just survive winters. Things will be nuts around here in a few months."

"Are you glad to be back on the ranch?" I ask.

"Yeah. I missed it. Seth loves every minute of it."

I glance over at Thor, whose ears have perked up at the sound of his young master's name. "Do you ever hear from his mother?" I can't say the woman's name out loud.

"No."

He doesn't elaborate.

"Never?"

"No." He won't meet my eyes, and instead just keeps shoveling food in his mouth. *Does it hurt him to think of her?*

The thought of *that* makes me ill.

"Is the divorce final?" I ask casually and reach for my wine. His fork stills in midair and he looks at me like I've just asked if he'd ever consider a sex change.

He lowers the fork back to the plate and wipes his mouth on his napkin, gathering his thoughts.

"The divorce was final before I ever touched you." The words are deceptively calm. His eyes are pinned to mine now, a slight frown pulled between his brows. "I would have never put my hands on you if it wasn't."

I nod once and carry on as though it's not that big a deal, but something in me that was worried before loosens.

When my plate is clean, I lean back in the chair and rub my hands up and down my flat belly.

"Dear God, I'm full."

"No dessert?" he asks with a chuckle.

"Not for a while. Maybe not for a month."

I stand and clear my plate and glass. "Are you finished?"

"Yeah, but I'll clean up."

"You cooked. I think there's a federal law somewhere that says that the cook doesn't clean." I wink and gather his dishes and carry them to the kitchen. I rinse and load the dishes into the dishwasher, wipe down the countertops, and then turn to find him standing on the other side of the island, leaning on his elbows.

He opens his mouth to speak, and just when I think he's going to say something profound, he says, "I have plans for this kitchen."

"You do?"

He nods and watches me carefully. "It hasn't been updated in about fifteen years."

I glance about the homey space. "I guess it could use some work."

*Why are we talking about the kitchen?*

"I think I might gut it and start from scratch."

"That's quite a project." I swallow hard as he walks around the island to me. I know I said no sex tonight, but frankly, if he boosted me up on this countertop and had his wicked way with me right now, I wouldn't turn him down.

I am a red-blooded woman, after all.

His hand glides down my arm and he links his fingers with mine, raises it to his mouth, and plants a soft kiss on my thumb.

"Shall we watch a movie?"

"Sure." My voice is high and squeaky, and I want to die. I clear my throat, but Zack grins and leads me out of the kitchen to the family room, where a huge TV dominates one wall and soft brown couches sit around the room. There are game systems situated on a unit under the TV, and controllers are lying on the ottoman, obviously left there from the last time the guys played.

"Seth and I spend a lot of time in here," he says sheepishly.

"It's a comfortable room." I flop down on a couch slouched in the corner and prop my sock-clad feet on the ottoman. "I like it."

"Make yourself at home," he says with a chuckle. "What do you want to watch?"

"Why don't we flip through the channels to see if there's anything on TV?"

"You're a channel flipper," he says accusingly and passes me the remote.

I begin flipping through the stations, pausing at the History channel to watch a show about secrets of museums.

"I have a thing for mummies," I say and glance over at Zack, who's watching me with a funny look on his face.

"What kind of thing? They've been dead for a while. It's not like you can date them or something."

"I think they're interesting, Captain Obvious." I throw the one pillow on the whole couch at him.

"Aren't there sports on? Or a show about murder?"

"Probably." I continue flipping through the channels and come to a stop. "*NCIS* is my favorite show!"

"Really?" He eyes me again. "Mine too."

"This is a marathon." I set the remote aside and settle in for a night with Zack King and Jethro Gibbs.

Not a bad way to spend some time.

"The ones from the beginning with Kate are the best."

Zack nods. "She was hot."

"She was?"

"Yeah, I have a thing for brunettes."

I roll my eyes and then startle when Zack pulls my feet into his lap and begins rubbing the left one, his eyes never leaving the TV. I sigh and settle deeper into the plush cushions of the couch. His thumb catches a particularly delicious spot in my arch and I moan, then slap my hand over my lips.

"Sorry."

He does it again and my eyes drift shut in ecstasy. "God, you're good at that."

I hear him swear under his breath, and when I open my eyes, his jaw is clenched shut, but his face is impassive as he watches his hands knead the muscles in my foot.

I have to get out of here. If I stay, I'll give in and rip his clothes off him and have my way with him.

"I should go."

"Stay," he says immediately and turns those dark

chocolate eyes on me. "It's a mess outside. The roads are most likely frozen over from the rain."

"I didn't bring anything with me . . ." *Am I seriously considering this?*

He pulls me into his lap and holds me against him, pushes my hair back over my shoulder, and drags his knuckles down my cheek.

"I won't ask you to do anything that you don't want to do, Jillian." His voice is soft. "But I'd love to have you here with me. We'll finish this *NCIS* marathon and take it from there. I have plenty of spare bedrooms."

"I just . . ."

"I don't want you to drive in this." He kisses my forehead, and I feel my resolve evaporating. I *want* to stay. I lay my hand on his cheek, and my stomach clenches when he turns his face and presses a wet kiss to my palm. "Didn't I hear that you remodeled the attic into a new master suite?"

He turns surprised eyes to mine and a slow smile spreads over his sexy lips. "I did."

"I'd love to see it."

"Are you sure?" He whispers and rests his forehead on mine. "I swear, there are no strings, sugar. You can have a room all to yourself."

I bite my lip and inhale deeply. He gently tugs the flesh out of my teeth with the tip of his thumb. "We've been circling around each other for months, Zack. I'm tired of it. I don't feel this with anyone else."

"What do you feel?"

I frown and try to look down, but he catches my chin with his finger and keeps me trapped in his gaze.

"I won't ask again."

"I feel . . . safe." I shrug. "Sexy. Turned on."

He stands easily with me in his arms and buries his face in my neck as he carries me to the stairs.

"You are all of those things, baby."

"I wasn't going to do this."

"You still don't have to."

I rest my hand on his cheek as he continues to climb the stairs without even an increase in his breathing.

He's so fucking strong.

"I want you." It's a whisper, but I feel it to my toes. His eyes dilate as he pushes open his bedroom door and carries me to his bed.

"I never stopped wanting you," he replies.

The bed is wide, king-size for a big man. The room is enormous, spanning the entire length of the house. There is a sitting area with bookshelves near a wide window that looks out to the back part of the property and the mountains, and I can just imagine what that view must look like early in the morning. The wood floor is covered in cozy rugs. There are two doors, both closed, on the opposite side of the space.

"Bathroom and closet over there," he murmurs when he sees me glance that way.

"This is beautiful."

"You are beautiful. Are you completely sure that this is what you want, Jillian?" He kisses my cheek and my neck then pulls back to watch my face.

I grin and lean in to press my lips against his. "Hell yes."

He growls and kisses me with restrained fervor. His hands grasp the hem of my sweater and tug it over my head, followed by the orange cami beneath it, leaving me in jeans and a bra.

I pull frantically on his T-shirt, dying to see and feel the muscles beneath.

Zack naked is a sight to behold, and it's been way too long since I last saw it.

He yanks the shirt off and returns his lips to mine, plundering, then reeling it back, tasting and nibbling.

"This isn't going to be fast, sugar," he murmurs as his lips drift down my jawline. "We have all night, and I'm going to take my time."

I push my fingers into his hair, loving the softness of the strands between them. "You don't have to go slow for me."

"I'm going slow for me." He reaches around with one hand and deftly unclasps my bra. I shrug out of it and toss it aside. "You are never going to forget all of the things I'm going to do to you tonight. Every inch of your amazing little body is going to feel me."

My breath hitches at his words. He boosts me up in the bed, unclasps my jeans, peels them down, and kneels between my legs, staring at me clad only in my tiny blue lace panties.

"Do you have any idea how fucking beautiful you are?" he growls and braces himself above me, holding his body away from mine as he brushes his lips over mine softly, barely touching me.

My hands glide across his smooth chest, over his sculpted stomach, to the button on his jeans.

"I need you naked," I breathe.

"Not yet."

"Please."

"Here's the thing," he whispers and pulls the lobe of my ear between his teeth, then soothes the bite with his tongue. "I only have one condom."

"Well, you're not very well prepared for this," I mutter grouchily.

"I wasn't trying to jinx anything," he replies with a chuckle. "But I do plan to make you come all night long, so we're going to have to be creative here, baby."

"All night?" I squeak. Dear God, I don't think I can do it.

"All." He kisses my collarbone. "Night."

# CHAPTER

### ZACK

Fuck yes I'm going to make love to her all night long.

"I'm going to make you feel things you've never imagined," I warn her as I trace her dusky brown nipple with my nose until it puckers. "I want to hear those sexy moans you make when I'm buried deep inside you, holding your legs down, making you stay still while I drive you nuts."

She moans and shimmies under me, trying to press her pussy against my stomach as I kiss across her chest, not quite reaching her sensitive nipples.

"And I want to feel you fall over the edge while I have my fingers deep inside your pussy and your clit between my lips."

"Jesus, Zack." Her sweet voice is raspy with lust now and she's breathing hard, her head thrashing on my pillow. Her gorgeous brown hair is fanned around her.

I can't wait to pull it while I fuck her from behind.

But that'll have to be another day because tonight, when I finally do sink into her hot, wet pussy, it'll be while she's under me, and I can see those amazing blue eyes while she comes around me.

I pull her nipple into my mouth and tug with my teeth, then soothe it with my tongue. She plunges her hands into my hair and holds on tight.

I make love to the other nipple, satisfied when it puckers, then pull back with a loud pop, glide my hands up her arms to her hands, still buried in my hair, and link my fingers with hers and guide them over her head.

"You taste so good," I whisper against her lips. She grins, panting, her blue eyes on fire, and circles her hips, pushing her pussy against my cock, making it throb even more.

"Zack," she murmurs. "I want you inside me."

"I'll get there," I reply and kiss her lightly, just tickling her lips with my own. God, she's so soft and sweet.

I let go of her hands and they go straight for my hair again, pulling me in deeper. This woman kisses like it's her sole mission in life, with 100 percent of her attention.

She's intoxicating.

Finally, I nip her little chin and down her neck

and begin the journey down her petite body. The first time I was with her, I was afraid I'd break her. But she's much stronger than she looks.

While kissing and nuzzling her belly button, I hook my fingers into her panties and pull them down her hips and legs, then throw them over my shoulder and settle between her spread thighs.

She's laid out before me like a feast. Her pussy lips are small and pink and dripping wet.

"Your clit is swollen," I murmur softly and trace a circle with my fingertip around the tight nub.

She gasps and squirms as I drag my finger down from her clit, between her folds, and push it inside her and amazingly, she clenches around my finger like a vise and I know that when my cock slides home, I won't last long.

Finally, I can't take it any longer. I *have* to taste her. I pull my finger out of her and suck it into my mouth. She bites her lip, watching me intently and I grin up at her, then lean in and pull her lips into my mouth, suck lightly, and then sink my tongue into her hot, tight pussy.

Her hips lift off the mattress, pushing unabashedly against my face. I plant my hands on her inner thighs and hold her down and lick from her entrance to her clit and back down again, and as I fuck her with my tongue, I press my thumb on her clit and watch as she explodes, her juices flowing around my mouth as she arches her back and screams my name.

I kiss her thighs and her soft, flat belly, running my fingertips up and down her skin, watching as goose bumps spread across her white skin.

"That was one," I inform her and climb back on top of her and kiss her, giving her taste to her. I love the way her pelvis cradles mine, and the feel of her strong thighs clenched around my hips, and I know I won't be able to hold out much longer.

I tug my wallet from my jeans, retrieve the condom, and shimmy out of my pants. My cock springs blessedly free, and I quickly sheath it in the rubber.

"You're sure?" I settle against her, not inside her yet, and gently brush strands of hair away from her forehead.

"If you stop now, I'll kick your ass." She reaches between us, takes my cock in her hand, and guides me inside her, and I swear to Jesus, I see stars.

"Holy fuck, Jilly."

"God, so good," she gasps.

I slide in as far as I can and stop, holding myself still. If I move, I'll pound in and out of her until I come hard, and I want to make this last.

"I missed you," I whisper. My heart stills. God, I missed her. I only had her for one night, and I thought I'd never be here again, and by some miracle, here she is.

"I'm sorry." She bites her lip. Tears form in her eyes, making my gut clench. "I shouldn't have left. I should have . . ."

"Shh." I kiss her softly and brush her tears away with my thumbs. "We had a rough year, sugar. I'm just so fucking thankful you're here now."

She nods and offers me a shy smile. "Me too."

I lean in and drag my nose down her jaw to her ear. "I have to move."

"So move," she replies and circles her hips again.

"I don't want it to be over too fast."

She drags those amazing hands of hers down my back to my ass and grabs a handful. "This is just the first time, Zack."

I pull back in surprise to gaze down at her nervous face. She's biting her lip again.

"I mean . . ."

"You're right." I pull my hips back and then slide right back in and it's all I can do to hold still again. "It's just the first time." I repeat the motion, and then slowly increase the pace.

"Oh God."

I hook her right leg around my elbow and spread her wide, and can't help but watch my hard, thick cock moving in and out of her small body.

"Amazing," I murmur and glance up at her face. "Your tiny body fits me like a glove."

Her body clenches around me, and I know she's on the edge again, ready to fall apart. I release her leg and cover her with my body and kiss her hard as her pussy milks my cock.

"Come, baby."

"Come with me," she purrs.

"I'm right here with you." I clench her hand in mine and kiss her fingers, then kiss her lips again. She nibbles my lower lip and suddenly, her hand tightens on mine and her pussy clenches around my cock like a fist.

"Holy shit!"

"Yes, baby." I hold my hips still, watching as she shudders around me, coming apart, and just as her orgasm is about to recede, I follow her over, pulsing inside her, and call out her name.

"Holy shit," she whispers, panting.

I laugh as my head clears, cup her face in my hands, and kiss her long and slow before pulling out of her to dispose of the condom and wash my hands.

"How do you feel?" I ask as I crawl back to the middle of my bed and kiss her cheek.

"Thoroughly fucked," she replies with a wide smile.

"Good." I kiss her cheek again and pull away. "I have to check the house. I'll be right back."

"Do you need help?"

The question makes me pause. When was the last time anyone asked me if I needed help?

"No, sweetheart. Get comfy. I'll only be a minute."

I pull on a pair of boxers and run into Thor, who is asleep right outside my door.

"Hey, buddy. Sorry about that." He whines and licks my hand as he jogs down the stairs next to me.

"I know, you miss your boy. He'll be home tomorrow. Here, go potty so we can all go to bed."

I open the back door and he flies outside, barks at the chickens just for form's sake, pees on a fence post, and then runs back to the house.

It's too damn cold out to fuck around.

I stoke the fire, add more wood, and make sure the house is locked up for the night, not that anyone is going to bother us out here. It's just habit now.

"Are you ready for bed, boy?" I ask Thor. He offers me a doggy grin and runs up the stairs ahead of me. He stops at Seth's room, but I shake my head. "You'll have to sleep in my room tonight. Come on."

When we enter the master, Thor jogs over to the bed, sniffs to see who's up there, and then jumps up on the bed.

"Thor, no."

"Awww, he wants to sleep with us." Jill scratches his ears as Thor curls up next to her, happy as a clam.

"Not a chance in hell are you going to sleep next to my woman, dog." Jill's eyes widen in surprise as I snap my fingers and point to Thor's bed. He whines, hangs his head for a moment, and then finally obeys, jumping off the bed and curling up on his dog bed in the corner.

I climb under the covers and pull Jill into my arms, settling her on my chest.

"Why do you look so shocked?"

"I'm not."

"Do you think that you're *not* my woman?" I ask calmly and kiss the top of her head.

"I hadn't thought about it."

I roll us to the side, so I can look her in the eye. "Think about it, Jill."

She drags her hand down my cheek. I turn my head to kiss her palm and guide that hand around my back, hugging her close.

"Think about it," I whisper again.

"Okay." She cuddles close to me and yawns.

"Go ahead and sleep, baby. You'll need your strength. I plan to wake you up several times tonight."

She laughs and shakes her head, tracing the tattoo on my bicep. "Yeah, right."

I don't bother to argue. She'll find out soon enough.

"Thank you for being here."

She yawns again and kisses my chest. "You're welcome. What is this tattoo for?"

"It's Seth." I feel her smile.

"How so?"

It's a tribal shamrock in green. "He was born on St. Patrick's Day."

"I love that. What about the eagle on your back?" She pulls away and pushes on my shoulder, making me turn over so she can get a better look.

"The eagle is red, white, and blue, so it's sort of

patriotic." I close my eyes as her sweet fingers trace the outline of the eagle.

"What do these stars mean? The ones that make the eagle look like it's in flight, leaving a trail of stars behind him?" She gently kisses each star. Her touch, her affection, is like a balm to my jagged heart.

"There is a star for each guy I lost in the field."

She presses another kiss to my back and nuzzles her cheek against me. "How many?"

"Sixteen." *Sixteen* good men who lost their lives.

I turn onto my back and scoop her against me, kissing her head and breathing in her delicious scent.

"Were you close to all of them?" she asks softly.

"Some. I witnessed nine of those deaths," I reply. I've never talked about this with anyone before, even Josh.

"What?" She braces herself on her elbows and stares down at me, her eyes wide with horror. "Are you telling me that it could have been *you* to die *nine times*?"

I pull my fingers down her cheek and brush her soft hair back off her face, tucking it behind her ear. "It wasn't me, Jilly."

"Oh my God," she whispers and kisses my cheek, then tucks herself against me as tightly as she can, burrowing her face into my neck and holding on tight. "Zack."

"I'm fine, sugar."

"I'm so sorry," she whispers. "I'm so sorry that you had to go through that."

I rest my lips on the top of her head and glide my fingers up and down her back, comforting her as much as me. "The worst was losing Miles."

"Who was he?" She doesn't pull away.

"I'd been in the same unit with him for years. We deployed together four times. I guess that besides Josh and Ty, he was my best friend."

"How did he die?"

My chest clenches when I think back to that hot day in the desert.

"I'll spare you the details," I whisper and wrap my arms around her, hugging her close. "But our convoy was driving into Baghdad to get more supplies, and we hit an IED. I barely got a scratch. Miles lost both legs and bled out in my arms."

"Zack," she whispers again and lifts her head to kiss me. God, she's so sweet, maybe the most loving woman I've ever met. "I'm so sorry," she repeats.

The feelings I've been fighting for months rise up and overwhelm me, and all I can do is hug her close.

"I'm home, and I'm safe, and that's all that matters."

"Thank God you're safe. Oh my God, Zack, I could have lost you before I ever really found you." She sniffles and I brush a tear off her cheek.

"Don't think that way, baby. You can *what if* all day

long, but the reality is, nothing happened to me, and we're here now."

She nods and settles back down onto my chest. She soon falls asleep. Thor is snoring from his bed in the corner. I wonder if Seth is having fun tonight at his friend's house. They're probably watching horror flicks and eating too much junk food. I'm just thrilled that he's made friends.

The guilt that grips my throat every time I think of my son has loosened with time, but it'll never fully go away.

Not now that I know the battle he survived while I was off fighting a war of my own. If I could kill my ex-wife and every son of a bitch she let lay a hand on my son, I would happily rip them apart, one limb at a time. The best thing that ever happened to Seth and me was the day she brought him here and filed for divorce.

Thank God for that.

Jill stirs in my arms. I kiss her head again and smile. I can't believe she's here. I've wanted her here for months. Hell, years, if I'm being honest.

I don't plan to let her go now.

"Zack, answer the phone," Jill mumbles and nudges my arm. I yawn and turn toward the soft, sleepy woman, wrapping myself around her.

"I can think of better things to do."

"It could be important." She chuckles and climbs

onto my chest as I check the time and answer the phone.

"Hello."

"Hey, Dad." Seth's voice is happy and he's clearly chewing on something crunchy.

"It's seven in the morning, Seth."

"I know. You're awake, right? It's, like, super late for you."

"Actually, I was asleep, but you're right, I should go check on some things. So what's up?" Jill kisses my chest and her hand is roaming over my stomach, and my morning semi-wood is no longer a semi.

"Josiah's dad says the roads are too icy to take me home today, so he said I should just stay here until tomorrow afternoon. Isn't that cool? Please say yes."

"That's fine with me if it's okay with Josiah's dad."

"It is. Cool. Thanks, Dad. How's Thor?"

"Thor misses you, but he's fine. Be good and call me if you need anything."

"Okay. Bye!"

I throw the phone onto the floor and roll Jill beneath me and run into a wall of warm fur.

"Thor jumped up here about an hour ago," Jill informs me with a laugh. I glance over at the dog's face. His chin is resting on his paws, his eyebrows shooting up and down as he looks about innocently.

"You're not innocent, you little mutt."

"Be nice to him," Jill insists and brushes her fingers through my hair. "He's just a baby."

"He's got you wrapped around his paw."

She grins and watches me with a sassy expression on her gorgeous face.

"It seems he's not the only male around here under your spell. I have to let him outside, but I don't want you to move from this exact spot. Understand?"

"Maybe I need to use the bathroom too."

"You have thirty seconds."

I run downstairs with the dog, let him out back, and set on a pot of coffee before returning to my bedroom. Jill is perched on the edge of the bed, the sheet wrapped around her. Her brown hair is tousled and falls around her face and shoulders, and her eyes are still sleepy.

She offers me a shy grin, and my gut clenches in lust and something else I'm not quite ready to recognize. "Hi."

"Hi yourself." I lean my shoulder on the doorjamb and cross my arms over my chest, watching her.

"Everything okay downstairs?"

"Fine," I confirm. "I started some coffee."

"Oh good, thanks." She stands to pull on her clothes, but I move quickly, grab her hand, and pull her behind me to the master bathroom.

"What are you doing?"

"We're going to take a shower."

"I thought we were going to have coffee."

"We will. After our shower. I owe you a few more orgasms." Her jaw drops and she watches as I tug my boxers down and step out of them. "Like what you see?"

To my surprise she reaches out and runs just the tip of her finger down the length of my cock to the tip and back again. "I love this."

I back away before I explode like a teenager and turn on the shower. "Stay with me this weekend."

"I have things to do . . ."

I pull her to me and tilt her chin back. "Stay."

"Okay."

"First things first." I pick her up and carry her into the shower. "I have to dirty you up before we get clean again."

"Oh good. I like getting dirty."

❀   ❀   ❀

"Hi, Max." Jill has Max on speakerphone and is typing furiously on the screen. We've been hanging out at the house today because it's just been too cold outside to show her the ranch. "Yes, I found a few places and was about to send you an email."

"Thanks, Jill. I appreciate it."

She grins and nods. "No problem. Let me know if any of these look good and we'll set up a time to go see them."

"Sounds like a plan," he replies.

"Great. See you soon." She hangs up and her fingers continue to fly over the screen.

"How's Max?" I ask.

"Fine. He's looking for property to buy here."

I nod and curse myself for being jealous. Who the fuck cares if Max wants to buy a house? I like Max. He's my friend.

But I don't love him calling Jillian.

"What have you been doing outside?" she asks while her nails click on her keyboard.

"Checking on things. It's actually warming up out there a bit."

"It's nine at night," she reminds me with a raised brow. "Is it clouding up?"

"Nope, but the ice is melting. In fact"—I walk to her and take her phone, set it aside, and pull her to her feet—"I have something to show you."

"Outside?"

"Yes." I help her step into her boots and bundle her up in her coat and scarf and take her hand in mine, leading her out the back door. We walk past the chicken coop, past the barn to the pasture beyond, where I've laid out a thick quilt to lie on and a quilt to cuddle up in.

"You want me to sit on the snow in the middle of winter at this time of night?"

"No," I reply and guide her onto the quilt. "I want you to lie on it."

She tilts her head, watching me, and I smile. "Trust me."

"Okay." We lie down, side by side, and I pull the heavy quilt over us and we gaze up at the sky.

"I love the sky at night." I turn my head to look at her profile as she stares up at the stars. "Everyone always talks about how big the Montana sky is, especially when it's blue, but honestly, I think it looks bigger, more magnificent, on a clear winter night."

"It's gorgeous," she whispers. "Look! A shooting star!"

"This is what I missed the most," I murmur. "Josh and I used to sneak out at night and come out here to lie in the grass and watch the stars. Of course,"—I laugh and take her hand in mine, linking our fingers—"Mom knew. She just didn't mind that we were sneaking out to look at stars rather than get in trouble."

"Yeah, sounds like you were real party animals."

"That came a bit later."

"Oh my God, Zack, look!" She points to the left, where the mountains loom in the darkness, and I see it too. "Are those the northern lights?"

"Looks like we're gonna get a light show." We watch raptly while green and blue streaks fill the sky above the mountain. "Amazing. I've never seen them before."

"Never?" she asks. I glance over at her. Her eyes are wide with wonder as the colorful lights fill the sky.

"What did you miss the most?" I ask her.

"Cara."

I nod and we lie silently for a long while, watching the night sky give us the best show around.

"Why did you stay away for so long?" she asks softly without looking at me. I didn't plan on this being the time when we'd share our secrets, but it's appropriate. Montana is coming to life around us, and this is the most honest, calm moment of my life.

"War sucked ass," I begin and point to another shooting star. "But living with Kensie was worse." Her hand tightens in mine, but otherwise there is no indication that she's uncomfortable, so I continue. "We got pregnant too young. Way too fucking young. It was a mistake, but I was taught to take care of my responsibilities, so I did. Married her. But with a wife and kid on the way, there was no way I could do college. The army was the best thing for all of us. So we left."

I take a deep breath and let the memories come, wishing it were different.

"It was never good. Kensie is a selfish mess. She was never a touchy-feely mom, and I knew that, but she met Seth's needs. He was just barely in school when I began the deployments, and when I came home on leave, he was always clean and happy."

"What happened?" she asks.

"I don't know for sure. I suspected for a while that Kensie was fucking around behind my back. I hadn't slept with her in years, even when I was home on leave, and that was on purpose. I couldn't stand her. I think that she saw that Seth was getting older, and able to fend for himself, so she left him to do just that. The kid can cook better than I can."

"But?"

*God, I don't want to talk about this part.*

I clear my throat and avoid her eyes when she turns on her side, watching my face.

"Zack?"

"I think she let the fuckers hurt him. Smack him around." I cover my face with my hands and struggle to breathe.

"How do you know?" she asks softly.

"He mentioned it a few times after he started working with Cara, so I put him in counseling."

"He's doing so great, Zack. He's happy and coming out of his shell."

"I know. Thank God. But how could I have left him with her for so long . . ."

"You didn't know."

"I knew she was a selfish bitch."

"You didn't know that she'd allow something so horrible to happen to your son. You don't have to be touchy-feely to be a decent human being, Zack. I'm just thankful that she doesn't have anything more to do with either of you."

"You and me both." I let out the breath I've been holding and kiss her forehead. We settle back on the blanket, watching the sky erupt in red, orange, and blue. "You really need to think about whether or not you want to be involved with me and all of my baggage, sugar. 'Cause I have quite a lot of it."

"Who doesn't?" she scoffs.

"You don't seem to."

She erupts in laughter. "I've learned to cope, Zack. So is this what we're doing? Spilling our guts?"

"I spilled some of mine. Maybe not all."

She nods and thinks about it for a minute, then begins in a soft voice.

"My dad beat the shit out of my mom my whole life, and when Ty was away at college, he almost killed her."

Rage boils up from my gut and my hands curl into fists. Ty is one of my oldest friends, so of course I knew some of what happened when he came home after graduation, but to hear it come from her lips, so matter-of-fact, it pisses me off all over again.

"Seeing Lauren in the hospital after Jack attacked her brought a lot of that baggage to the surface for me. I've had a few bad nights."

"I'm sorry, baby. I wish I'd known."

"I don't think I was ready for you yet," she admits. "And there's more. It's a long story, but the gist of it is, my ex-husband was a cheating bastard. He couldn't keep it in his pants, and I realize now that that wasn't my fault. But one thing you should know is . . ."

She pauses and bites her lip and then glances over at me with scared eyes.

"What?"

"I can't ever have babies, Zack. I can't get pregnant. We tried for years, worked with doctors, and it's just not ever going to happen."

The grief in her voice is my undoing. I pull her into my arms and kiss her head. "I'm sorry. Are you okay?"

"I'm healthy," she confirms. "There's no medical reason for it, it just is. So if you want to run, now might be the right time to do it."

"Stop." I pull back to look her in the eye. "We are going to take this one day at a time, sugar. See where it goes. I haven't really given having more kids much thought. Seth is awesome, and a handful. I just want to enjoy you, continue spending time with you." I lean in to whisper in her ear. "Be inside you as often as humanly possible."

She giggles and kisses my cheek.

"We'll figure the rest out."

"Okay."

"Now, lie back and watch this amazing show I arranged just for you."

"This is pretty impressive," she agrees and snuggles up to my side to watch the sky. We lie in silence for a long while until something suddenly occurs to me.

"Wait. Does this mean we don't need condoms?"

She shrugs nonchalantly and grins. "Maybe."

I cover her body with mine and bury my fingers in her spectacular hair. "Maybe what?"

Her eyes narrow and she suddenly looks uncertain.

"Until our amazing night this summer"—I kiss her lips—"I hadn't been with a woman in close to

FALLING FOR JILLIAN 99

four years. I didn't cheat on my wife, Jill. I've had plenty of workups while in the army and I'm as healthy as can be."

"I had myself checked too, especially after I found out Todd had been . . ." She can't finish the sentence and I smooth my hand down her cheek.

"So, we don't need them?" I ask hopefully.

"I guess not."

I jump up to my feet and tug her up with me, roll the blankets up into a ball, and pull her behind me to the house.

"Hey! What about the big, amazing Montana winter sky?"

"Fuck the sky. I get to sink into you without a barrier between us, and I'm not waiting another minute."

"Thank God."

# CHAPTER

*Seven*

## JILLIAN

"Dad! I'm home!" Seth stomps through the house, greeted by a very excited Thor. "Hey, buddy! Where's Dad?"

"Hey, Seth." It's Sunday morning and Zack and I are in the game room, me working some more on my phone, which makes me crazy—I wish I'd brought my computer—and Zack reading on his iPad. "You're home early."

"Josiah's dad said the roads were good enough, so he brought me home. Why is Jill's car here?" He spies me sitting on the couch and he smiles shyly. "Hi, Jill."

"Hi," I reply with a smile, wondering how Zack is going to explain this. We had agreed that I'd leave before Seth returned home.

"Jill was out here yesterday to see Cara and she

got stuck here because of the weather, just like you got stuck in town. She's waiting for the roads to clear up."

"Oh." He shrugs and pets his dog. "What are we gonna do today?"

"Good question." Zack grins over at me. "Can you stay for the afternoon?"

"If you would both like me to," I reply carefully. "What do you have in mind?"

"It's warm enough to take the snowmobiles out," Zack suggests.

"Woo-hoo!" Seth exclaims and thrusts his fist in the air. "Can I drive?"

"You can drive in the field, where there are no fences or animals," Zack says with a smile. "What do you say?"

Both of them stare at me hopefully. Even Thor looks hopeful with his tongue lolling out of his mouth. They're so handsome, how can I refuse them?

"Come on, Jill," Seth says while bouncing on his toes. "It's so fun! You can ride with me. I'll keep you safe."

Zack's gaze swings down at his son and then back to me with pride. I wink at him and then shrug. "Well, how can I resist that offer? Sounds like fun."

"Go put your stuff in your room, Seth, and then we'll go."

Seth takes off like a shot up the stairs to his room, his dog running with him.

"You don't have to take me along," I say quietly. "I can just go on home and you can spend the afternoon with Seth."

I push my phone in my pocket, and then Zack steps to me and tugs me to my feet and into his arms for a big hug.

"I want you to come with us. It'll be fun."

I lower my voice to a whisper as I hear Seth clomp down the hallway upstairs. "Do you really think you're ready for me to start hanging out with your kid?"

"My kid already knows you, Jillian." He kisses my forehead and then steps away as Seth runs back into the room, dressed in snow pants and jacket.

He stops on a dime and looks back and forth between us with narrowed eyes. Just when I'm sure he's going to ask what's going on, he says, "Can we go now?"

"Let's go," Zack confirms. Seth and Thor run out the back door toward a big garage beside the barn. Zack and I take our time with our coats and boots, gloves and scarves. He tugs the ends of my scarf until I'm plastered up against him so he can steal a quick kiss. "Not gonna be able to do that for a while."

"I think you'll survive it." I shake my head and chuckle when he pushes his fingers into my hair and combs through it.

"Let's go before I carry you upstairs, sugar."

"Dad, are you coming?" Seth yells from inside

the garage. He's already opened the big door and is standing next to the snowmobiles. "Can I take Grandma's? Please?"

Zack looks between Seth and the smaller of the four snowmobiles sitting in the garage.

"I don't know, Seth . . ."

"I've driven it a lot, Dad. I know how to drive it. I'll be very careful, I promise."

"No showing off," Zack warns sternly.

"No way," Seth agrees and hands me a pretty purple helmet. "You can wear Grandma's helmet."

"Thanks." I slip on the helmet and Zack helps me buckle it under my chin before securing his own helmet, then checks to make sure that Seth's is secure as well. Zack pulls the smaller snowmobile out of the garage and sets it up for Seth, then pulls a bigger two-seater out for us.

"Are you ready?" Zack hops on and pats the backseat for me to join him.

"Let's go!" Seth exclaims and drives away carefully.

I wrap my hands around Zack's waist and hold on tight as he sets off after his son. Thor is running through the snow beside his boy, grinning happily. We drive through an empty pasture, where Seth makes several circles, laughing loudly.

His face is red from the cold and bright with happiness, and my stomach clenches at the sight of him. He looks just like his dad, and the change in him from when he first came here is remarkable.

Zack parks and laughs at Seth as he plays in the snow. Thor chases him, barking and bouncing.

"He's wonderful," I tell Zack honestly.

"Yeah, he is. I'm getting him his own snowmobile for Christmas."

"Oh, he's going to *love* that." I grin happily and lean my cheek against Zack's shoulder as we watch his son with the happy dog. "He's the perfect age for it."

"I agree. Plus, it's my first Christmas with him in a long time. I want it to be special."

Seth makes a wide circle, then drives toward us, and when he's about ten yards away, he makes a sharp turn, sending snow spraying up onto us.

"Oh that's cold!" I laugh and wipe the snow off my face with my glove.

"And he's just declared war." Zack laughs and hops off his seat, scoops up some snow, and throws it at his son, hitting him square in the face.

Seth stops, shuts off his vehicle, and we all proceed to have a snowball fight. Seth hides behind his snowmobile, throws snow, then ducks back for safety.

"You can't hide forever!" I yell just before Zack stuffs a handful of snow down the back of my jacket. "Ooh, Zack, you're a dead man."

I chase Zack down and tackle him in the snow. It's knee-deep and difficult to run in. My plan to smear snow in his face once I tackle him backfires when he rolls me onto my back and tickles me mercilessly.

"Stop!" I cry, giggling so hard it's impossible to understand the word.

"I'll save you, Jill!" Seth cries and jumps on his dad's back, knocking him off me. I scramble to my knees and scoop up snow and throw it at Zack, hitting him in the face.

"My hero!"

"That's right!" Seth laughs and then tosses a snowball for Thor to chase after. "I saved her."

Zack runs after Seth now, lifts him up off the ground and spins around, then dumps him in the snow.

"You ganged up on me," Zack accuses.

"Well, duh," I reply with a smirk.

"You're the one who told me not to pick on girls, Dad." Seth rolls his eyes and lies back on the snow, panting. "This is fun."

I join Seth, lying on my back, looking around at the trees around the pasture. "Are there bears out here?"

Seth giggles. "They're hibernating."

"What about mountain lions?"

"The snowmobiles scared them off, if there were any," Zack informs me.

"What about Bigfoot?"

Both boys grow quiet and I look around to find them both smiling at me.

"You're such a *girl*," Seth accuses and giggles again. "There's no such thing as Bigfoot."

"I've seen movies on TV that say there is," I inform him. "There's footage."

"There's footage of a moron in a gorilla suit, Jilly," Zack says with a laugh.

"Okay, what about wolves?"

Seth glances around with suddenly sober eyes. "We had wolves last summer."

"There aren't any here now," Zack assures him.

"Are you really afraid of animals?" Seth asks.

"Nah, I just wanted to know if there were any."

"Good." Seth tosses a ball of snow in the air and sputters when it falls into his face.

"That was smart." I laugh. "What goes up must come down."

Thor lies next to Seth, tongue hanging out as he pants happily.

"It's so quiet out here," I comment and watch my breath come in feathery puffs. The earth is still around us. Every once in a while, a patch of snow will fall off a tree branch, but aside from our breathing, that's the only sound.

"So this is turning to naptime in the pasture?" Zack asks. "I thought we were going to ride snowmobiles."

"Let's go!" Seth jumps up and tightens the strap on his helmet before sitting on his vehicle.

"I want to drive." I bat my eyes up at Zack. "Please."

"Have you driven one of these before?"

"Of course," I scoff. "You can sit behind me and hold on tight."

Seth starts his engine and Zack leans in to speak directly into my ear. "I know how I'd like to hold on to you, sugar."

"Stop." I giggle and glance over at Seth, who is happily driving in circles and calling out to his dog.

"He's not paying us any attention," Zack replies with a smile. "And I kind of like that blush on your cheeks."

I shake my head and climb on, start the engine, and motion for Zack to climb on behind me.

"I'm ready," he says with a smile in his voice.

"Hold on!" I call over my shoulder and then set off across the pasture. Seth whoops and follows. We drive past an old, huge tree, circle around, and head back the way we came. Poor Thor is getting tired, so Seth and Zack switch places. Seth holds on to me and Zack pulls the dog up on the seat in front of him, caging him with his arms, and we all ride back to the garage.

"That was awesome!" Seth exclaims as he hops off. "You drive pretty good for a girl."

I pull my helmet off and shake my hair out, laughing. "Gee, thanks. I think. You drive pretty well for a little kid."

"I'm not little," he disagrees and stands next to me when I climb off the seat. "See? I'm as tall as you."

"You are getting tall. You're going to be as tall as your dad and your uncle." I push my fingers through his dark hair and smile at him. "And just as handsome."

"Dad's not handsome." Seth winces and sticks his tongue out. "He's the ugliest ever."

"And now you're grounded for a year, brat." Zack chimes in.

Seth laughs and pats his dog on the head. "No I'm not."

"Are too."

"Not."

"Admit it. I'm good-lookin'."

"You're gross!" Seth laughs and runs out of the garage toward the house.

"Did you have fun?" Zack cups my face in his hands and lowers his head to kiss me lightly.

"I had a great time."

"Stay for dinner."

"I should go home before it freezes up again and I'm stuck out here."

Zack sighs and drags his thumb over my bottom lip, sending shivers down my spine. "We'll eat early. I promise."

"Well, twist my arm." He smiles and pulls me out of the garage, locking up behind us, and leads me back to the house. Seth and Thor are already settled in the living room. Seth has stripped out of his wet gear and is sitting on the floor, controller in hand, playing a video game. Thor is curled up snoring before the fire.

"Jill! Come play with me."

"Do you need help with dinner?" I ask Zack, but he's already shaking his head no. "Go play. I'm just going to put on a pot of chili and mix up some corn bread. Nothing fancy."

"Just call me if you need me."

"Will do." He kisses my forehead and then leaves me alone with his son.

"What are we playing today?"

"LEGO Batman," Seth replies and passes me a controller.

"No racing today?"

"We can race if you wanna." He shrugs, like it doesn't matter at all to him.

"No, this is fine. I'll watch you first and be player two."

"Okay."

We scoot onto our bellies and Seth teaches me how to maneuver around the LEGO world of Gotham City.

"Ha!" I exclaim and offer my fist for a bump. "This game rocks."

"You're good," Seth admits with admiration. "You're a fast learner."

"Thanks."

"Are you guys having fun?"

I glance back over my shoulder to find Zack leaning against the back of the couch.

"How long have you been there?" I ask.

"Long enough to see you kick my son's butt at this game."

"She did not! I let her win."

"I creamed you, squirt." I laugh evilly, climb to my feet, and stretch my arms up over my head.

"Rematch!" Seth declares.

"Dinner's ready," Zack says and shakes his head. "Rematch after dinner!"

"I have to drive back to town. I don't want to get stuck out here again."

"It's cool out here." Seth wanders into the kitchen to scout out dinner, leaving Zack and me alone. Thor wakes and trots after his boy, not ready to let him out of his sight yet.

"Yeah, it's cool out here," Zack whispers and kisses my cheek.

"You know I can't stay."

He sighs and nods, takes my hand in his, kisses my knuckles, and then leads me into the kitchen.

"Smells great, Dad."

Seth and Zack set the table and move easily about the kitchen together, clearly used to their own special rhythm. I can picture them like this every night at dinnertime, and a part of me yearns to be a part of it every day.

And that's just silly.

Isn't it?

"What did you and your friend do this weekend, Seth?" I ask as he sits at the table and Zack sets a pot of steaming chili on a cast-iron trivet and then sits next to me.

"Mostly annoyed his older brother." Seth shrugs and then grins. "He's sixteen and has a girlfriend. So we stole his cell phone and made prank calls to her."

I cover my mouth with my hand and do my best

not to laugh, but I can't help the giggle that escapes.
"That's not very nice."

"He got us back."

"What did he do?" Zack asks and passes me the
corn bread.

"He spit in our sodas." Seth shrugs like it's no big
deal and I cringe. "We drank them anyway."

"Ew."

"Don't do that again, Seth." Zack chuckles and
covers his face with his hand.

"It's just spit."

"We're at the dinner table," Zack reminds him
sternly. "Don't talk about that here."

"You asked." He shrugs again and slips a piece
of corn bread to Thor. "Other than that, we played
games and watched TV and stuff."

"Did you have fun?" I ask.

"Yeah, Josiah's mom made cookies and she let us
eat them when they were still hot from the oven." He
sets his spoon in his bowl and frowns up at Zack. "I
don't think Mom ever made cookies."

Zack stiffens beside me and I lay my hand on his
thigh. He clears his throat. "She didn't like to cook
much."

Seth nods and then frowns again. "Jill, do you like
to cook?"

"Yeah, when I have time to."

"Do you make cookies like Josiah's mom and
Grandma?"

"Sometimes. I like to make sugar cookies at Christmastime." I grin, an idea forming in my head. "Speaking of which, it's almost Christmas and I haven't made any cookies yet this year. Maybe you and your dad can come to my place sometime soon to make some."

"Can we, Dad?"

I glance up into Zack's deep brown gaze and smile encouragingly.

"Are you sure?"

"Of course. I can't eat all those cookies by myself."

"Cool."

"Thanks," Zack murmurs with a grin. "That sounds like fun."

For the rest of the meal, Seth fills us in on happenings at school, and reminds his dad that baseball tryouts are in March.

"Yes, I know. You've told me five times, and March is still almost four months away, so we have plenty of time."

"I don't want you to forget."

"Trust me, I won't."

"Okay." Seth slurps his chili and when he's finished, he immediately rinses his bowl and loads the dishwasher. "Are you finished, Jill?"

"Yes, thank you."

He clears the table, loads the dishes, and then stops next to his father.

"Can I go back to my game, Dad?"

"After you hug me."

Seth rolls his eyes, but hugs his dad tight around his neck.

"I'll see you soon, Seth. I think I'm going to head home."

"Okay. Thanks for playing with me."

"I had fun," I say and smile widely, meaning every word.

Seth and Thor walk into the living room and within seconds we hear the game resume.

"I'll walk you out. I don't want you to get stuck driving on icy roads."

"I don't want that either," I reply while Zack helps me with my jacket. He follows me out to my car, waits for me to throw my purse inside and start the engine, then pulls me into his arms. He tucks me against his chest and rocks me slowly back and forth. His heart is beating steadily against my cheek and he smells so delicious, I just want to climb him.

"I had the best weekend I've had in a long, long time. Thank you for that." His words are softly spoken against my head. He presses a kiss to the crown of my head and leans back to look into my face.

"I enjoyed it too. Thank you for everything."

"I'm not quite ready to let you go home."

I chuckle and push my fingers through his brown hair. "It'll be okay. Go spend some time with your boy. You obviously missed him."

He nods and kisses my forehead. "I'll call you tonight to check in. I want to see you this week."

"Yes, sir." I offer him a mock salute and then smile softly. "I'd like that too."

He kisses me sweetly, then holds my door open for me.

"Text me when you get home. I'll worry."

I nod and wave before putting my new car in gear and pulling away from Zack's house, knowing full well that everything has changed.

I'm falling for those two men.

# CHAPTER

*Eight*

It's been three days since I spoke to Zack. I called when I arrived home from the ranch Sunday night to let him know I was safe, we spoke for a few minutes, and that's been it.

My phone isn't malfunctioning. I called my cell carrier to check.

*Pathetic.*

On my way home from my last home showing of the day, I call Cara.

"Hello?"

"Hey, please tell me you're still in town."

"I'm just leaving the school now. What's up?"

"Wanna come over to my place for coffee? I have information that I'm pretty sure you'll enjoy." I pull into my driveway and bite my lip. I'm going nuts. It's time to bring in the girlfriends to yank me back from the ledge.

"Sure. Should I pick Lo up on my way?"

"Sounds good. I'll put the coffee on now."

"See you in a few."

I tromp through the freshly fallen snow and into the house. Thank God it's warm in here. Whatever magic the furnace guy used has worked.

I set the coffee on, change out of my work clothes into jeans and an old sweatshirt, and pile my hair into a knot just as my doorbell rings.

"We're here!" Cara calls.

"And we brought brownies!" Lauren says in a sing-song, making me grin.

"You're lifesavers," I assure them and lead them into the kitchen. I pour us all a cup of coffee, set cream and sugar on the table, and we dig into the brownies without plates or forks. They won't survive long enough for that.

"So, what's going on?" Lo asks around a large bite of chocolaty goodness.

"I'm being a girl."

Cara rolls her eyes and sips her coffee. "Oh good. 'Cause you *are* a girl."

I sit back in my chair and lick chocolate off my lip. "I sort of have news."

My friends share a glance and then both lean in closer to me.

"Spill," Lo commands.

"I slept with Zack."

They blink at me for a moment before breaking out in wide grins.

"You owe me twenty," Cara tells Lo. "I told you it would happen before Christmas."

"You had a fucking *bet* going on whether or not I'd bang Zack?"

"Of course. The sexual chemistry between you two is off the charts. It was just a matter of time." Lo shakes her head.

"When did you say it would happen?" I ask her.

"I thought you'd hold out until New Year's."

I laugh and then shrug, already feeling better. "Well, it happened."

"When?" Cara asks and dives back into the pan of brownies.

"Last weekend. Seth spent the weekend at a friend's house, so I went to the ranch."

"Hold up." Cara holds up a hand and then shoves it through her hair. "You were at the ranch all weekend and I never saw you once?"

"It's a big ranch, Cara."

"Okay, so get to the good stuff," Lauren interrupts. "Tell us everything."

"Well, at first I wasn't going to sleep with him. We were just going to hang out."

"Yeah, I tried that with Josh," Cara says. "It obviously didn't work for me either. The King boys are just too hot for that."

"Yeah, and then the roads got too icy for me to drive back to town, and then one thing led to another, and then next thing I knew it was Sunday and Seth was home and we were snowmobiling and playing video games and having dinner." I pull my knees up to my chest and wrap my arms around my legs.

"So it didn't suck," Cara says.

"No, it was fun."

"What's the problem?" Lo asks.

"Well, I spoke with Zack that night after I got home, but haven't heard a word from him since then. I've texted him a couple of times, but nothing." I shrug in exasperation.

"It's only been three days," Cara says with a frown.

"He said he wanted to see me this week and would call." I sound ridiculous. "Am I becoming one of those girls who checks her phone every three seconds and stalks his social media?"

"Zack doesn't do any social media," Cara replies with a grin.

"I know, I checked—and that makes me a tiny bit psycho."

Lauren laughs. "Did you drive past his house? Call his mom? Hire a PI?"

"Of course not."

"Then I'd say you're good."

"Why didn't you just call one of us to talk it out?" Cara asks. "I live on the same property. I have the inside scoop, you know."

"What do you know?" I lower my legs and help myself to a brownie.

"Well, he probably didn't call because he's been in the barn with a sick horse for the best part of the last few days." Cara sips her coffee and I feel like the biggest idiot on the face of the earth.

"I'm a moron," I whisper.

"No, you're just a woman who wants attention from the man she's currently sleeping with," Lauren replies and pats my shoulder. "That's understandable."

"He said he'd call, and when he didn't, it pissed me off. Most men promise the world and then typically end up disappointing you."

"Not always. You've just had shitty luck with men." Cara crosses to the coffeepot to refill our cups. "He'll call. He and Josh have been out with the vet and that horse almost nonstop. The poor thing."

I take a deep breath and let it out slowly. "He could have at least returned my texts."

"Zack's famous for forgetting his phone in the house. It's not yet habit to grab it—he spent too many years in the field and they didn't have cell phones out there."

I nod thoughtfully. She's right. Of course he was too busy being worried about getting blown up by a roadside bomb to think about carrying a cell phone.

And I'm acting like a lovesick teenager. "I need to get a grip," I mutter in disgust.

"I think it's great." Lauren stirs her coffee and then props her elbows on the table and takes a sip. "I hope it works out."

"We're just getting to know each other better."

"Yeah, while nekkid," Cara says with a giggle.

"That's the best part," Lo agrees. "What about Seth?"

"What about him?"

"How is he reacting to it?"

"Good question," Cara agrees.

"He doesn't know that we're seeing each other. We all hung out together on Sunday and it went really well." I shrug and smile. "Zack's a great dad. They're adorable together. I don't know who's more endearing: Zack, Seth, or that sweet dog of theirs."

"So you're cool with hanging out with Seth. It's not just about the sex with his dad." Lauren is watching me calmly and Cara tips her head to the side, waiting for my answer.

"I don't know what this is yet, but it's not just sex," I admit softly. "If that was the case, I wouldn't have stayed around after Seth got home. The sex is great, but so is just being with them. I like them."

"Awesome." Cara grins as Lo yawns.

"I'm sorry," Lo says and blinks rapidly. "I'm not sure why, but I get so tired around this time of day."

"Late nights with Ty?" Cara asks with a knowing smile.

"That must be it."

"Ew." I wrinkle my nose and shudder. "I do not want to hear about my brother and late nights."

"It's not just late at night," Lo adds with an evil grin.

"Yuck." I cover my ears with my hands and laugh. "Stop talking."

"Okay, okay, since you've had a rough week, I'll go easy on you." Lo laughs and then claps her hands. "Oh! The torchlight parade up at the Whitetail Mountain ski resort is happening next weekend! We're all going, right?"

"Absolutely," Cara replies immediately as I nod. "Grace and Jacob invited us all to join them at the lodge for the best seats up there."

"I love it when we know the right people." I sigh happily and sip the last of my coffee. "How are they, anyway? I haven't talked to Grace in a while."

"They seem to be having fun," Cara says. Grace was a college classmate of Cara's and they've been good friends ever since. After we all gave Grace lessons at the ski resort last month, Grace fell in love with the owner of the resort, Jacob Baxter.

"They make such a cute couple," Lo says with a sigh. "I love a sweet love story."

"Of course you do. You write them," I remind her. Lauren is a successful author. We couldn't be more proud of her.

"I wouldn't say I write *sweet* love stories."

"You write sexy love stories," Cara agrees. "And we appreciate them."

As the conversation segues to Lo's current project, I sit back and nibble a brownie, thankful for these two women and their amazing friendship.

Men may come and go, but my friends will be a part of my life forever, and that is the best thing I could ever ask for.

❈  ❈  ❈

The girls have just left and I pop the last bite of brownie in my mouth just as my phone rings. I grin when I see Zack's name.

"Hello?"

"Fuck, it's good to hear your voice," he replies. His voice is rough and low, and my thighs immediately clench.

"How are you?" I ask and bite my lip as I lower myself onto my couch.

"It's been a shitty few days. I'm sorry I didn't respond to your texts, sugar."

"Is everything okay now?" I ask, trying to keep my voice level.

"We had a very sick horse on our hands, but it looks like she's out of the woods now." He sighs deeply and I can hear the fatigue in his voice. "I just woke up from a few hours' sleep, and I'd like to come to town and take you out to dinner."

"I can hear how exhausted you are, Zack," I say softly. "You should rest."

"The only thing I need right now is food and you."

"What about Seth?" I ask tentatively. "I don't want to take you away from time with him."

"He's been staying with Mom and Dad for the past few days because I've been in and out so sporadically. He's happy as can be, getting spoiled by my mom and decorating his bedroom over there."

"They gave him his own room?"

"He's the only grandchild. Of course they did." He chuckles softly. "So, Seth is fine, and I want to spend some time with you."

"I'd like that," I admit quietly. "I just have to change my clothes and I'll be ready to go."

"I'm on my way." Just as I think he's going to hang up, he says, "And Jilly? Don't bother with panties. You won't need them."

The line goes dead and I stare at my phone for several seconds before laughing and rushing to the bathroom to take a very quick shower. I touch up my makeup and brush out my hair, then dress in a tight pair of jeans and a black low-cut blouse with a push-up bra that shows the girls off to their fullest potential.

I slip on a pair of boots with four-inch heels and take a twirl in front of the mirror.

Not bad, if I do say so myself.

I walk into the living room just as the doorbell rings.

"Hey, handsome." I grin and step back as Zack's jaw drops and his eyes roam from the top of my head down to the heels on my feet.

"Fuck me, you're beautiful, Jilly." He pulls me into his arms and kisses me, urgently. "I missed you this week."

"I missed you too. I thought maybe you weren't going to call."

"Fuck," he whispers and leans his forehead on mine. "I'm sorry. The days just got away from me, and I was in the barn more than I was at the house."

"It's okay." I shake my head and push my fingers through his soft, dark hair. "I hope the horse is better now?"

"So far, yeah." He nods and then grins down at me before gently brushing his lips over mine one more time. "Are you really going to try to walk through the snow in these fuck-me boots?"

"I'll be fine," I insist. "I was going for sexy."

"You've achieved it. I can't get much harder." I cock a brow and boldly glide my hand down his chest to cup his hard-on in my hand. "I stand corrected. That did it."

"Very nice, Sergeant King."

"Dinner first," he growls and cups my face in his hands, kissing me yet again.

"Let's go."

He helps me out to his truck, patiently guiding me through the snow in my heels.

"I can't believe you're wearing those in this weather."

"I won't fall," I assure him and then damned if I don't slip. I catch myself, but Zack turns and lifts me into his arms, carrying me the rest of the way to his truck. "This is excellent service."

"Yes, ma'am," he says with a grin. "I can't have you falling. You'll break your neck in those things."

"You don't like them?" I pout.

"I fucking love them, sugar. Wear them anytime

you want. I'll carry you." He winks and kisses my cheek before setting me gently in the cab of his truck.

"What are you in the mood for?" Zack asks as he pulls out of my driveway.

"I already ate a third of a pan of brownies today, so we might as well indulge in some greasy bar food."

"Bar food it is." He takes my hand and kisses my knuckles as he easily maneuvers through the streets to downtown Cunningham Falls.

"My house is so close, we almost could have walked here."

"Not in those boots." He laughs and parks, helps me out of the truck, and leads me into the dimly lit bar. There is a small kitchen immediately to the left, where we place our order, then go to find a table in the heart of the bar.

Because it's a weeknight, it's relatively quiet. We choose a table near the back, by the pool tables.

"Shall we play?" Zack asks, pointing to the table.

"I don't really know how." I shrug and bat my eyes innocently. "But I guess we can play. Will you show me?"

"Sure." He grins widely and hangs our coats on the backs of our chairs before choosing two pool cues. He's delicious in another pair of faded blue jeans and a fitted blue T-shirt. He's wearing Chucks, which surprises me but completes his outfit perfectly.

He's just yummy.

"I'll break," he offers and sets up the balls while I order us both a beer from the waitress.

"Good idea."

He takes his shot and scatters the balls, and when a solid goes in the corner pocket, he says, "Looks like I'm solids."

"You are solid, yes," I agree and run my hand down his arm, feeling his muscles. "I like it."

"Are you going to be trouble all night?" he growls in my ear.

"I don't know what you mean." I smile serenely and point to the table. "Your shot."

He chalks his cue and watches me with narrowed eyes, and a half smile on his lips, then takes a shot, missing the pocket.

"My turn." I circle the table, looking for my shot. Of course, I lied through my teeth to Zack. I played pool all the time in college, and I'm damn good at it.

Not that he needs to know that.

I make sure I find a shot that puts my ass in his line of vision as I bend over the table and take a shot, sinking the ball.

"Oh, yay! That must have been a lucky shot." I wink at him and then bite my lip at the look of lust in his eyes. He's leaning against his stool, his arms crossed over his chest, showing off the bulge in his arms.

Christ on a crutch, I want to attack him.

I circle the table and find my next shot, on the opposite side of the table, bend deep so he can see my cleavage, and shoot the ball, missing the pocket.

"Don't think I'm not onto your game, sugar."

"I'm playing pool." I shrug and smile at the waitress who delivers our food. Zack takes a huge bite of his burger and then walks around the table and takes several shots, sinking all of the balls.

I nibble on my buffalo chicken fingers with sour cream and chive fries—really, I'll be eating yogurt for a month to make up for this meal—and watch the sexiness that is Zack move around the table.

"Nice shot," I say when he sinks his fourth ball in a row.

"Thanks." He shoves some fries in his mouth and wanders back to the table. And for the next while, we eat and play in companionable silence, high-fiving when we sink the ball, and rooting for each other.

When we've finished eating, and begun our third game, someone puts some money in the old-fashioned jukebox and a classic Aerosmith song comes on. I shake my hips to the rhythm and dance around the table, looking for a shot. I lean over the table, still swaying my hips and shoot, missing the hole.

"Stay where you are," Zack commands in a low voice.

I look up at him, startled, to find his brown eyes feral and trained on my ass. He walks around the table, glides one hand down my hip and butt cheek, then pulls my back against his chest and presses his mouth to my ear.

"Do you enjoy torturing me like that, Jilly?"

"Like what?" I ask breathlessly.

"Swaying your hips, walking around in these boots, bending over the table to show me your chest. I'm permanently hard here, sweetheart."

I sigh against him and smile when he wraps both arms around me, hugging me tightly. "Let me stay with you tonight."

"Absolutely."

"I'm telling you now, I'll have to leave very early to get back to the ranch. Josh is covering for me tonight, but I'll need to be back early to help and to drive Seth down to the bus stop because it's too far to walk in the snow—"

"Zack, I don't mean to sound like an insensitive ass right now, but it's been three days since we had sex, and I'm having a hard time focusing here. I won't be mad that you're leaving early in the morning."

He groans and presses a kiss to my cheek, then retrieves our coats, throws some bills on the table for our waitress, and leads me out to the truck.

"By the way," I mention casually as he drives as quickly as he can while still staying safe, which is faster than I would have thought, back to my place. "I'm not wearing any panties."

He throws me a glance and then presses down on the accelerator even more, cussing under his breath.

"Stay put," he instructs me when we pull up to my house. He comes around to my door, lifts me out of the truck, and carries me through the yard to the front door.

"And they say chivalry is dead." My voice is dripping with sarcasm, but Zack laughs and waits patiently as I unlock the door.

When we're finally inside, Zack bolts the door behind us, then turns to me, and we immediately start tearing at each other's clothes, scattering them about the room. I have to unzip and yank off my boots to get my tight jeans down my legs.

"Next time, you keep the boots on," Zack murmurs. "They're fucking hot."

"So noted," I reply and jump up into his arms, wrap my legs around his waist, and hold on as he carries me to my bedroom. "God, you feel good."

My hands won't stop roaming over his skin, his shoulders, his arms. I can't wait to feel his back and stomach.

His cock.

"So do you, baby." He lowers me to the bed and joins me, covering me with his large body. He rests his full cock against my folds, but doesn't enter me as he kisses me with a fever unlike any I've ever seen. We've been starved for each other, and it's only been a few days since we were last together.

With one hand in his hair, I glide the other down his back to his ass and hold on tightly, loving the way the muscles clench and move under my hand as he rocks his pelvis against my own.

"You're so fucking wet," he growls as his cock slides effortlessly through my dripping lips.

"Since the moment I saw you," I agree and then

bite my lip when he pulls up to look down at me. "Should I not have said that?"

"I love that you said that," he says as he pulls his knuckles down my cheek. "I've had a hard-on since the moment I heard your voice today."

"Can you turn onto your back please?"

He frowns for a moment and then complies, dragging me with him. I shimmy down his body and before he can blink, I take his cock in my hand and wrap my lips around the head, sucking firmly.

"Holy fucking hell, Jilly!"

"Mmm," I reply and begin to move quickly up and down, pumping my hand in sync with my mouth, making him crazy. He plunges his hands in my hair and holds on for dear life as I fuck him with my mouth.

"That's right, sugar. Suck it." He groans and flops his head back on the bed, then looks back down at me, watching. His abs tighten with the movement, begging me to brush my hand over them, up to his chest, over his nipples, and back down the small trail of dark hair that leads to his dick. "You look amazing, Jill."

I kiss his thighs and work my way up his body, straddling him, then guide his thick cock to my entrance, and sink down onto him.

"Ah shit," I moan as I sink down as far as I can. He's filling me, completely. His hands glide from my breasts to my hips and back again, as though they can't decide where they most want to be.

"You're so fucking gorgeous," he growls, watching me with hot eyes as I begin to ride him. I circle my clit with one hand and ride him earnestly, and his eyes glaze over. "That's right. Touch yourself, baby. Oh God, you're clenching around me like a fist."

He sucks in a breath and watches as I continue to masturbate while riding him. His eyes finally meet mine and he bites his lip as he grips my wrist in his hand and brings the fingers to his own lips, licks them, and then kisses them as he sits up straight and wraps his arms around me. He takes control, holding me still as he thrusts in and out of me, his eyes never leaving mine.

"I fucking love your pussy," he whispers and nibbles at my lips. "Your mouth. Your tits."

"I love it when you talk dirty," I reply and moan when he pulls me down onto him, so hard I almost see stars. "Fuck me, Zack."

"I am," he replies with a wolfish grin. "And I plan to for a while yet."

"Oh God, I'm going to come, baby."

"The only thing better than watching you come is making you come, Jilly." He kisses me hard and thrusts deep and I come apart, shivering. I wrap my arms around his neck and hug him close.

"I missed you," I whisper into his ear.

# CHAPTER

*Nine*

## ZACK

"She's doin' better, boss," Louie assures me as he runs his hand down Lily's flank. Louie has been a ranch hand at the Lazy K since I was a kid. I trust him completely—with our animals, our land, and our family.

"You gave us a scare, didn't you, girl?" I pet her neck and smile when she nudges my face with her muzzle, asking for apples. "You can have apples in a few more days."

"Nothin' more frustrating than watching a horse with colic," Louie says with a shake of the head.

"Or more exhausting," I agree. "I'm pretty strong, but I'm not built to make a horse stand on her feet when she doesn't want to."

"You did good, son." Louie scratches his head and nods at my dad and Josh as they come into the barn.

"How's our Lily this morning?" Dad asks as he claps Louie on the shoulder. The two men have had an employer/employee relationship for close to thirty years and are also the best of friends.

"She's holding her own, finally."

Josh steps into the stall to give the horse some attention. Dad watches with pride in his eyes, takes a quick glance around, and then says, "I'd like to steal Louie away for a few hours and mend some fence in the west pasture. That last snowstorm was a bitch."

"So much for retirement," Josh says tauntingly.

"Your mother has me signing up for exercise classes at that new fancy gym in town and volunteered me to help with the winter carnival. For God's sake, son, cut an old man a break."

"This is your ranch, Dad." I laugh and carry tack to the other side of the barn. "You're welcome to do whatever you want."

"Exactly," he agrees with a grumble. "And if I have to watch one more episode of *Diners, Drive-Ins and Dives*, I'm going to lose my mind. Now your mother wants to buy an RV and drive around the country, trying all those places to eat. I'll weigh four hundred pounds before a month is out."

Josh is laughing in earnest now, and Louie is coughing, masking his own laughter.

"Mom just wants you to enjoy retirement, Dad," I assure him.

"I'll enjoy it just fine right here, riding my damn horses and checking the fence."

"Well then, let's see to it." Louie motions for Dad to lead him outside. "Call if you need us, boys."

When the barn door closes, Josh and I shake our heads at each other and grin. "I hope he never retires," I say.

"He'd go crazy, and Mom knows it. She just likes to rile him up."

"Seems all the King women enjoy doing that."

Josh nods and pats Lily on the neck, then walks out of the stall and closes it behind him. "So how is Jilly?"

"She's doing well."

"Okay, stubborn ass, how are things with *you* and Jilly?"

I fold a saddle blanket and throw it on a pile of blankets and then prop my hands on my hips. "It's going . . . really well."

"That's great."

"Is it?" I rub my fingers over my lips as I think about the beautiful woman that has managed to capture my heart in such a short amount of time.

"Why wouldn't it be? Jill's awesome."

"I feel like a selfish bastard, J."

"Why?" He frowns at me and leans his hips against the wall. "Does she think it's more than you do?"

"No, it's not just sex for me, man. She's amazing. Funny. Smart as hell and yeah, she's sexy as fuck. But

Jesus, is it fair to ask her to take on all of my fucking baggage?"

"Did you ask *her* that?"

"Yeah."

"What did she say?"

"That she has baggage of her own." I shrug and pace around the barn. "But seriously, I have a kid who is about to be a teenager, and we all know how hard that's gonna be."

"Seth is great, and he'll be easier than you think."

"I have a bitch of an ex-wife . . ."

"Who you never hear from, thank God."

"I have guilt issues from when I was deployed . . ."

"That you're working through."

I stop and glare at my brother.

"Seems to me," he continues, "that you have a lot of excuses, but I think you're just scared."

"I'm not scared of a girl," I scoff and then I swallow hard. "Holy fuck, I'm terrified. This is worse than taking fire in the red zone."

"Yeah, Cara still scares the shit out of me," Josh agrees with a grin. "But she's so damn worth it." He sobers, watching me closely. "Are you planning to end it?"

"No," I reply quickly. "I don't want to end it. I tried to stay away from her for months, and it was torture."

"You need to talk to Seth. This is a small town and word travels fast."

"What have you heard?"

"Just that you two were getting pretty cozy at the bar last week."

An image of Jillian in those fucking amazing boots, her ass showcased in her tight jeans and that rich, dark hair cascading down her back has my dick on full alert. Has it already been a week?

"And," he continues, "I know that you've seen her a few times since then. Eventually someone will say something in front of Seth."

"You're right." I nod and walk back to Lily, who is hanging her head over her stall door, begging for some attention. "I'll talk to him today. It's either going to go very well or fucking horribly."

"I think he'll be okay." Josh shrugs and offers me a smile. "He likes Jill."

"Thanks, man." My phone rings in my pocket, startling me. "Still not used to carrying this bastard."

"I'm surprised you do," Josh says.

"I missed some texts from Jill last week. Don't want to repeat that."

"You're already whipped." Josh grins as I flip him off and answer the phone.

"Hey, sugar."

"Hi," she replies with a smile in her voice. "Do you and Seth have plans for after school?"

"It's Friday, but he's not going to Josiah's this weekend. I'm sick of sharing custody of my kid with that family."

Jill laughs and my heart tightens in my chest.

Josh continues to grin, watching me unabashedly, clearly listening to every word she says, like he used to do when we were teenagers and a girl I liked was on the phone. So I flip him off again, making him laugh.

"Well, why don't you and Seth meet me at my house and we'll bake those cookies I promised him?"

"We'd enjoy that. I'll order in pizza for dinner."

"My hero." She laughs and I can imagine her tucking her hair behind her ear in that way she does that makes me want to lean in and nibble on her earlobe.

"Seth gets out at two thirty. Does that work?"

"Perfectly. I'll see you then. Bye, handsome."

"Bye, Jilly."

I hang up and turn to find Josh standing with his arms crossed over his chest and a shit-eating grin on his face.

"God, you're ugly," I toss at him for lack of anything else.

"You look just like me, brother."

"Impossible. I'm much better looking." Josh laughs and slaps me on the shoulder.

"Gonna go bake some cookies?" He wiggles his eyebrows at me suggestively and I punch him in the arm. Hard.

"Don't be an asshole. My kid will be there."

"Hi, guys!" Jill opens the door wide to let us in. Her cheeks are flushed and her hair is tucked up into some kind of knot on the top of her head. She's in a red T-shirt and black stretchy pants. She's barefoot, so I see that her red toenail polish matches her shirt, and I want to scoop her up and make that flush on her cheeks spread all over her body.

But instead of throwing herself into my arms, she ruffles Seth's hair and smiles at him happily.

"Where's Thor?"

"In the truck," I reply.

"Why?" she asks.

"Dad said he couldn't come inside and ruin all of your nice things."

"Nonsense. Thor won't ruin anything. Go get him."

Seth turns to me excitedly. "Can I, Dad?"

"Her house, her rules." I grin down at my boy as he runs back outside to fetch his pup, then turn and pull Jill into my arms. "Hey, sugar."

"It's good to see you," she replies with a soft smile. "You did that on purpose, didn't you?"

"I had to have a reason to get to do this," I reply and lean down to take her sweet lips with mine. God, she tastes like chocolate and coffee and *Jill* and I know I could get drunk off her lips alone.

"Okay, Thor peed outside already!" Seth announces as he stumbles inside with the happy dog. "About three times."

"Hi, Thor." Jill greets the clumsy black Lab with ear rubs and a kiss to the head, then motions for us all to follow her to the kitchen after we hang our coats on the coat tree and slip out of our boots. "I put a blanket on the floor for Thor so he'd have a comfy spot."

"Thor is a spoiled dog," I murmur and smile down at her. "And thank you."

"What kind of cookies are we making?" Seth asks as he boosts himself onto a stool at the breakfast bar.

"All different kinds, and don't get too comfy there, mister, 'cause you're helping." She smiles at Seth and then at me. "We're all worker bees around here."

"Okay, Sergeant King and Private King reporting for duty, ma'am," I say and stand at attention. Seth follows suit and we both salute her, making her laugh.

"First order of business for both of you is to wash your hands. God only knows where they've been. Especially you." She points at Seth, who laughs as he turns on the faucet.

"Yeah, you don't wanna know," he says.

"I'm going to slip an apron on," she continues and pulls a white apron over her head and tries to tie it in the back, but her hands get tangled. I turn her away from me and tie the apron strings, then lean down and kiss her cheek while Seth washes his hands.

"You look beautiful," I whisper.

She smiles at me and turns to the countertop behind her. "I've pulled out pretty much everything we're going to need. We'll start with the sugar cookies, then the chocolate chip, peanut butter, and we'll do the Chex Mix last."

"Wow." Seth's eyes are wide as he wipes his hand on a towel.

"I already made the sugar cookie dough because it had to set up in the fridge for a couple hours before we can roll it out." She pulls it out of the fridge and motions for us to follow her to the kitchen table. "Who wants to roll it?"

"Me!" Seth exclaims and listens carefully as Jill shows him how to roll the dough with the rolling pin.

"Zack, would you please grab the cookie cutters over there?"

"Sure thing."

There's a small mess bag full of at least twenty different cookie cutters in all shapes and sizes. "Let's do the palm trees," I suggest, holding it up.

"It's Christmas, Dad," Seth reminds me with a roll of the eyes.

"Starfish?" I ask.

"I'm sensing a theme here," Jill replies dryly. "Looking forward to summer?"

"I'm just teasing," I reply and fish out the reindeer, Santa, and a gingerbread man.

"Go ahead and pull out the beach ball. We can make it into an ornament."

Realizing he's not going to get scraps anytime soon, Thor moseys over to his blanket and lies down with a loud sigh.

Jill watches Seth roll out the dough, stepping in now and again to give him some tips. Seth is grinning when the dough is ready to be cut.

"I wanna do the gingerbread men."

I raise my brows at him, and he bites his lip then looks over at Jilly and adds, "Please."

"Go ahead." She nods and then steps next to him to show him the best way to position the cutter to get the maximum number of cookies from the dough.

"Dad, are you gonna cut some?" Seth hands me the beach ball with a smile.

"Sure."

Jill takes the soft cookies from us and arranges them on cookie sheets as we cut them, then puts them in her double ovens when we're done.

"Okay, sugar cookies are done. Next up: chocolate chip."

"My favorite!" Seth exclaims and fist-bumps her. "Can we eat them hot from the oven?"

"Is there any other way to eat them?" she asks in a loud whisper.

Seth laughs and helps her clean up the sugar cookie mess on the table and all I can do is watch silently. My stomach is clenched, my chest aching, and it's in this moment, as I watch this amazing woman with my son, that I know that I love her.

She's it for me.

Now I just have to convince *her* of that.

Jill and Seth return to the kitchen to mix the dough for the next batch of cookies, and I know that this is as good a time as any to talk to Seth.

"You have flour on your cheek," Jill says and rubs the white powder off Seth's cheek.

"Seth, I have a question for you," I begin softly and join them, pulling eggs out of the carton.

"I didn't leave the lid off the orange juice again this morning. I promise."

"Not about that." I laugh and tousle his hair and then decide *what the fuck* and kiss his head.

"Yuck, Dad. Jill is here."

Jill laughs and pulls Seth to her to plant her own lips on his head.

"There, we're even."

"You're both weird." His lips twitch as he fights his smile and he ducks his head, measuring the sugar like Jill showed him.

"I want to ask you what you think about me and Jill dating each other."

Jill's eyes widen as they whip up to mine and I offer her a reassuring smile.

"I don't care." He shrugs like it's no big thing at all and continues measuring.

"Well, I'd like to date Jill, and I want to know how you feel about that."

"Dad," Seth replies with a long-suffering sigh, as though he's the dad and I'm the kid, "I already know that you and Jill are dating."

"You do?" Jill asks. "How?"

"I'm not stupid. You guys make gross googly eyes at each other all the time." He rolls his eyes and then makes fun of the way we look at each other before dissolving in a fit of giggles. "Plus, if you really got caught at the ranch in the storm a few weeks ago, you would have stayed at Uncle Josh's house."

*This kid is too smart for his own good.*

"I don't want you to be uncomfortable, Seth." Jill frowns as she watches Seth mix the eggs and sugar in the bowl.

"Why would I be uncomfortable? Are you going to kiss and stuff like Uncle Josh and Cara do?"

"Absolutely," I reply before Jill can and grin at her reassuringly. "I will kiss Jill."

"Ugh, can you keep trying to do it when you think I can't see you?"

I let out a loud laugh and pull my kid in for a quick hug. "I love you, son."

"You have a girlfriend," Seth taunts Zack, backing out of his grasp.

"I want you to know," I begin seriously and hold Seth's face in the palm of my hand, "Jill is very special to me, Seth. This isn't like what you saw with your mom."

"I'm not a little kid," Seth replies with a shrug as Jill frowns at him, curious to hear more about what Seth saw, I'm sure. "But it's cool. Jill's fun and you're happy, so . . ." He shrugs again, because shrugging is Seth's favorite form of communication, and then frowns. "Are we going to bake cookies or talk about mushy stuff?"

"I want cookies," I reply and pull the flour toward me. "Here, I don't think you had enough flour on your cheek." I dip my fingers in the white powder and wipe them on Seth's cheek, making him giggle.

"Do *not* have a flour fight in my kitchen," Jill warns us. Seth and I grin at each other, then each take a small handful and throw it at Jilly, making her hair and red T-shirt white.

"I'm sorry, did you say something, sugar?"

"You're both brats!" She laughs and brushes the flour out of her hair. Thor comes running over to see what all the ruckus is about, and manages to get coated in flour too.

"Thor looks old." Seth giggles.

"He looks very distinguished with his gray hair," Jill agrees and then pours the chocolate chips into the batter, giving it a good stir. "Let's drop these onto the cookie sheets and then we can bake them."

She pulls the sugar cookies out of the oven and sets them on a rack to cool as we replace them with a batch of chocolate chip cookies.

Finally, when those are in the oven, she sighs and blows a wayward strand of hair out of her face. "You know, maybe we can bake the peanut butter another day. This is hard work."

"Pansy," Seth taunts her and then laughs his head off.

"No chocolate milk for you," Jill replies, throwing him a mock glare.

He quickly recovers. "I was just kidding."

While the cookies bake, I order pizza, and when

the first batch of chocolate chip is done, we all sit at Jill's table and sip chocolate milk and nibble the hot cookies.

"So good," Jill moans.

"These are even better than Grandma's!"

"Don't tell her that," I warn him with a laugh.

"Nah, that would just hurt her feelings."

There are moments when my kid can be the most compassionate person I've ever met. He's always worried about hurting the feelings of those he loves. I hope he never loses that.

"I accidently farted in class today."

"Aaaand we're back to being twelve," I mutter under my breath as Jill chokes on her chocolate milk, laughing her ass off.

"I didn't mean to!"

"Dude, really?"

"You asked how my day was." He grins and stuffs a whole cookie in his mouth.

"No, I don't believe we did, actually."

"Well, you were gonna. I could feel it."

"Never a dull moment with you two, that's for sure." Jill wipes the tears from her eyes and then coos down to Thor, "No, buddy, you can't have these cookies. Chocolate is very bad for puppies. Yes it is." She cups the canine's face in her hands and kisses his forehead, points to his blanket, and turns around when Thor obeys her, lying down.

"I'm glad we're here," I murmur to her and brush

my knuckles down her cheek, wiping a speck of flour away with my thumb.

"Pizza!" Seth exclaims when the doorbell rings and he runs to the front door to retrieve the food.

"I'm glad you're here too," Jill replies softly. "I'm having fun."

"We are having a blast, sugar."

"Jill, can we eat our pizza in the living room and watch a movie?" Seth calls out.

"That sounds perfect," Jill calls back and then turns to me. "Snuggle up on the couch with me?"

"There's nowhere else I'd rather be," I reply.

Jill loads *Transformers* into her DVD player. Seth and Thor settle on the floor with blankets and pillows, and Jill and I are on the couch. The pizza is devoured within minutes, so we settle back to watch the movie.

"We have to frost the sugar cookies," Jill announces halfway into the movie, then glances down and laughs. Both Seth and Thor are out cold, snoring deeply. "Or not."

"Can we stay tonight?" I ask without thinking, and then decide *fuck it*. I want to be with her.

"We can't . . ." she begins, but I hush her with my fingers on her lips.

"No, we can't. But I can hold you, and Seth and Thor are out for the count. They won't stir until morning."

"I've missed sleeping beside you," she admits with

a whisper, and the tension I didn't know I was holding melts out of me. I hug her close and bury my nose in her hair, breathing in scents of vanilla and chocolate.

"Me too, baby. I say we take it where we can get it. I want to hold you tonight."

"Okay." She smiles up at me and finally presses her lips to mine. She drags her small hand down my face, and before I can push the kiss any further, she backs away, leans her forehead to mine, and brushes her fingers through my hair. "I'd love nothing more."

# CHAPTER

*Ten*

## JILLIAN

"So what you're saying is, you like bacon," I say dryly while Seth chomps on his sixth strip of crispy bacon.

"Yeah." He nods. "Bacon should be on everything."

"I've seen it on doughnuts. And ice cream," Zack mentions, pouring me another cup of coffee.

"Really?" Seth perks up and slips half a slice of bacon to Thor, who is sitting patiently at Seth's feet. "Did you try it?"

"I tried the doughnut. It was good."

"That sounds . . . interesting," I reply with a laugh and sip my coffee. "It's snowing pretty hard out there."

"It dumped another eight inches, easy," Zack agrees and grins knowingly at me as I stretch my lower back. We ended up falling asleep on the couch before the movie ended. At some point in the night,

Zack turned off the TV, covered Seth with a blanket, and just tucked me against him on the couch, and we had our own version of a slumber party in my living room.

We woke to Seth and Thor both peering at us with wide smiles, demanding to be fed.

"My lower back is a little sore," I murmur.

"You're too old to sleep on the couch," Seth remarks matter-of-factly and stuffs more bacon in his mouth.

"How old do you think I am, Seth?" I grin and watch while he narrows his eyes, giving his answer a lot of thought.

"Maybe twenty-six? You know, old."

"Well, I'm twenty-nine," I inform him with a sniff and then tickle his ribs. "And I'm not old!"

"Old lady!" He giggles. "What are we doing today?"

"We have to frost those cookies we baked last night."

"I'm going to take Thor outside with me and shovel." Zack walks around the table to me and kisses me softly. "Have fun with your cookies."

"Have fun in the snow," I reply. "And thanks."

"Be good, brat." Zack ruffles Seth's hair, then whistles for Thor to follow him outside.

"Are you about finished?" I ask Seth. He nods and immediately helps me clear the table and load the dishwasher. "You're good at cleaning up."

"Dad and I share the cleanup, since it's just us guys now." He takes a plate out of my hands, rinses it under the faucet, and sets it in the dishwasher. "It's kind of fun to talk to Dad while we do KP duty."

"Kind of catch up on your day?" I ask and hand him a glass.

"Yeah." He shrugs and places the glass in the dishwasher.

"Your dad loves you very much."

He nods, fills the soap compartment, and starts the washer. I gather the frosting, knives, and the trays of cookies and carry them to the table.

"Red or green?"

"Green, please." Seth dives for the green frosting and begins coloring his cookies. He sticks his tongue out as he concentrates on outlining a gingerbread man with the frosting, doing a pretty good job of it.

He looks so much like his dad it's startling. The only difference really is that Seth's eyes are a light hazel rather than chocolate brown. He has the same dark hair, dimple in his left cheek, and square jaw. He's going to be a knockout someday.

I reach over to ruffle his hair, but he flinches out of my reach, his eyes suddenly wide and wary.

"Sorry, buddy. I was just gonna touch your hair."

His shoulder jerks up in a shrug, and then he pins his eyes back on his cookie, avoiding my gaze. "Sorry," he mumbles.

"You didn't seem to mind being touched last night," I comment casually and frost an ornament in red.

"Yeah."

Geez, what do I say? The playful, carefree boy from just a few moments ago is gone and has been replaced with a pensive, wary kid, and my heart breaks for him.

"Wanna talk about it?" I ask and set the finished cookie aside, then reach for another. My voice is calm and casual, as if I asked him what he thought about the movie we watched last night.

"You just surprised me," he whispers. I glance over to see his lower lip wobbling, but I don't offer him comfort, sensing that it wouldn't be welcomed.

"You know," I begin, "when I was a kid, my dad beat on my mom."

From the corner of my eye, I see Seth's head whip up, his eyes wide.

"He did?"

"Yeah." I nod and continue to frost. "He was a really mean man. Sometimes he'd pound on Ty too."

"Did he hit you too?"

"Not really. He mostly just ignored me. My mom and dad both just sort of ignored me. I hid in the closet a lot." The pain that I grew up with has long since healed, and in its place is a numbness that I find equally sad. I feel nothing at all when I think of my parents.

"My mom ignored me too."

I nod and work to keep my hands steady as anger washes through me. Who in their right mind could ever mistreat this gorgeous boy?

"For a long time after Dad went away, she would leave me with babysitters and just go have fun," he tells me, his voice low.

"Were the babysitters nice?" I bite my lip, not sure that I really want to know the answer.

"Some were." He shrugs again. "Most of the time, they made me watch a lot of TV. Then she started bringing men home with her."

He swallows hard and lowers his frosting to the table. His eyes are fixed on his cookie, but that's not what he's seeing. Instead the horror of the last few years with his mother is playing through his mind. I want desperately to pull him into my arms but I wait, sensing his need to talk.

"Most of the time, they just liked to yell a lot. I was in the way." The last few words are said with a whisper. "Then one day, this one guy slapped me."

A tear slips down his cheek and without thinking, I reach over and cover his hand in mine. "What did your mom do?"

"Nothing." He raises his head and meets my eyes with his bright hazel ones. "She didn't tell him he couldn't do that. She just . . . laughed."

I swipe at my own tears and clench his hand in mine even more tightly.

"And she always said really horrible things about my dad. She said he left on purpose because he didn't love me. And lots of other things too. I didn't know that he asked to talk to me when he called. She didn't tell me."

I didn't know it was possible to feel the physical pain of your heart breaking until this moment with this amazing boy. She had the gift of a beautiful child, something I would have given *anything* for, and she treated him like trash.

I want to rip her apart.

"Seth," I say softly and scoot close to him so I can wrap my arms around him. I tuck his head under my chin and kiss his head, soothingly rub circles on his back. "I want you to hear something very important. Are you listening?"

He nods.

"You are loved very, very much. Your dad talks about you all the time, and you are the most important person in his life. That will never, ever change." I press my lips to his head and breathe in his shampoo. "Your mom was a shitty mom, Seth."

"I know. Cara said that too."

I grin and nod. "Cara is a smart woman. That's why she's my best friend." I lean back so I can cup Seth's face in my hands, wiping his tears with my thumbs. "You're with all of us now. Your dad, grandparents, Josh and Cara, Ty and Lo and me, we all love you and best of all, Seth, we *like* you. We like having you with us. You make us laugh and there is nowhere else we'll ever want you to be. Got it?"

His lips twist and fresh tears fall from his eyes as he nods. "Yeah."

"Good." I kiss his cheek and pull away and we

both busy ourselves wiping up our faces and sniffling, then look at each other and laugh a little.

"Jill?" Seth asks tentatively as he chooses another cookie to frost.

"Yes, sweetie."

"I really like it that you're with my dad."

I raise my eyes to his and offer him a wide smile. "I like it too."

Suddenly the front door opens and Thor comes clomping into the kitchen, covered in snow. He hops his front paws onto Seth and then me, licking, tail wagging furiously, happy to be back inside. He backs onto all fours and shakes frantically, sending snow and water all over us.

"Thor, no!"

"Damn dog!" Zack comes running behind him into the kitchen, scowling and holding an old towel. "I went to get a towel to wipe him down and he ran away from me."

"It's okay." I take the towel from him and run it down Thor's back, rubbing him vigorously. "Did you have fun in the snow?"

"He did," Zack confirms and sniffs. "It's damn wet out there."

"Here." I hand the towel to Seth. "You help Thor get dry. I'm going to help your dad."

"Okay," Seth agrees happily and falls to his knees on the floor to wipe down his dog. Thor sits on his haunches, his tongue hanging happily out of his mouth, and enjoys the massage from his young master.

I stand and take Zack's hand and lead him through my bedroom to the master bath.

"You're freezing." I lean against the sink and hold his hands between mine, rubbing them. "You didn't have to do all of that."

"Why have you been crying, sugar?" he asks quietly. He tips my chin up with his cold finger and cups my face in his chilly hand. "What happened?"

"Seth and I had a heart-to-heart," I reply softly. Zack's brow wrinkles in confusion.

"Did he say something to hurt your feelings?"

"No, not at all, babe. He just confided in me about some things that happened when he lived with his mom." Zack's eyes close on a sigh. I hold his face in my hands and kiss his chin in comfort. "We're fine. *He's* fine. In fact . . ." I grin up at him when he opens his eyes and gazes down at me. "He said he's happy that you and I are seeing each other."

"Good." He boosts me up onto the sink and leans down to brace his forehead on mine. Even his head is cold from being outside so long. "Death is too good for her, Jilly."

I brace my hands on his rib cage and stay silent, letting him talk.

"For a while, I wished her dead for what she put him through, but honestly, that's too good for her. I want her to suffer. God help me, I know it makes me a monster, but I want her to feel every bit of pain she ever put him through times a million."

"You're no monster, babe." I kiss his lips and then wrap myself around his torso, holding him close. "You're a daddy. She hurt your boy."

He hugs me tight, then backs away, helps me off the sink, and accepts the towel I pass to him. He rubs it over his head and tosses it into the hamper.

"You're sure everything is okay?"

"Yep, perfectly fine."

He nods and kisses my forehead, then leads me back to the kitchen, where Seth is talking to Thor and frosting the last of the cookies.

"And then Josiah said, 'There's no way you can climb to the top of that snowbank and jump onto the roof!' So I did."

My heart stops as I halt beside the table and gape down at Seth. "You did *what*?"

"Oh, hi. I didn't know you were back. I figured you were doing mushy stuff."

"No, we were talking, and what did you just say?"

Zack grins and crosses his arms over his chest, watching me with his son. "Did you hear him?" I ask.

"I did."

"What are you going to do about it?" I demand.

"It sounds like you're about to do something about it," he replies calmly.

"It wasn't that far of a jump," Seth assures me. "It was like, super short. And not that far off the ground."

"It was a *roof*, Seth."

He bites his lip, aware that he's been caught. "Well, the snow was super high."

"I'm super mad at you," I reply.

"Why?" Seth asks, confusion written across his face.

"You could have been hurt! Didn't you think of that?"

"I didn't get hurt." He sounds so calm, like I'm the one being unreasonable.

"You *could have*."

"But I *didn't*."

"No more jumping on roofs, and that's all there is to it," I insist.

Seth looks over at his dad, who shrugs and nods.

"Fine." His shoulders droop in defeat.

"I don't want you to get hurt, buddy. You just took ten years off my life."

His lips twitch as he tries to fight a satisfied smile. "You're already old."

"No more cookies for you," I inform him sternly, fighting a grin.

"But you're pretty," he quickly adds.

Zack bursts out laughing and ruffles his son's hair as he saunters past him to the kitchen to pour more coffee. "You're just like your uncle. Always the charmer."

"I don't know." I pick up a green-frosted sugar cookie and take a bite. "I think he sounds a lot like his dad."

My phone pings with an incoming text.

Grace: **Jacob has reserved rooms for you all here at the lodge tonight after the parade. So bring an overnight bag! His treat. Xo**

"That's Grace," I inform Zack. "She says we're all to bring overnight bags tonight to stay at the lodge, on Jacob."

"Does this mean I get to stay with Grandma and Grandpa again?" Seth asks hopefully.

"Looks like," Zack replies with a grin.

"Yessss!" Seth pumps his fist and does a happy dance in his chair. "Grandma said the next time I stay over, she'll help me order some Christmas presents online."

"I told you I'd take you shopping," Zack says with a frown. His dark hair is messy from the towel, and he just looks delicious leaning against my kitchen counter with a coffee mug in his hand. It occurs to me that I've done hardly any shopping yet this year, and make a note to take care of that this afternoon after Zack and Seth leave.

"I know, but what I want to buy I can't find around here, so she's gonna help me order it."

"What is it?" Zack asks.

"Can't tell," Seth replies with a grin. "But it really sucks. Whoever gets it is gonna hate it."

I laugh and shake my head at the silly boy. "I doubt that."

"We'll see." He grins widely and bites a cookie. "This Christmas is gonna be the funnest ever."

"What did you ask for?" I ask Seth.

"Nothing." He frowns like it didn't occur to him to ask for anything.

"You didn't ask Santa for anything?"

He rolls his eyes and gives a long-suffering sigh. "Santa isn't real."

"Oh yes, my friend, he is." I give him a stern look and nibble my cookie. "So, what would you ask him for?"

"My own snowmobile," he says and blushes. Zack's lips twitch, but he keeps his face sober as he sits back and listens.

"Is that all?" I ask.

"That's a lot!"

"But what if you're daydreaming? What else would you ask for?"

He blinks and thinks hard. "Maybe some high-powered binoculars to look at the birds and stuff when we're in the woods."

"That's cool," I say with a grin.

"And Josiah has a Kindle Fire that's cool. I like to read."

"You do?"

"Yeah, Cara got me started on some fantasy books that are cool."

I nod, making rapid mental notes.

"What about you, Dad?" Seth turns the question to his father, whose face goes blank.

"I don't need anything. Everything I need is right here."

His eyes shine as he gazes over at me, then to his son and, well, if I wasn't already in love with him, I would have fallen hard right then.

"It's a daydream, Dad."

"I'm daydreaming about getting you home so I can do my chores and take my woman out on a date."

"I can help with chores." Seth jumps up and runs around the table to me and hugs me hard. "Thanks for the cookies and letting Thor and me sleep on your floor."

"You're welcome." I hug him back and whisper in his ear, "Thanks for our talk."

He smiles at me and takes his coat from his dad.

"I'll see you tonight," Zack murmurs and pulls me into his arms for a full-blown kiss, right there in front of Seth and the dog.

"I'm looking forward to it."

"Ugh," Seth groans. "Come on, Thor, let's go out to the truck."

Zack and I laugh as we hear the front door close behind the boy and his dog.

"Thanks for staying over. I had a lot of fun."

"We did too." He nuzzles my nose with his and nibbles the side of my mouth. "I'm going to do a lot of naughty things to you in that hotel room tonight, sugar."

"Promise?"

"Absolutely."

❀   ❀   ❀

"At least we got a break in the snow," I comment as Zack leads me out to his truck six hours later.

"You're going to break your ankle in those shoes,"

Zack mutters moodily and eyes my Jimmy Choos warily.

"I am not. It's a party, Zack."

"We'll be outside."

"I'm quite sure Jacob has outdoor heaters," I reply and study his face as he lifts me into the passenger seat. He looks tired and like he's aged five years since this morning. "What's going on?"

"Nothing, I'm just worried about the health of your legs."

"My legs and I are fine."

He shakes his head, slams the door, and trudges around to the other side. He pulls away from my house and is quiet all the way through town. He rubs his fingers over his mouth, the way he does when he's agitated.

Do my shoes really piss him off? I think they're hot. He liked the boots, so I figured these would turn him on too.

"Did I do something wrong?" I ask softly. His gaze turns to mine and softens. He pulls my hand to his lips and kisses my knuckles, sending electricity to my core.

"No, baby."

I shrug and chalk his mood up to hormone changes. Even though they deny it, we all know men have their own version of their period.

The snow has stopped, leaving a beautiful blanket of white over everything. It's past dark now, and I love looking at the lights on our neighbors' homes, the fun lawn decorations, and of course, the beautiful trimmings through downtown.

Before long, we approach the turnoff to head up the mountain to the ski resort. The road has been freshly plowed and sanded, and with Zack's 4×4, I have no doubt that we'll make it to the top safely.

"I hear all of the Hulls are coming," I say casually as we pass the Hideaway, the bed-and-breakfast owned by Brad and Max's younger sister, Jenna. "And Hannah, the new OB/GYN. She's Grace's roommate."

"Great," Zack replies. His voice is monotone.

"Are you sure you're okay?"

"Fine."

"You're not terribly chatty."

"I'm driving up a bitch of a road, Jilly. Cut me some slack."

I sink back into my seat and blink at him in surprise. Zack can be moody, we all know this, but he doesn't usually snap at me.

"Sorry."

He sighs and rubs his hand over his lips again, but doesn't say another word until we've reached the lodge. It's a good thing we came a bit early because the parking lot is already full. Zack pulls into the valet slot right behind Josh and Cara and Ty and Lo, who all rode together.

"Hey, girl!" Cara waves and comes running to me, as quickly as her own heels will carry her.

"Hi! I love your shoes!"

"Thanks. Your jeans are awesome."

I grin and turn around to show her my backside. "I love my ass in them."

"You have a gorgeous ass," Lo adds as she joins us and then leans down to hug me close.

"Holy shit, you're tall." I laugh and glance down at her own feet, also in heels.

"She's perfect," Ty says and buries his face in Lo's neck as he wraps his arms around her waist. My brother is in a thick cable-knit sweater with the sleeves pulled up on his forearms, showing off the tats on his right arm. He's in jeans and Chucks, and after the conversation with Seth today, I feel a softness toward the pain in the ass, so I walk to him and slide into the comfort of his arms when Lo steps away.

"You okay?" he asks softly.

"Yep, just love you."

He pulls back to look into my face and offers me half a smile. "Love you back. Just stop showing off your ass."

"No." I smirk and turn away, running smack into Zack. He's grinning lazily down at me, and right here, in front of my brother, his brother, and the girls, he pulls me into his arms and kisses the breath right out of me. His hands dive into my hair, holding me firmly, as he plunders my mouth, and when I go weak in the knees, he steadies me against him.

When he pulls back, he smiles up at my brother and says, "She has a great ass."

"Oh God," I groan and lean my forehead against Zack's sternum. "Don't start something."

Ty's quiet for a long moment, then leans in above me and shoves his face close to Zack's. "Hurt her and I'll kill you."

"Understood."

"Hey, everyone! Why are you out here in the cold?" Grace and her boyfriend, Jacob, come out the front doors of the lodge, hand in hand. "Come in! We have heaters upstairs."

"See?" I whisper to Zack. "I told you they'd have heaters."

"I still think you're crazy. Gorgeous, but crazy."

I glance back at him and my eyes take a trip up and down his long, lean body. He's in his usual jeans, but instead of a T-shirt and coat, he's wearing a long-sleeved, gray V-neck shirt under a red puffy vest. Hello, hot stuff.

"I think you're crazy gorgeous, soldier." I wink and lead him into the lodge behind our friends. We're guided into an elevator and up to the penthouse.

"Make yourselves comfortable," Jacob says as he leads us into the wide space. The river-rock fireplace that mirrors the one in the lobby is aglow and surrounded by plush furniture. The dining table is set buffet-style, the kitchen bustling with kitchen staff, and the sliding glass door that leads out to the balcony is open, inviting us to wander outside.

We grab drinks and a bite to eat on our way out the door to the enormous balcony. It spans the width of the room, and is just as deep, boasting a fire pit in the center, which is lit, and couches arranged in a circle around the fire. There are outdoor heaters in each corner of the balcony, so no space is too cold to be without a coat.

"This is beautiful," Cara breathes as she gazes up at the ski hill that is currently awash in light from the night-skiing lights.

"Stunning," I agree. "Thank you for inviting us," I say to Jacob and Grace, who still haven't let go of each other. They really are the cutest couple ever; she's got pretty blond hair and hazel eyes, and Jacob is the handsomest Englishman I've ever seen, tall with blond, wavy hair and bright green eyes that he rarely pulls away from Grace.

He's completely in love with her, and I couldn't be happier for them.

"We're happy to have you," Jacob replies with a smile. "This is the best view on the mountain. You'll be able to see the torchlight parade without fighting the crowd."

"Oh! Before I forget," Grace adds, "here are the keys to your rooms." She hands them out gleefully, like a giddy Christmas elf.

"Thanks for this, man," Ty says to Jacob. "You didn't have to."

"It's nothing, really. This way you can relax and enjoy without having to worry about driving down this bloody mountain in the wee hours of the morning."

"Is this where the party is?" A pretty redheaded

woman sticks her head out of the door and glances about until she finds Grace. "There you are!"

"Hey! Come on out." Grace takes Hannah by the hand and turns to all of us. "Do you know everyone?"

"Not quite." She laughs and waves at us all.

"I'm Jillian," I begin and shake her hand. "This is my boyfriend, Zack King, and his brother, Josh. You've met Josh's fiancée, Cara, right?"

Hannah nods and smiles at Cara.

"And this is Ty, my brother, and his beautiful fiancée, Lauren."

"You can call me Lo," she says and smiles warmly.

"Oh good, the rest are here!" Cara exclaims and hugs Brad as he comes through the door. "Hey you!"

"Hey, young lady," Brad replies with a grin. Max and Jenna follow him out onto the balcony.

"That's Brad, one of Cunningham Falls' finest, followed by his younger brother, Max, and their sister, Jenna."

"Holy shit, don't expect me to remember everyone's names," Hannah replies but laughs and shakes everyone's hands.

The guys all shake hands, and Max's eyebrow raises when he sees Zack's arm around my shoulders, holding me to his side. I smile and shrug, and Max offers me a silent thumbs-up.

I love my friends.

# CHAPTER

## *Eleven*

### ZACK

I don't want to be here. Not with all of these people. I love my brother, and hell, I like everyone here, but I just had the shittiest afternoon of my life.

Worse than watching young men get blown to bits. Worse than having to hold their moms and wives while they grieve.

But Jilly wanted to be here tonight, so here we are. And I'm fucking pissed at myself because I snapped at her and she didn't deserve it. I'll make it up to her tonight.

"What time does the parade start?" Jenna asks and wanders over to the edge of the balcony, looking up at the hill.

"In about thirty minutes," Jacob replies. "So in the meantime, please, grab some food and drinks and enjoy."

"What, exactly, is a torchlight parade?" Hannah asks. Brad offers her a glass of champagne, and I tilt my head to the side, watching my friend. Seems he might be interested in the new doc in town. Can't say I blame him. She's a pretty woman.

"Exactly what it sounds like," Brad answers her. "They dim the lights, and skiers come down the hill holding torches."

"It makes me nervous." Grace shudders delicately. "I'd fall and break all my bones."

Jilly laughs next to me, catching my attention.

"I love your shoes, Jill," Jenna comments. "Jimmy Choo?"

"Yes." Jill nods and looks down at her sexy-as-fuck shoes. Seems they cost a fortune and she's wearing them out in the fucking snow.

Women.

"I wish we could get stuff like that here," Lo says and sips her drink.

"Yes, it's one of the things I miss about LA," Jill replies, and my heart stops. *She misses LA?* "I have to shop online more than anything."

"Oh, I'm sure that's not a hardship," Ty says. "You like to shop any way you can get it."

"True." Jill giggles and shrugs. "Thank God for the internet."

"Where are you from, Hannah?" Cara asks.

I glance around the balcony, looking for my brother and see that he's talking with Jacob, Max, Brad, and Grace.

"Excuse me, sugar," I whisper into Jill's ear. "I'll be right over there if you need me." I kiss her cheek and walk away toward my brother.

"Max was just telling us about the ranching software he sold to Google," Josh says excitedly.

"Seriously?" I turn to Max and shake his hand. "Congrats, man."

"Thank you."

"Jilly says you're moving back to town," I reply and sip my beer.

"Yeah, she's going to sell me a house." He cringes and leans in to talk quietly. "I don't want any weirdness between us. I didn't know you were dating her when I asked her out."

"I wasn't then, man. If we were, Jill wouldn't have gone with you. It's all good."

He nods and we're sucked back into the conversation with the others. Finally, Grace yawns.

"Sorry guys, I love you all, but this is boring. I'm going to go talk about sexy shoes with the girls, even though I can never wear shoes like theirs because I would die a very violent, painful death."

"Enjoy, darling."

"Cheerio, love," she calls back to him in a horrible accent, making us all laugh.

"She's always doing that," Jacob murmurs as he watches Grace with lovesick eyes.

Ty and Brad wander over to join us, and now we are officially split, men versus women.

"Couldn't take the shoe talk anymore?" I ask Ty.

"Dude, they're on to purses now."

"Handbags," Brad corrects him with a shudder. "We got schooled on the whole, 'they're not purses, they're handbags' thing. So we came over here where it's safe."

"Who the fuck spends a thousand dollars on a purse?" Ty asks.

"Handbag," Brad says again. "We don't ever want that lecture again."

"Oh, some spend more than that," Jacob adds with a wince. "It's ridiculous."

"Cara spends hundreds on her *hair*, just to keep it straight. I don't get it. It's hair. Wash it and be done with it." Josh shakes his head in confusion.

"I pay fifteen dollars to get my hair cut," I reply with a shake of the head. Is this what will keep Jillian happy? Thousands of dollars' worth of accessories and designer clothes and hair and nails? I'm not a poor man, but I can't give her that. I glance over at her and see her laughing with Jenna, with her designer shoes and jeans, the *handbag* with the MK emblem on the side.

"My apologies, mates, but if spoiling my Grace with a trip to the hair salon makes her smile, I'm happy to do it." Jacob shrugs but doesn't look in the least bit embarrassed.

I take a deep breath to clear my head, then feel Jill's small hand on my arm. "Zack?"

"Hey, sugar." I turn to smile at her, and my heart

stills in my chest at the happy grin on her gorgeous face. Her blue eyes are big and bright, and she bites that luscious lower lip of hers as she slips her arm through mine and presses her round breast to my arm.

*Fuck, I love her tits.*

"What are you guys talking about?"

"Women," I reply honestly and tweak her nose with my fingertip.

"Oh good, I came at the right time." She laughs and leans her cheek against my upper arm.

"Actually," Jacob begins as he checks his watch, "it looks like things are about to start."

The night-skiing lights on the mountain go out, leaving the small ski village in utter darkness. Suddenly, music begins to play from a DJ booth near the ski lift. As Rihanna sings, asking someone to stay, an MC takes a mike.

"Welcome to the annual torchlight parade! In just a few moments you'll be able to see the skiers come down the mountain with their red torches. There will also be a fireworks show, courtesy of Jacob Paxton, the generous sponsor of this event!"

A round of applause is heard, then the music volume goes up and we all gather around the railing, watching the dark hill.

I pull Jill in front of me and wrap my arms around her shoulders. She holds on to my arms and leans against my chest. I plant my lips in her hair and breathe her in, her scent, her warmth, mentally counting the hours until I can scoop her up and carry her down to our room and bury myself inside her for the night, forgetting about everything but her.

But us.

"Look!" Jill points to the top of the hill, where we can barely see a warm red glow as the skiers begin to ski down the mountain.

They ski down in a crisscross pattern at a relatively slow pace. When the skiers in the front reach the halfway mark down the mountain, the fireworks begin.

And this is the part I've been dreading all night. Jill looks up at me to watch my face. I kiss her forehead and murmur, "I'm fine."

And I will be.

But while everyone around me enjoys the fireworks display, it's a private hell for me. The sounds, the bursts of light, are all too reminiscent of warfare, and I've seen enough of that to last me a fucking lifetime.

If I never saw fireworks again, it would be too soon.

I keep my eyes trained on the lights of the pyrotechnics. It helps if I can keep my eyes on them, rather than just hearing the loud boom, wondering where it's coming from. I let go of Jill and brace my hands on the railing before her, still caging her in, but now I'm able to tighten my fists without her knowing.

I bury my nose in Jill's hair, take a long, deep breath, and pray that it's almost over.

The skiers are almost all down the mountain now, and the fireworks are coming faster and bigger now, signaling the finale.

Thank fucking Christ.

Finally, the last burst of light is ignited and the crowd roars with excited yells and applause. Some of the spectators will file into the few bars up here on the mountain, while still more will drive down to town and party it up down there.

"That was beautiful!" Cara exclaims. "Why have I never come up here to watch this before?"

"Locals rarely experience all of the fun things in a tourist town," Max reminds her.

"True," Lo agrees. "We should do more of them."

Jill turns in my arms and wraps herself around my torso, hugging me tightly, rubbing her small hands up and down my back soothingly.

"Are you okay?" she murmurs softly.

I kiss her forehead tenderly and take a deep breath of the fresh mountain air. "I'm fine, baby."

She can feel the tension rolling through me and frowns up at me, but I shake my head and kiss her lips gently. "I'm okay. We'll talk later, okay? Just enjoy the party."

She studies me for a moment and then nods.

"I'll go get us a couple of drinks," I offer.

"Perfect, thank you." She smiles widely as I walk into the kitchen to grab two fresh drinks. Jacob went all out for this small party. If I hadn't met him, I would think it was just to impress us all, but I have a feeling it was purely for the convenience of having the food prepared, and staff on hand to help so he and Grace could enjoy their guests.

I can respect that.

When I walk back out to the balcony, I hear Jill's laughter tickling the air, and my dick immediately hardens. Jesus, I have it bad. Just the sound of her voice turns me on. I survey the small crowd and find Jill and Max, their heads together, laughing loudly. Max wraps his arm around her shoulders and pulls her into his side in a half hug, and that's it. The lack of sleep, the stress from the day, the fireworks, and now seeing Max with his hands on my woman all just push me over the edge.

I stalk over to Jill, glaring at my friend, and hand her her drink.

"Are you ready to go back to the room?" My voice is hard and distant. Jill's eyes widen before she glares at me and props her hands on her hips.

"No, I'm not."

"I think it's time we have a talk, Jilly."

Max shakes his head and mutters under his breath. "Zack." His voice is low so he doesn't draw attention from the others. "We were just talking about—"

"I don't care," I reply calmly, but fist my hands at my sides. "This really isn't about you, Max."

The other man shrugs and pats Jill on the back before walking away.

"What is wrong with you tonight?" Jill's face is worried now, and I don't know how to soothe her. Fuck, I'm just a jumbled mess, and I know that I'm done being in this crowd of people, and I need to get her out of here.

"I'd like to leave now, please."

"Babe, are you . . . ?"

"Let's go, Jilly."

She shrugs and we say our good-byes to our hosts and friends. Josh stares at me with questions in his eyes, but I just shrug and keep walking.

The walk to the room is quiet and tense. The valet delivered our overnight bags to the room while we were upstairs. When I close the door behind me and lock the dead bolt, Jill immediately turns on me.

"Tell me what's going on."

"Just drop it, Jill."

"Fuck that." She's pissed now, her cheeks flushed with anger, her blue eyes burning with fire.

Good.

I prowl around the room as I peel off my vest and throw it on a chair.

"You've been in a pisser of a mood since you picked me up, and then you insulted both Max and me up on that balcony. What the fuck, Zack?

Did you think we were planning a secret time to screw each other's brains out and laughing about it?"

The thought of it sends me into a rage. I advance on her and take her shoulders in my hands and push her up against the wall, caging her. I'm breathing hard as I take in her gorgeous face, her hair, and I know I'm a fucking bastard for what I'm about to say.

"I know I'm not fucking good enough for you, Jillian. I get it. You deserve so much better than the likes of me. I'm just a broken soldier with a kid and a fucking bitch of an ex-wife, but God damn it, you're *mine*. I'm not letting you go back to LA."

Her mouth opens and closes and her brow furrows in confusion.

"What are you talking about?"

"I know that I can't just run out and spoil you with all of those fancy things you love. We're simple here, Jill. And I'm okay with that, but I see it eating at you. I heard you say that you miss LA."

She pushes on my chest, and begins to pace the room when I back away from her, giving her space. The loss of her heat against me is painful.

"You think I want to move back to LA so I can go shopping?" she asks incredulously.

"I think—"

"You're a fucking idiot, Zack King." She props her hands on her hips and glares at me. "I've made it pretty clear that I want to be here, with *you*. So if that's not what you want, you need to say so now and stop playing these damn games with me."

"It's not a damn game!" I pull her to me again, plant my hands on her ass, and lift her, wrapping her legs around my waist, then brace her against the wall so I can look into her eyes.

"Just tell me what's happening! Talk to me!"

I brush my fingers down her smooth face and then bury my face in her neck, holding on tight.

"Kensie called today," I murmur softly. Jill stills and I can feel her pulse speed up.

"What did she want?" Her voice is low and hard.

"Seth." I pull back and meet her gaze with mine. "She says things didn't work out with the fucker she was with and she misses Seth."

"Fuck that!" Jill's lips peel back from her teeth, and I swear to God, she snarls. "She'll never touch him again."

"I told her that she couldn't have him and she'd best not set one foot on my property or she'd land her ass in jail."

Jill cups my face in her hands. "Is this what had you so upset?"

"I can't have her make Seth's life any more difficult than she already has."

"She can't. She gave up custody. Right?"

"Yeah, I have full custody. She didn't even ask for visitation. In the court's eyes, she abandoned him."

Jill's nodding and pushes her fingers into my hair. "You have all the power here, babe."

I nod and rest my forehead on Jill's, drawing strength from her. Jesus, she's so fucking strong.

"Now, about the rest of it. Why in the bloody hell would you think I'd want to move back to LA?"

"You deserve nice things, Jill. You deserve—"

"I deserve *you*. And Seth. And even that silly dog of yours. I don't want LA. I left there for a reason, Zack."

I sigh, knowing I've fucked up. "It was a mother-fucker of a day, sugar. Between the lack of sleep last night, that call, the fireworks, seeing you in Max's arms . . ."

Jill throws her head back and laughs. "In Max's arms? He hugged me, Zack. That happens some-times."

"He had his hands on you."

"That happens when a person hugs you."

"I didn't like it," I growl.

I turn with Jill in my arms, cross to the bed, and crawl onto it with her still clinging to me. I kneel between her legs and tug her expensive shoes off her feet, and toss them on the side of the bed as she pulls her shirt over her head.

"I think I should remind you who you belong to, sugar."

"Is that so?" She cocks a brow and pulls at the hem of my shirt until I tug it over my head and toss it aside. Her hands glide over my stomach and to the button on my jeans.

I peel her sexy jeans down her legs and take in the sight of her lying on the bed in a sexy lacy bra and matching panties, and my tongue sticks to the roof of my mouth.

"Holy fuck, Jill."

"Back at you, soldier." Her eyes are taking in my torso, my shoulders. "Take your pants off."

"Not yet," I reply and cover her sex with my hand. She hisses in a breath and stares up at me with wide eyes as I yank her panties down her hips and legs, toss them aside, spread her legs, and look my fill. "Do you know how gorgeous your pussy is, sugar?" I scoot down to my belly, shoulder between her thighs, and run one finger through her already wet folds. "God, it's so beautiful. Pink. Puffy." I raise her clitoral hood with my thumb and blow on her clit and grin wickedly when it swells. "So fucking responsive."

"Zack," she whimpers.

"That's right, Jilly. Mine." I lean in and lick her, from her opening to her clit and back down again. "This is *mine*."

I push two fingers inside her and press my tongue to her clit, barely moving it back and forth to give her just a tiny bit of friction. Her hips buck and she grips my hair in her strong hands.

"Oh my God!"

"Whose pussy is this, Jilly?" My fingertips brush over that rough sweet spot and I feel her tighten around me like a fist. My cock twitches in anticipation, throbbing with want for her. "Tell me, baby."

"Yours," she whispers and moves her hips, trying desperately to make me increase the friction against her clit, but I pull back.

"Say it again, Jill."

"Yours," she repeats, stronger now.

I wrap my lips around her clit and pull gently, and my fingers increase speed, fucking her harder. "Again."

"Yours!"

"Fucking right," I growl and then pull on her clit again until she comes violently, bucking and trembling, panting, chanting my name.

I stand and drop my jeans, then pull Jill off the bed and into my arms again.

"Wrap your legs around me."

She obeys, wraps those toned, slender legs around my waist and arms around my neck and kisses me for all she's worth, not giving a shit that her juices are still all over my mouth.

I groan against her lips and push her against the wall again, pull my hips back, and slide home, impaling myself completely inside her. With her eyes level with mine, I pin her in my gaze as we both gasp for breath.

"You are mine, Jillian. Do you hear me? Mine."

"Yes," she sobs as I begin to move in hard, quick strokes. This isn't soft and slow like before, it's hard and urgent, and I know exactly what I'm doing.

I'm claiming my woman.

My cock is harder than it's ever been, pulsing and throbbing inside this amazing woman. Every time I pull back, she whimpers.

"Dragging against your sweet spot, sugar?"

"God, yes!" Her legs tighten on my hips as her pussy clenches around me.

"Do not come yet," I command. Her eyes burst open with surprise and she bites her plump lower lip. "Not yet."

"Please," she whispers and circles her hips again, almost frantically. "I'm almost there."

I plunge inside her and stop abruptly, holding her against the wall with my body, filling her with my cock. I watch her for a moment as her breath heaves in and out, pressing her hard nipples against my chest.

"Zack."

"Yes, Jilly."

"I need to fucking come!" She makes a small fist and gently pounds it on the top of my shoulder in frustration. "Please."

I hook an arm under her knee, cup her ass with my hand, opening her wider, and push against her even more tightly.

"I love the way you feel wrapped around me," I

murmur. "I love the way you taste and smell. I can smell how fucking turned on you are. Do you have any idea what that does to me?"

She shakes her head. I pull back then slam home again, making her cry out.

"It makes me fucking crazy. It makes me want to fuck you all night long. Would you like that, Jilly?"

"Yes!"

I begin to pound in and out of her again, my pace quicker now. She's so fucking slick, her wetness pouring down over my cock and balls, and her entire body is clenched around me like a vise.

She's fucking amazing.

"Oh my God, Zack, please, I can't wait . . ."

I watch her face in awe as she begins to succumb to her release. "Do it, baby. Come."

Instead of screaming like I expected, she grows silent, bites her lip, and her body is racked with shudders as she pulses and contracts around me. It's the most beautiful thing I've ever seen. My spine tingles and balls lift as I surrender to my own release, rocking into her. She cradles me in her arms as I bury my face in her neck and come harder than I can ever remember coming before, my entire body stiff, feeling like it's going to turn inside out.

After a few long moments of us clinging to each other, supported by the wall, Jill giggles softly.

"We made a mess."

"We'll clean it up." I brush a few strands of her hair back from her face. "You're mine, Jilly."

"I get it." She grins and kisses me softly. "And you're mine, soldier."

"Damn right."

# CHAPTER
## *Twelve*

### JILLIAN

Someone is nibbling on my neck. I stretch under the soft sheets and smile sleepily, not opening my eyes yet. Zack's pressed to my back, leaving damp kisses down my shoulder, then back to my spine. His hand drifts down my arm to my hip, up my side, then around to cup my breast.

I moan softly and wiggle my hips, pressing against his hard erection.

"Good morning, sugar," he whispers against my ear. "Did you sleep okay?"

"Mm."

He pulls me onto my back and smiles down at me. His dark hair is mussed and his big brown eyes are heavy with sleep. The dimple in his cheek winks at me.

"You're gorgeous in the morning," he murmurs and kisses my forehead, and just that press of lips to my skin has my body on full alert. My hand glides from his naked hip, up his side to his shoulder.

"You're sexy all the time."

He chuckles and shakes his head. "Doubtful."

"I love this dimple." I rub it with my fingertip, enjoying this lazy, relaxed time with him. We don't get it often. "I love when you smile at me like this, because you don't smile very often."

"I seem to be smiling more and more now that you're in my life," he replies softly. His fingertips are tracing small circles around my belly.

"I love your arms," I continue. "They're strong. And your tattoo is supercool."

"*Super*cool?" he asks with a grin.

"I've been hanging out with Seth a lot," I say and shrug. "I love your flat abs and this line right here." I trace the V in his hip and watch with fascination as he bites his lip and holds his breath. "Is that sensitive?"

"You tell me," he whispers and repeats the motion on my own hip.

"That . . . tickles." I wrinkle my nose at him and gasp when he does it again.

"You know what I love about your body, sugar?" He kisses my cheek, then effortlessly moves over me, covering me with his large, hard body. He rests his cock against my folds, his pelvis against mine, and his elbows at either side of my head. "I love your big blue eyes. They can make me feel like the only man in the world, or they can cut me to the core, in just one look."

He kisses my lips and pushes his fingers into my hair, massaging my scalp. Dear sweet God, he's good with his hands.

"I love your ass. I thought I was going to have to kill Josh and the other guys last night when you were showing off your jeans. You have an ass that's just the right size for a nice handful, and fuck me if it doesn't look amazing in jeans."

"So you're an ass man." My voice is raspy and heavy with desire.

"I'm not finished," he replies and kisses down my jawline to my neck. "I love your hands. They feel amazing on me. They can be comforting and gentle, or they can grab onto my hair and clench so tight I don't think you'll ever let go."

His words are intoxicating. My body is humming, moving slowly beneath him. He's rocking his hips, sliding his cock between my wet folds, and continuing to massage my scalp while kissing his way down my neck and across my collarbones.

"But Jesus, Jilly, your pussy is just fucking amazing." He pulls his hips back and then slides deep inside me and when he's seated completely, he drags his lips up my jawline back to my lips. "You fit me perfectly. Like you were made for me."

He moves leisurely in and out of me. The only sound in the room is our panting breaths as we slowly make love, as though we have all day to explore each other's bodies.

I cup his face in my hands and bring his lips down to mine to nibble and tease, until he kisses both of my palms, laces his fingers with mine, and pulls my hands up over my head. He keeps them there as he begins to move more quickly, his eyes pinned to mine, and I can't tell where he ends and I begin.

He presses all the way in and rocks his pubis against my clit and grins as he watches me begin to come apart beneath him.

"Yes, baby, come." He kisses my lips and nuzzles my nose. "Come for me."

And I do. Quietly, intensely, the orgasm shakes through me, and as my pussy is gripping him in the throes of my release, Zack follows me, grunting with his own climax.

We lie still for several minutes, caressing each other's bodies, kissing shoulders and cheeks and palms.

"When do we have to be downstairs for brunch?" he asks finally.

"At ten thirty," I reply softly and glance over at the clock. "We have about an hour."

"Good. We need a shower."

"We took a shower last night."

He cocks a brow. "I've dirtied you up at least three times since then."

"Good point." Before he can move away to lead me into the bathroom, I wrap my arms around his shoulders and hug him tightly to me.

"Baby?" He hugs me back, but his voice sounds a little confused. "Are you okay?"

"Yes. I just think this might be one of the best moments of my life, and I want to take a minute to enjoy it."

"God, Jilly, you destroy me when you say shit like that." He rolls us to our sides and tucks me more securely against him, rubbing my back soothingly and kissing my forehead.

"We need to get in the shower," I remind him with a whisper.

"It'll wait. This is more important." He kisses my forehead again and takes a deep breath. "You're always more important. Don't ever forget that."

❋   ❋   ❋

"So what is everyone doing for Christmas?" Cara asks. We're back up in the penthouse, seated around a huge dining room table and too stuffed to move after the incredible brunch Grace and Jacob provided. I'm not ready to have to go back down the mountain yet. "It's less than a week away already!"

"We'll be at our mom and dad's," Jenna replies. Brad and Max both nod. Hannah yawns, catching Brad's attention, and given the hot looks that pass back and forth, I can't help but wonder what's going on there.

"What are we doing for Christmas?" Grace asks Jacob with a frown.

"I may have something up my sleeve, darling." He winks at her and all of us girls sigh at the romance of it all.

"I think that accent is what gets you all of the attention," Josh comments. "I mean, I could say to Cara, 'I may have something up my sleeve, darling.' And she'd say, 'You forgot again, didn't you?'" He shakes his head in disgust as we all laugh.

"You're probably right," Ty agrees.

"Aye, the accent works. He's full of the blarney, he is!" Grace giggles as she attempts the worst Irish accent any of us have ever heard.

"I'm not Irish, love," Jacob reminds her and kisses her forehead.

"You two are too adorable." I wrinkle my nose and tilt my head. "I'm happy for you. Okay, what are you doing for the holiday, Hannah?"

"I'm working," she replies with a sigh. "People don't stop having babies just because it's a holiday."

"Surely your office isn't open," I say.

"No, but I'll be on call for labor and delivery. I'll probably be at the hospital all day."

"We're having Christmas at the big house, right, Zack?" Cara asks and nibbles a strawberry.

"Absolutely, and I wanted to ask you all a favor. I was hoping everyone could stay Christmas Eve at my place. We have more than enough bedrooms. That way, you'll all be there Christmas morning."

"Are you sure?" Ty asks. "Lo and I can drive out both days."

"No, we want you there." Zack glances down at me and leans in to whisper in my ear, "You'll be sleeping in my bed, sugar."

I feel my cheeks heat as I give him a subtle nod.

"We can get started on Christmas dinner early that way too," I offer. "Cara, can we use your oven for the side dishes?"

"Great idea!" she agrees excitedly. "This is going to be so fun."

"What are we doing Christmas Eve?" I ask the boys.

Josh and Zack share a wide smile and Ty's eyes widen. "The fire pit!"

"Yep," Zack confirms.

"What about the fire pit?" I ask with a frown. "Wait. You have a fire pit?"

"You'll see, sugar." He kisses my temple and smiles down at me.

"This has been so fun," Jenna says and smiles at all of us. "It's so good to see you guys."

"Thanks for inviting us up," Josh agrees.

"It was our pleasure," Jacob says. "You are all welcome up here anytime."

"We should go check in on Seth," I murmur to Zack. Josh and Ty both hear me and toss me surprised glances. Zack nods and kisses my hand.

"It was good to see you all," he says sincerely. "Happy holidays."

"Happy holidays!" The gang all waves as we stand to leave.

"Did you really have fun?" I ask Zack when we're in his truck and headed down the mountain.

"I always have a great time with you, sugar. Thanks for being patient with me."

"I don't know if I'd call it patient." I chuckle and squeeze his hand in mine.

"Come back to the ranch with me." It's not a question.

"Are you cooking dinner?" I raise a brow and feel my lips twitch.

"I'll cook you anything you want."

"I'm in then. A nice steak and salad would be *super*cool."

He laughs and shakes his head as he approaches the stoplight at the bottom of the mountain. "Been hanging out with Seth a lot, huh?"

"Yeah. Maybe he's rubbing off on me."

"I would say so. You fart like crazy in your sleep."

My jaw drops in outrage and I smack his shoulder as hard as I can. "I do not!"

"No." He shakes his head as he laughs. "But your reaction was *super* worth it."

"You're a *super* ass."

He laughs even harder as he drives toward town.

# CHAPTER

## *Thirteen*

"Why didn't you trim the tree weeks ago?" I ask Zack as he passes me another ornament for the tree. Josh and Cara are stringing popcorn while Ty and Lo fight over the pros and cons of tinsel.

"I haven't had much time," he replies with a chuckle. "A certain woman has kept me busy."

"Plus," Seth adds and hangs bulbs on the tree, "we had to cut the tree down ourselves, and it's been too snowy. But I got to drive the snowmobile and drag it behind us back to the house."

"I still say fake trees are better," Lo says with a grimace, eyeing the tree like it's evil.

"I agree," Cara says and glares at Josh. "He made me have a real tree."

"I can cut them down for free on my own property," he insists, as though this is an argument they've had a hundred times.

"I like the smell of the real ones," I say and take a deep breath. "You bring the outside inside."

"Along with spiders and who knows what else," Lo says.

"Oh God." I feel my eyes grow wide and turn to Zack. "Did you shake it? What if there's a squirrel? Or birds?"

"There is no wildlife in this tree," he insists as his dad, Jeff, laughs hysterically.

"It would be so cool if there was a squirrel!" Seth exclaims.

"I'm sure Thor would appreciate that too," I murmur. Thor's ears perk up at his name and he tilts head. "No squirrels for you."

"Oh, Joshy, remember this one?" Nancy says as she pulls an ornament out of the ancient box that Zack rescued from the attic.

"*Joshy*?" Ty echoes, earning the flip of the bird from Josh.

"I made that in the second grade," he replies and rolls his eyes.

"Where are its legs?" Seth asks, eyeing the old gingerbread man with a string through its head. "Did you eat them?"

"No, they probably fell off," Nancy says with a laugh. "It's about twenty-five years old."

"You're such an artist," Zack taunts his brother.

"You don't have much room to talk, son," Jeff says and holds up a photo that's been choppily cut into a circle and glued to red construction paper that has faded to a light rust color. "I do believe this is you. *Zacky*."

"That's Josh," Zack lies and laughs.

"Nope, it's you," Josh confirms.

"Oh, your first Christmas ornaments," Nancy announces with tears in her eyes. "Look!"

"Oh God, Mom's gonna cry," Zack mutters.

"You were just tiny little things," she chokes and Ty laughs while pinching the bridge of his nose.

"I love this so much." He laughs.

"Shut up, man." Josh punches Ty in the shoulder.

"I think it's wonderful." Lo glares at her fiancé.

"Don't cry, darlin'." Jeff kisses his wife's cheek and pats her back. "Just hand the ornaments to the kids to hang on the tree."

"Can I put the angel on top?" Seth asks excitedly.

"Yes," I reply and smile at him. He's been so fun today, so excited for Christmas. It's been a challenge keeping him away from all of the wrapped gifts with his name on them, because he wants to shake them and try to guess what's inside.

I can't wait for tomorrow morning.

The tree that Zack, Jeff, and Seth chose is at least eight feet tall, almost meeting the ceiling of the grand family room. Zack and Jeff strung the lights and garland around it this afternoon before the rest of us arrived, so it would be ready to dress right after dinner.

"Hey, boys, let's go get the fire started outside." Jeff motions for all of the guys to follow him outside.

"Be right back, sugar." Zack kisses my cheek and follows the guys out the back.

"Does it take four grown men to start that fire?" Cara asks with a laugh.

"I'm going too!" Seth cries and runs for his boots to follow the men.

"Make that four and a half," Lo says.

"Yes, because they have to choose the perfect wood and argue about the best way to start the fire and then admire it once it's been started," Nancy informs us. "It's a man thing."

"I suppose so." I step back to admire the huge Christmas tree. "This is pretty."

"I like the red and white lights," Lo says, also admiring the tree.

"I do too," Cara agrees.

"Those are new," Nancy says. "Zack got them for Jilly."

"For me?" *Holy shit!* "Why would he get special lights for me?"

"Because he knows your favorite color is red," she replies and offers me a soft smile. "I do believe my son is in love with you, darling."

"Oh." I wave her off and shake my head. "There have been no exchanges of the *L* word."

"It won't be long," she replies. "How did your little project turn out?"

"What project?" Lo asks and hangs a pretty red bulb on the tree.

"Nancy found a photo of Zack with Seth when Seth was a tiny baby for me. You'll see what I did with it in the morning when he opens his gift." I hug Nancy and kiss her cheek. "Thanks again."

"You're welcome."

"What did Ty get you?" I ask Lo.

"He says we're exchanging our gifts tomorrow night when we get home. He won't tell me what it is." She rolls her eyes. "How about you, Cara?"

"Josh says I can open it tomorrow morning." She shrugs and continues to string her popcorn. "It doesn't really matter to me, though. I have everything I need. What do you and Jeff usually do for each other, Nancy?"

"We typically don't exchange gifts, but this year Jeff bought us tickets on an Alaskan cruise."

"Awesome!" I exclaim. "You'll love that."

"It will be fun. I was surprised he thought of it. He likes to stick close to home."

"I wonder what Zack got you," Cara says.

"Oh, I don't need anything. We've been seeing each other for less than a month."

"That doesn't matter," Cara insists.

I shrug and smile softly. "As long as Seth has a good Christmas, that's all that matters. He deserves it."

"I agree," Zack says as he walks into the room, clearly hearing the last part of the conversation. "And thank you." He pulls me in for a big hug, and when my breasts press against his chest, I have to catch my breath. They've been so sore the past couple of days. I must be about to start my period.

Merry Christmas to me.

"Are you guys ready to go outside? The fire's roaring."

"We're not done trimming the tree," I remind him.

"How much is left?"

"The popcorn is done," Cara announces and begins draping it around the tree. Lo jumps in to help her, and within seconds they're finished. "Now it's just the angel on top."

"Seth can do that when we come back in."

"I'll grab some extra blankets," Nancy offers and opens a hall linen closet as we all bundle up into our jackets and boots. "Zack, will you grab the bags in the kitchen?"

"Sure, Mom."

"I'll be right out," I say and set a pot on the stove and fill it with milk. "I'm going to make some hot chocolate real quick. I brought a thermos."

"We have dozens of thermoses, sugar." Zack kisses my cheek. "I'll be right back to help."

Zack and the girls go outside, leaving me alone in the kitchen. It smells fantastic, since Nancy and I baked pies this afternoon for tomorrow's dessert. When the milk is on its way to a boil, I add the chocolate and vanilla—my secret ingredient—and mix constantly, not wanting the milk to scorch.

"How's it going?" Zack asks as he rejoins me.

"Fine. Almost ready. I think I'll need one of your thermoses too. I made a lot."

He fetches me the thermos as I fill the first, then helps me fill the second.

"I brought disposable cups with lids too."

"Thought of everything, didn't you?"

"I'm a planner, can't help it." I turn to carry the hot drinks outside, but Zack stops me, sets everything back on the kitchen counter, and pulls me in for a long, firm hug.

"I'm so glad you're here, Jilly."

"Me too." I grin and breathe him in.

"You spoiled the shit out of my kid."

"How do you know? Everything's still wrapped."

"Because there are at least ten gifts over there for him from you." He massages my lower back gently. "You didn't have to do that."

"Once I started with that damn one-click button I couldn't quit. It was fun, and I really want him to be spoiled rotten this year."

Zack kisses my forehead then leans his forehead against mine. "Thank you."

"You're welcome. Tomorrow morning is going to be fun." I kiss him quickly before pulling out of his arms. "Let's go. I want s'mores."

"How do you know we're having s'mores?"

"I saw the chocolate. I'm no dummy." I wink and lead him out the back door, through the trampled snow to the side of the house where everyone else is already huddled around the fire, sticks of marshmallows in the fire.

"I can't believe I didn't know you guys did this every year," I say as I sit next to Seth and Zack settles next to me. I grin to myself. I love being sandwiched between my guys.

"Can I have some hot chocolate?" Seth asks. "Please?"

"Of course." I pour him a cup, then everyone else too, passing the cups around the circle.

"What do you do if it's snowing?" Cara asks around a bite full of s'mores.

"This," Josh replies with a shrug.

"What if it's a blizzard?" Lo asks.

"This," Zack confirms.

"Well," Nancy adds, "the one year that we had twenty-below weather we had to take it inside and roast the marshmallows in the woodstove." She grins as her gaze circles about the fire. "I've truly missed this. Think of how different last Christmas was."

We all fall quiet lost in our own thoughts as Zack leans over and kisses my temple.

"So how did s'mores become a Christmas Eve tradition?" I ask as Zack blows the fire out on my marshmallows and helps me place them on my chocolate and graham crackers.

"I don't remember," he replies. "Do you, Dad?"

"I'm out of marshmallows!" Seth announces and licks his fingers.

"Stop sharing with Thor," Ty says with a laugh, earning a wide grin from the boy.

"The boys were about five," Jeff begins and passes a fresh bag to Seth. "And they wanted to sit outside to watch for Santa."

"That's right." Nancy nods with a laugh. I've always loved the King family. Nancy is slim with dark hair like her boys. Jeff is tall and broad, but where his boys are dark, he's got light hair, sprinkled with gray. They had the twins in their thirties after many years of struggling to have children. "They refused to sit inside and watch out the window. They didn't want to miss it. So, Jeff built the fire and we bundled up and made s'mores to pass the time."

"Did you ever see Santa?" Cara asks with a nudge to Josh's arm.

"We always fell asleep," he replies with a grin.

"And how did you know about this?" I ask Ty with a frown.

"The guys invited me out here on Christmas Eve in high school, and we'd hang out here, make the s'mores that Mama King bought for us, and lie to each other about girls."

"You never mentioned it," I reply.

"It wasn't a secret," he says with a laugh. "I guess I never thought to tell you."

"Hey! I never lied about girls," Zack insists.

"Right." Ty rolls his eyes and then kisses Lo on the temple. "Do you need anything, sweetness?"

"Nope, I'm good."

"Warm enough?"

"Mm." She nods and smiles happily. "The fire is nice."

"So, Seth," I say and tousle the boy's hair. "Are you going to stay up long enough to see Santa with me?"

"There's no Santa," he insists as he blows out a burning marshmallow.

"What did I say last week in my kitchen? Yes, there is. If you keep saying there isn't, he won't show up tonight, and I for one want to see what he brings you."

Seth raises a brow and stares at me like I'm crazy. Conversation swirls around us as I scoot closer to the boy and wrap my arm around his shoulders and speak softly to him.

"Even if you don't believe in the man himself, you have to believe in the magic of Christmas, Seth. That's what Santa is."

"What do you mean?"

"It's the whole season. The lights and decorations and good food. It's sitting right here, by this fire in the middle of a snowy Montana winter, eating s'mores and slipping marshmallows to your dog."

Seth smirks and flips another marshmallow to Thor as I continue.

"Christmas is the magic of being generous to others. And it's about remembering that a little baby was born so that you and I are forgiven our sins. Christmas is special."

I lean back to find that everyone sitting around the fire is watching us, listening. Nancy is smiling widely and nodding, and murmurs simply, "Well said."

I shrug and feel my cheeks heat. "I like Christmas."

"And that's saying something, considering how shitty Christmases were in our house," Ty mutters with a grimace.

I shake my head in warning. I don't want to talk about Mom and Dad now, here in this special place. We're having too much fun to bring old, bad memories into it.

Zack pulls me into his arms, cradles my face in his hands, and kisses me long and slow, right here in front of all of our family. When he finally pulls away, Josh yells, "Get a room!"

"What was that for?" I ask breathlessly.

"You're a special woman, Jillian Sullivan."

"I'm just a girl who loves Christmas. And s'mores. Give me some of those marshmallows, brat." I steal the bag from Seth and giggle when he sticks his lower lip out in a pout.

Jeff stands to throw more logs on the fire and glances around the yard, taking in a deep breath. "We lucked out on the weather. Stopped snowing just in time."

"And it's not too cold," Cara agrees. "It's just perfect."

"Keep an eye on the sky," I warn everyone. "Wait. I'm gonna download that Santa tracker app on my phone."

I pull my phone from my pocket to download the app and see that I've missed a text.

"Shit," I whisper.

"What's wrong?" Zack asks.

I look up into his brown gaze and then shake my head and look over at my brother, who is also watching me. "Did you check your phone?"

He pulls his phone out of his pocket, frowning down at it. He swears under his breath, kisses a troubled Lo on the cheek, then stands and pulls me into a hug.

"It's okay, princess."

"I don't ever want to hear from her, Ty. She knows that."

He drags his hand up and down my back soothingly, murmuring in my ear. "Just delete it and go about your holiday."

"What is going on?" Zack demands.

"It's my mom," I reply softly and glance over at Cara. "She texted."

"What did she say?" Cara asks quietly.

"Just merry Christmas," I mumble. *And that she's sure to remind us that she's spending it without my dad because we killed him.* "I don't like hearing from her."

"It's okay," Seth speaks up and surprises me by rubbing my shoulder. "I don't like hearing from my mom either."

We all still and watch Seth carefully.

"When did you last hear from her?" I ask calmly.

"Today."

"What the—" Zack begins, but I hold my hand up to stop him.

"Did she call you?"

"Yeah, she called my cell phone." He nibbles his s'more as though it's no big deal at all. "She said merry Christmas."

"I wonder how she got your number."

"Jill should have been a lawyer," Ty mutters to Lo.

"She said the school gave it to her." Seth shrugs and then frowns.

"Did she say anything else?" I ask. Zack has begun pacing behind us in the trampled snow. Jeff and Josh both look like they're ready to punch someone out and Nancy is wringing her hands in agitation.

Seth nods uncertainly and glances over at me. "But I'm not supposed to say."

"It's okay." I rub his back and shake my head at Zack when he opens his mouth. "You know you can tell us anything, Seth."

"She said she might make a trip up here from Vegas soon to see me."

"Oh." I raise my eyebrows as though I'm surprised. "She's living in Vegas, huh?"

"I guess." He scowls. "I told her not to come here."

I nod thoughtfully. "That was probably a good idea. Will you do me a favor?"

"Sure."

"If she calls again, please tell your dad right away, okay? She's not supposed to be calling you."

"Oh." He looks back at Zack and frowns. "I'm sorry, Dad. I didn't know."

"It's not your fault, buddy." Zack ruffles his hair and smiles reassuringly. "Just let me know next time, okay?"

"Okay."

"Stick a marshmallow on my stick, will ya?" Lo asks Seth with a grin.

Everyone exchanges looks, and I know there will be a discussion about Kensie after Seth goes to bed. If that woman so much as steps foot on this property, I'll beat the crap out of her myself.

"I wish we could have piped Christmas music out here," Nancy murmurs softly as she snuggles into her husband's side.

"Here!" I wake my phone up and pull up Pandora, set it to a classic Christmas music station, and turn the volume up before setting it in the cup holder of my camping chair. "There you go, Mama King."

"Thank you, sweet girl." Nancy sighs happily as "O Holy Night" plays sweetly around us. Zack pulls me in for a snuggle, tucking me against his chest. Lo and Ty have their heads together, whispering intimately, while Josh and Cara lean against each other, watching the fire.

Thor is lying in a sugar coma on a blanket in the

snow and Seth is leaning against him, looking at his phone.

"Are you texting someone?" Zack asks him.

"No, I'm reading," he replies.

I smile to myself and wink at Nancy, who catches my eye.

"I don't see Santa yet." I lean back to look up at the sky that has magically cleared, putting on a grand display of stars.

"I think he hits us up last, on his way back up to the North Pole," Jeff replies with a smile.

"That makes sense." I nod. "Seth, you still have to put the angel on the tree."

"I won't forget," he answers absentmindedly.

"I think we're going to head up to bed," Ty announces and pulls Lo to her feet.

"Sorry guys," she says with a yawn. "I've just been extra sleepy lately."

"Working long hours?" I ask with a frown, worried about my friend.

"Yeah." She smiles softly and glances up at Ty, and I have a feeling that work's not the reason she's tired at all.

"Us too," Josh announces as he and Cara climb out of their chairs and gather their garbage to carry in with them.

"Come on, Seth, let's go put that angel on the tree." Nancy and Jeff stand and motion for a sleepy Seth and Thor to join them.

"But I'm not tired."

"The sooner you sleep, the sooner Christmas morning will be here," I remind him. "Good night."

"See you in the morning." Nancy leans down to kiss her son's cheek, then, to my surprise, kisses mine as well then whispers in my ear, "So happy to have you as part of our family, Jilly."

I blink back tears as she pats my cheek and follows her husband and Seth into the house.

On my phone, Kelly Clarkson is singing about having a merry little Christmas, and Zack and I are alone with the fire in the clear Christmas Eve night.

"Are you ready to go in?" I ask him quietly.

"I'm ready to do this," he replies and stands before me. He offers me his hand and tugs me to my feet, and then to my utter shock, wraps one arm around the small of my back, kisses my cheek, and begins to sway with the music. His brown eyes look almost amber in the firelight. He has the beginnings of stubble on his chin. I desperately want to push my fingers through his hair, so I reach up with my free hand and tug his hat off his head, toss it on the chair, and finger-comb his hair gently.

"How are you feeling, Mr. King?"

"Like the luckiest man in the world." He kisses my forehead and sighs contentedly.

"This is starting to be the best Christmas I can remember." I smile and graze my knuckles down his cheek. "Seth is having a blast."

"He's excited," he agrees. "Wanna help me bring his snowmobile out of the garage and set it up for him?"

"Where are you going to put it?"

He grins widely and suddenly looks like a young kid on Christmas morning himself. "You'll see."

# CHAPTER

## *Fourteen*

### ZACK

This is the best fucking dream I've ever had.

I'm lying on my back on the softest bed I've ever been in and I'm naked. Jill is with me, stroking my cock until it throbs and pulses with the beat of my heart. Her small hands roam up and down my body. I push her hair off her face and watch raptly as she gazes up at me with happy blue eyes and runs the tip of her tongue up the underside of my dick.

"Zack."

I hear her sweet voice, but I don't want to wake up. This is just too damn good. But as I surface, I realize, I'm not dreaming.

Jill's hand is cupping my sac and she's licking my cock like it's an ice cream cone.

"Merry Christmas, babe."

"Merry Christmas," I mumble sleepily and tangle my fingers in her rich brown hair. She smiles widely up at me, then takes me into her mouth, sinking down on me until I can feel the back of her throat.

I about jackknife up off the bed. Fucking A, I've never felt anything better than Jilly's amazing mouth wrapped around me.

Except when it's her pussy.

Her hand glides up to circle my cock and she tightens around me, just the way she knows I love it, and begins to jerk me off into her mouth.

Dear sweet mother of God, I fucking love this woman.

She hums and it's like lighting a fuse. My balls tighten and I harden even more.

"Baby, you know I fucking love this." I try to keep my voice low so no one else in the house can hear me.

"Mm-hmm," she agrees.

"But if you keep this up—ah, fuck, sugar—I'm going to come in your mouth."

She pulls off me long enough to say, "Good," licks the tip, and then sinks over me again and sucks hard.

Good God, she could suck the rust off a bumper.

*And she's all mine.*

I thrust my hips up off the bed and begin to fuck her face in earnest and she growls deep in her throat.

*Growls.*

I groan as I surrender to my release, coming in her mouth, and damn if she doesn't lap up every drop, then kisses up my body, my neck and cheek, and whispers in my ear, "Merry Christmas, Zack."

"That might be the best damn Christmas present I've ever received." I can't catch my damn breath. I'm panting and sweating and the gorgeous woman draped over me has a very smug, catlike smile on her face. "Proud of yourself, aren't you?"

"Very," she agrees readily, making me chuckle. She rubs the dimple in my cheek with her fingertip. "That was fun."

"You won't get an argument out of me." I kiss her forehead softly. "What time is it?"

"Six," she replies. "I figure the rest of the house will start waking up anytime."

"My parents are probably already down in the kitchen." I thrum my fingers up and down her soft back. "They're early risers."

"You all are," she replies.

"It's habit. In fact ..." I kiss her again and then slide out from under her. "I'm going to grab Josh and run out to the barn to feed the animals and get a few things done before we open presents."

"I guess ranchers don't get holidays, huh?" She's pulled the sheet around her and is resting her head on her hand, watching me pull my jeans and shirt on.

"Nope."

"While you do that, I'll get breakfast started."

"Do you honestly think Seth will let us all eat breakfast before diving into his presents?"

"He can open his stocking while we eat and then he can open the rest," she decides. "And we'll make it a quick breakfast. If I move fast enough, I can get most of it done before he wakes up."

"Good luck with that."

She slides out of bed and stretches her arms high above her head, and I can't help myself. I walk to her and bend my head to take one perfectly puckered nipple between my lips and suck it softly. Jill gasps, as if in pain.

"Does that hurt?"

"I'm a little tender."

"I'm sorry, sugar." I kiss up her chest to her neck.

"This isn't getting stuff done, Zack." She giggles and brushes her fingers through my hair.

"Your fault," I murmur and back away. "You're naked."

"Go feed your horses," she says with a laugh. "Then you're mine."

I kiss her quickly then leave the master suite and jog down the steps to the bedroom Josh and Cara are using. I knock softly, but Josh pulls it open, already dressed.

"Headed to the barn?" he asks.

"Yeah. Let's get it done so we can enjoy the rest of the day."

"My thoughts exactly."

Mom and Dad are sitting in the kitchen, reading a newspaper and munching on bacon.

"Merry Christmas, boys." Mom wraps an arm

around each of our necks as we bend down to kiss her cheeks.

"Merry Christmas," we murmur back to her.

"Heading out to the barn?" Dad asks.

"Yes, sir." Josh nods.

"I'll join you."

"The girls and Ty are still in bed," I say to Mom and grin when I hear Jill's footsteps on the stairs. "Jill's coming down to help make breakfast."

"Oh good." Mom grins and hugs Jill as she comes into the room. "Shoo, guys, we have work to do."

"We'll be back soon."

❀  ❀  ❀

"Thank God you're back!" Seth exclaims as Josh, Dad, and I walk through the back door. "We've been waiting forever."

"You've been up for ten minutes," Jill reminds him dryly.

"That's forever on Christmas morning," Dad says with a laugh. "It smells great in here."

"We saved breakfast for you guys, and already put the turkey in the oven." Cara looks proud as she wraps her arms around my brother's waist and hugs him tight.

"You guys could have woken me up. I would have been happy to help," Ty says with a frown.

"We weren't out that long," I reply.

"Can we do presents now? Pleeeeeease?" Seth asks me with hopeful hazel eyes.

"I suppose so," I say and hang my coat up. "But don't go tearing into everything!"

"I won't! I'm just gonna get ready. Come on, Thor!"

"He's been very patient," Mom says with a smile. "When are you going to take him outside?"

"That'll be last," I say and rub my hands together. I'm almost as excited as my boy.

"Let's go!" Jill bounces into the family room behind Seth, and we all join her. Seth is already separating presents.

"Here's one for you, Jill!"

"Just divvy them up, and then we'll all open them," I murmur to him, sitting in my big recliner and tugging Jill onto my lap.

"Um, how am I supposed to help from here?" she asks.

"There's nothing for you to help with, sugar. Sit back and watch."

She settles against me and a small pile of presents for each of us grows in her lap as Seth hands out the gifts under the tree. When they're all passed out, Mom says, "Seth, go get one of those chew bones that Thor loves, so he has something to enjoy too."

"Okay!" He runs into the kitchen and retrieves the bone for Thor, who curls up happily before the fire.

"Go ahead and dig in, Seth."

The adults all set their gifts aside, excited to watch Seth tear into his loot. For the next twenty minutes he opens everything from new clothes from

Josh to a Kindle Fire from Jilly and video games from Mom and Dad.

"Holy crap!" Seth exclaims. "A rifle?"

"That," Dad says with a stern voice, "is only to be used when you're with your dad. But yes, you're old enough to start learning."

"Thank you!"

He continues through his pile, coming away with the binoculars he told Jill he wanted and a whole slew of crap that he didn't need, but that every twelve-year-old loves.

"This is so cool," he whispers as he sits back on his feet and takes in all the loot before him. He looks up at me with wide eyes, and his lip quivers. I stand with Jill in my arms, then lower her into the chair and turn to my boy.

"Come here, bud." Seth throws his arms around me and hugs me close. "You okay?"

"Yeah." He nods against my chest. "Just ... I didn't expect all this."

"You deserve it," Cara says with a grin. "You've worked your butt off this year."

"Definitely," Josh says.

"No one deserves it more," Ty agrees as Lo nods.

"We love you, sweet boy," Mom tells him with tears in her eyes.

Seth sniffs and pulls away from me with a watery smile. "Thanks, everyone."

"I think maybe we forgot to do something outside," I say with a sudden frown.

"What's that?" Dad asks.

"I think Seth should go check."

"I have to go outside? I thought you said I didn't have to do any chores on Christmas."

"It's not a chore."

"I'll go with you," Jill offers.

Seth looks at us all with a frown. "You're all weird. You haven't opened your presents."

"We will in a minute," Josh assures him.

"Okay." Seth shrugs and stuffs his feet in his boots, throws his jacket on, and stomps outside. We all hurriedly shove our feet in shoes and clamber outside after him, and just as we round the house, we hear, "No freaking way!"

I have Jill's hand in mine as we join Seth, who is standing next to a black-and-yellow snowmobile with a bright red bow stuck to the hood.

"Are you serious right now?" he asks me. He has the biggest smile I've ever seen on his face, and his whole body is vibrating in excitement.

"I'm completely serious."

"Holy crap!" He jumps up and down and throws himself in my arms to hug me tight. "I love it! It's so supercool!"

"I got you a new helmet too, and you *will* be careful."

"I promise," he says. "Can we take it out now?"

"Let's finish up with presents and while we cook dinner, maybe your dad and your uncles can take you out for a ride," Mom suggests.

"Okay!" Seth hugs me hard again. "Thanks, Dad. It's the best present ever."

"You're welcome, buddy." I kiss his head and we all file back into the house. After shedding boots and coats, we settle back in the family room to open the rest of the gifts. I pull Jilly back in my lap and settle in to watch her.

"Open this," she murmurs softly. Everyone else is opening gifts from each other, gasping and laughing and hugging. "This is from me."

"You didn't have to get me anything, sugar."

"Of course I did," she argues with a frown. "It's Christmas."

I chuckle and open the large box, and then my heart stills when I see what's inside. It's a picture frame with a two-photo mat.

On the left is a photo of me and Seth when Seth was just a tiny baby, maybe a week old. I'm holding him against my chest and my lips are planted on his tiny head.

"God, I look young in this photo," I murmur.

"You were young in that photo," Jill says.

The photo on the right is of Seth and me and Thor, playing and laughing in the snow. Jill was standing over us and we were all smiling up at the camera. Even Thor looks like he has a big grin on his dopey face.

"I took that the day we went snowmobiling," she says.

I nod and look into her eyes. "Thank you. It's perfect."

"Your mom helped," she says shyly and smiles over at my mom, who is, of course, watching us raptly.

"I love it." I kiss her lips chastely then reach down at the side of the chair and lift her gift into her lap. "This is for you."

She smiles in excitement and tears the paper away then pauses with her jaw dropped as her eyes take in every inch of the framed photo before her.

"He's a local artist," I begin. "This was taken in Glacier National Park last year."

The photo is of the mountains during winter, with a lake cradled between them, and lighting up the sky are the northern lights, spreading across the sky in streaks of green and blue, just like the ones we saw a few weeks ago out in the pasture.

"It's so beautiful." Her eyes fill with tears and she turns her face into my chest.

"Hey, it's okay, sugar. It's just a photo."

"I'm hormonal," she mutters, but leans up to whisper in my ear, "but this was the moment, Zack. Our special moment. And I'll treasure this forever."

I hug her tight and kiss her temple, and I want to tell her how much I love her. It's Christmas, and God knows I'm so in love with her I can barely breathe. But just as I'm about to whisper in her ear, Cara comes running over to us with a squeal to hug Jill and thank her for the earrings Jill gave her.

"You're welcome," Jill says brightly. "They reminded me of you."

"You went nuts this year, girl," Cara says as she rejoins Josh.

"I couldn't help it," Jill replies. "I had the best time shopping for Seth." She winks down at him and then focuses on Cara again. "You two need to start having babies so I can spoil them rotten."

Ty and Lo suddenly share a glance and it's not missed by Jill.

"What's up with you two?" Jill demands.

"Well, we weren't going to tell yet, because it's still pretty early, but we just found out the day before yesterday that . . ." Lo clears her throat and glances up at Ty.

"We're gonna have a baby," Ty finishes with a proud smile.

"Oh my God," Jill breathes. "Honest?"

Ty nods and then looks at Jill with uncertainty, but she jumps up off my lap and he stands just in time to catch her midair. "Oh my God!" she yells.

"Are you okay?" Ty asks.

"Why in the hell wouldn't I be okay?" she demands and hugs him tightly around the neck. "You're having a baby!"

"I think I'm the one who gets to actually *have* it," Lo says.

"I'm so excited." Jill hugs Lo tightly too, then pulls her brother back into her arms. "This is the best Christmas ever."

"You're sure?"

"Ty," she says and wipes the tears off her face. Fuck,

she's crying again. I can't stand it when she cries. "You deserve a dozen babies, if that's what you want."

"So do you," he replies softly and my heart trembles. Jill can't have babies.

"Stop it," Jill insists. "I couldn't be happier for you."

Cara leaps to her feet and hugs Lo close to her and suddenly the room is a flurry of activity of hugs and well-wishes.

"I'm happy for you, man," I say to Ty as I shake his hand and pull him in for a hug. "You're going to be a hell of a father."

"I have a good teacher," he replies, and if I'm not mistaken, his eyes mist over as he looks from me to my dad. "You and Jeff have taught me everything I know about being a dad, man. I'm terrified, but knowing I have you guys makes it a little easier."

"You won't need us," I assure him, but then pull him in for another hug. "But I'm happy to help out in any way I can."

"Thanks." He looks a bit shell-shocked, and I can't blame him. Being a father may be the best thing that's ever happened to me, but it's scary as hell too.

"There's going to be a new baby around here to snuggle," Mom exclaims excitedly. "If you need me to, I'll come stay with you after he or she arrives to help out."

Lauren's jaw drops and her eyes water as she stares at my mom. "You would do that?"

"Of course. You're our family." She hugs Lo close

and then pats her cheeks, in that way she does with those of us she loves. "This baby is our family too. I'm happy to help."

"I might take you up on that," Lo admits and smiles shyly. "I don't know what in the hell I'm doing."

"I get to help too!" Jill exclaims.

"And me," Cara adds. "This baby won't be lacking for women to love on it."

"Thank you, everyone," Ty says and hugs his sister again. "Thanks for including us in your family."

"You've been a member of this family since you were a teenager, son," Dad says and claps Ty on the shoulder. "Don't you forget that. Now, when are you going to marry this beautiful woman?"

"Well, we've decided to move the wedding up to Valentine's Day. It's going to be a small wedding anyway."

"And this way, I won't be showing yet so I can still wear a beautiful dress," Lo adds.

"Great idea," Cara says. "Jill and I can help."

Jill nods enthusiastically and then yawns.

"You okay, baby?" I murmur down to her as I wrap my arms around her from behind.

"Yeah, I'm fine. Don't know why I'm suddenly tired." She shrugs and when I tighten my arms under her breasts, she flinches. "Hormonal, I guess."

"Do you want to take a nap?"

She shakes her head and smiles happily up at me. "No way, we have to get dinner started."

"Can we go ride my new snowmobile?" Seth asks.

"You guys go play in the snow," Jill says. "We're going to cook and talk about you now."

"Oh good," I reply dryly. "Thanks for the warning."

"I only say nice things, babe."

# CHAPTER

## *Fifteen*

### JILLIAN

I roll over in bed and cringe when my breast is pressed against the mattress. Holy shit, what time is it? I glance at my phone and groan. Since when do I take naps at noon? I've never been a napper. Yet today, I was so exhausted after showing a house that I had to come home and sleep before my mid-afternoon appointment.

This is the second time this week that I couldn't make it through the day without catching at least an hour of sleep.

I frown, my breast still cradled gently in my hand, and think back over the past couple of months. Huh. I haven't had a period in a while. Which isn't anything unusual since all of the extensive fertility treatments I went through.

Maybe I should make an appointment with Hannah.

I google the phone number for the new OB/GYN's office and click SEND.

"Dr. Malone's office, how many I help you?"

"Hi, this is Jillian Sullivan. I have a history of abnormal menstrual cycles and my doctor in California used to prescribe me progesterone to regulate them. Is it possible to have a prescription written for that?"

"Are you a patient of Dr. Malone?"

"No, I've never seen her before, but I can give you the name of my doctor in California so you can get my records if that helps."

"That would be helpful, but even with those records, Dr. Malone will have to see you in the office. She won't prescribe anything without establishing care with you first."

*Damn! I was worried about that.*

"But," she continues, "you can come in to give us a blood and urine sample anytime, and that way by the time your appointment rolls around, you should be all set."

"Okay, can she see me Friday afternoon? That's the best time with my work schedule."

"Let's see. Today's Wednesday . . . Hmm . . . yes, she can see you at two o'clock."

"Perfect. Thanks."

The receptionist keeps me on the line for a few more minutes to gather demographic information and when we hang up, I'm already exhausted again.

Geez, talk about PMS.

I groan as I pull myself out of bed and pull my work clothes back on, already daydreaming about coming home after work and crashing again.

Pitiful.

I plug the address for the house I'm showing this afternoon into my GPS and set off across town. Today, I'm showing a home to the Petersons. This is a couple who knows exactly what they want, and I've been trying for six months to find the house that fits that bill.

I pull into the long driveway of the beautiful, two-year-old craftsman home on the outskirts of town and smile when I see Mr. and Mrs. Peterson already standing on the covered porch, looking in the windows.

"Hi!" I call as I step out of the car and approach the young couple.

"Hi, Jill," Whitney Peterson replies and opens her arms for a hug. "How was your Christmas?"

"I had a great Christmas, thank you."

Bryan Peterson smiles and shakes my hand. "Fifteenth try's the charm, right?"

"Right." I wink and unlock the front door then lead them inside. "This one hasn't even hit the listings yet. When I saw it come through this morning, I had a feeling about it. And it's priced exactly right." I tell them the listing price and feel my heart quicken when they glance at each other and nod. "Let's have a look."

The further through the house we go, the more excited the young couple seems to get. The bedrooms are spacious, the bathrooms equipped with exactly what they want. Even the master bathroom, which has been a bone of contention in past houses they've seen.

"We'll take it," Bryan announces when we wander back down to the kitchen.

"Just like that?" I ask with a laugh.

"Just like that," Whitney replies. "This is exactly what we've been looking for."

"What do you want to offer them?" I pull my iPad out of my purse and open my notes.

"The asking price." I raise a brow and do a quick mental calculation. Holy shit, that's going to be an awesome commission.

"You really want this house," I reply.

"We've been waiting a long time to find exactly what we want, and I don't want anyone to come in and snatch it out from under us," Bryan says with a shake of the head.

"I can arrange for an inspection this week and get the paperwork in motion. I'll send the offer as soon as I get back to the office."

Whitney squeals and jumps up and down, clapping her hands, then launches herself into her husband's arms. This is my favorite part of my job, helping my clients find a home they love.

"It's been such a pleasure working with you both," I say as I lock up behind us and we walk to our cars. "I'll be in touch when I hear from the seller."

"Thank you so much."

I pull away with a wide grin on my face and I immediately push the button on my Bluetooth. I need to tell Zack.

"Hey, sugar," he says as he answers. He sounds out of breath, and my mind immediately shifts to the way he feels when he's over me, inside me, making exactly that noise.

"Jilly?" he asks.

"I'm here. Sorry. Do you have plans tonight?"

"What do you have in mind?"

"I need to celebrate. I just sold a house to a couple that I thought I'd never find the right house for. I want to take you out to dinner."

"*I'll* take *you* out for dinner. Do I have to wear a monkey suit?" I hear the smile in his voice.

"You'll look hot in your monkey suit." I chuckle and pull into the parking lot of my office. "I have some paperwork to take care of this afternoon and then I'm heading home."

"I'll pick you up at six."

"Great. See you soon."

"Bye, sugar."

❁  ❁  ❁

After adjusting my boobs in my push-up bra, I check my lipstick and grin when I hear the doorbell, then

Zack coming inside. I love that he feels comfortable enough to make himself at home here.

"I'm almost ready!" I call out and stuff my lipstick, phone, and debit card in a small clutch bag then smooth my hands down my long, black fitted dress. It falls to my feet, but is strapless, so I added a simple necklace and earrings. My hair is held on my head with about fifty pins.

"Jesus Christ, Jilly." I turn to find Zack leaning against the door frame, his arms crossed over his chest, as his eyes take me in from head to toe. He's delicious in a dark gray suit and royal-blue tie. He's clean-shaven and his hair has been tamed, begging for my fingers to mess it up.

"You look fantastic." I cross the room to him and reach up to adjust his tie, although it doesn't need to be adjusted at all. I just want to touch him.

"You are the most beautiful woman I've ever seen." He cradles my face gently in his hands and lowers his face to mine, tenderly sweeping his lips back and forth, barely touching them, and it drives me crazy. My thighs clench and I grab onto his tie, pulling him in closer.

"Say stuff like that and we won't leave my house," I whisper.

"I'm okay with that," he replies with a wolfish smile.

"I have lots to celebrate," I reply and pull away.

He holds my black peacoat up for me and then

lifts me in his arms and carries me out to his truck so I don't have to trudge through the snow in heels.

"You're very chivalrous," I comment and plant a kiss on his cheek.

"No need to get your fancy shoes wet." He sets me in the truck and drives us to a restaurant that sits on the lake. It's one of the more expensive places in town, with white tablecloths and excellent food.

"Swanky." I wink at him as he leads me inside.

"I'm in a tie, sugar. And you're celebrating." The hostess guides us to a table in the corner, looking out on the lake. It's dark now, but the lights from the houses along the shoreline reflect in the water.

It's romantic.

After taking our wine order, the waitress leaves us to read over the menu.

"So what, exactly, are we celebrating? I've been in suspense all day."

"Do you know Bryan and Whitney Peterson?" I ask. Zack frowns and moves his head side to side, thinking.

"I don't think so."

"They moved to town about a year ago, and started looking for a house to buy last summer. I've shown them fifteen houses, and they didn't like any of them. I think all of us had given up hope that we'd ever find the right one. Then, this morning, I saw a house that was just put on the market today, and I had a gut feeling."

"So you showed it to them . . ."

"And they bought it!" I announce and clap my hands. "They *loved* it. Jumped right on it. I'm so happy for them."

"Well done, baby." He smiles widely and clinks his wine glass to mine. "I'm proud of you."

"Thank you." I feel my cheeks heat as the waitress returns to take our order.

"So what happens now?" Zack asks and takes my hand in his.

"Well, I already sent over their offer. There will be an inspection, and if all goes well, they should be proud new homeowners soon."

"Talk to me about your job."

I cock my head to the side and think about his request. "What do you want to know?"

"Everything. Why you chose it. What you enjoy about it."

"I got into it because I like looking at houses. Always have. Maybe I'm just naturally nosy." I wrinkle my brow as I think about it. "So it seemed natural to sell houses. It's a puzzle."

I lean in, getting excited as I describe my job to Zack.

"Finding the perfect home for a family or couple is fun. Everyone has different expectations. Different needs. So, I enjoy talking with those I'm working for, get a feel for what they want, and find the perfect home for them."

"So it's about the people you work with."

"It really is." I nod as I think about it from that perspective. "When I'm working with a client, I speak with them frequently. Whitney Peterson and I email back and forth at least once a day. I develop a relationship with these people. Of course," I add and sip my wine, "some people are weird. Those I don't speak to as frequently."

"Your eyes light up when you talk about your job," he murmurs. "I love you, sugar."

I feel my eyes grow wide as I stare at this dear man before me and feel the floor drop out from under me.

*Did he just say what I think he did?*

He blinks, as though coming out of a trance, and begins to look embarrassed, but before he can apologize or say anything else, I lean way out over the top of the table to plant my lips on his. He grips my wrists, as though grounding us both, and kisses me back with all of the passion and love that were just in his eyes. I pull back just an inch and stare into his deep chocolate gaze.

"Say it again."

"I love you so much it hurts." He raises a hand and brushes his fingertips down my cheek to my jaw. "You are the most amazing person I've ever met, sugar."

"I love you too," I whisper. "And it scares the shit out of me."

He kisses me again and suddenly I hear someone clearing their throat from beside us.

"Your ass is in the air. You know that, right?" Zack asks.

I pull away and glance around the busy restaurant, which has now gone quiet. Everyone is watching us raptly.

"He just said he loves me!" I announce with a wide smile. There are smiles and cheers and applause. Zack laughs and stands to guide me back to my chair. From across the room, I can see my eighth-grade history teacher. "Hi, Mrs. Anderson!"

She waves and I turn my attention back to my handsome date. "Did you have Mrs. Anderson for history?"

"No."

"I liked her." I brace my chin on my fist and watch Zack happily. "What's wrong?"

"Absolutely nothing. Aside from your ass being in the air for everyone to see for longer than I'm comfortable with."

"Who gives a shit if anyone could see my ass?" I shake my head and sip my wine. "My man just told me he loved me. I had to get to you as quickly as possible."

"And right over the top of the table was the quickest route?" He offers me a half smile, his brown eyes shining with happiness.

"Yes."

"Good to know." Our dishes are served and my stomach growls in anticipation. "Hungry?"

"Oh my God, so hungry." I dive into my chicken marsala with gusto.

"Didn't you have lunch?"

"Yes, I ate a whole foot-long sandwich. I don't know why I'm so hungry lately."

"Speaking of feet," Zack says dryly, "Seth needs new boots. Since you have Friday afternoon off, do you want to ride with us to pick some out?"

"Sure," I reply and take another bite of food and then I remember my appointment. "Oh, crap. I can't."

He cocks a brow in question.

"I just made a doctor's appointment."

"Are you okay?" He lowers his fork to his plate and frowns at me, giving me his undivided attention.

"Oh, I'm fine." I take another bite of food and shake my head. "I have issues regulating my cycles, so sometimes I have to go in and have it taken care of."

He grimaces and then takes a swig of wine. "That's a little TMI, baby. A simple 'I need a checkup' would have sufficed."

"Sorry." I laugh and butter a piece of warm bread. "I need a checkup. But if you want to come to my place after, I can make you guys dinner."

"I think Seth is going to go to Josiah's for the night.

They seem to be inseparable these days. Plus, Seth needs something to do. This whole being on winter break thing is getting old."

"Ready to go back to school, is he?" I ask with a laugh.

"Yeah, we're both ready. If I hear 'Dad, I'm bored' one more time, I might kill him."

I giggle and finish my dinner. "I doubt that. Does he go back Monday?"

"Yes, thankfully. But if Josiah's family decides to adopt him over the weekend, I won't put up a fight."

"I might put up a fight," I reply seriously. "I'd miss him."

"I love that you love my kid," Zack says softly and takes my hand in his, lacing our fingers.

"This wouldn't work if I wasn't fond of Seth, Zack. You're a package deal, and I wouldn't have it any other way."

"I know, and that's just one of the things I love about you."

"I like hearing that." The waitress returns with our paid check, and without another word, Zack stands and helps me into my coat and out to his truck.

"When I heard that we were celebrating, I asked Josh and Cara if they'd let Seth bunk with them tonight."

"Does that mean . . . ?"

"It means," he says as he pulls into my driveway and cuts the engine, "that I don't have to race out of here in the middle of the night."

I smile widely and watch him with hungry eyes as he walks around the truck and lifts me out of the passenger seat and holds me close to him as he carries me up to the front door.

He sets me down and waits patiently while I unlock the door, step inside, and shed my coat. He's not speaking, and he seems calm, but there's a new intensity to him. When I turn around to face him, he's removed his suit jacket, and he backs me up against the wall without touching me. He pulls at his tie, loosening it, staring down at my lips, my eyes.

My breasts.

"Do you have any idea," he murmurs softly, "how fucking gorgeous you look tonight?"

My breathing quickens as he unbuttons the cuffs of his shirt and then down the front, pulls it out of his pants, and peels it off his broad, muscled shoulders and drops it to the floor.

"What are you wearing under that dress?" he whispers.

"Why don't you take it off me and find out?" I reply with a saucy smile.

"I'm going to touch you, Jilly," he breathes and barely drags the tip of his nose down my cheek to my neck. "I'm going to explore every amazing fucking inch of your body."

"Oh my."

"And baby?"

"Yeah?"

"Keep those shoes on."

I smile as his nose glides back up my neck to my ear. If the wall weren't at my back, I'd be on the floor because I'm pretty sure my knees gave out on me a while ago.

He wraps his arms around my waist and lifts me straight up off the floor, so my feet are dangling and his face is pressed to my throat. He's panting now, as turned on as I am. I want to cry out when my breasts press against his chest, but suddenly, he sets me back on my feet next to my bed and turns me away from him so he can lower my zipper. The motion is so fucking slow, I want to scream at him to hurry up.

"Zack, hurry," I whisper instead.

"Oh no. This isn't going to be fast." When the zipper is down, the dress falls and pools at my feet. "Fucking A, Jilly, it's like unwrapping the most amazing Christmas present."

My lips twitch into a smile. "Can I turn back around now?"

"Not yet." His hands glide from my shoulders down to the hooks of my bra. He unfastens it and it falls away, making me gasp softly.

"Okay?" he asks.

"I'm a little tender," I reply.

"I'll be gentle." His hands journey down my back, my sides, to my hips, where he hooks his fingers into my black lace panties and tugs them down until they also pool at my feet. "I fucking love your ass."

"It's a little round," I murmur and bite my lip when I feel him squat behind me, cup my ass, and place wet, sucking kisses on either cheek.

"Perfect." He spreads the cheeks of my ass and presses his face to my core, licking my pussy lips, up and down and back and forth, and I have no choice but to lean forward against the tall mattress.

"Holy shit." I reach behind me to bury my fingers in his hair, but he takes my wrist in his grasp and holds my hand against the small of my back, rendering me helpless as he stands, and, keeping me pressed to the mattress and my arm behind my back, unbuckles his belt, and releases his pants. I hear them hit the floor with a clang and suddenly, he's guiding his hard erection through my folds and pushes inside me. I gasp in surprise and then moan with the intensity of it all.

"You are stunning," he growls and kisses my shoulder as he begins moving in and out of me fiercely. "I can't take my eyes off you. Even in a roomful of people, you're all I see."

"Oh my God, Zack," I whimper, trying to thrust my hips back to meet his hips, but he has me held still.

"You make me crazy. I dream of you, whether I'm asleep or wide awake trying to work." He suddenly pulls out, turns me around, and boosts me up onto the bed, lying back so my hips are at the edge. He wraps my legs around his hips and dives right back in, locking my gaze with his own.

I cup his cheek in my palm and guide his lips to mine.

"You are the best part of my life," he whispers gently. "I didn't know it was possible to feel this fucking fiercely about anyone aside from Seth. To want to protect and love anyone the way I do you."

"I love you too." I wrap my arms and legs around him tightly and hold on with all my might as he pounds in and out of me, riding me hard as though he's been swept away with too much emotion and just can't hold it in anymore.

He pushes a hand between us, presses his thumb against my clit, and sends me right over the edge into oblivion. I cry out with the surprise of the intense orgasm wracking my body.

"Jilly," he breathes and stills, his whole body clenched hard, as he comes, surrendering to his own climax.

He's sweating, panting, and his heart is pounding a fast beat as he braces himself over me and tries to compose himself.

"Did I hurt you?" he asks softly.

"Never." I hold him closer and kiss his cheek. "You'd never hurt me."

He stands and pulls out of me, then leads me to the bathroom. I reach for the pins in my hair, but he stills my hands. "Wait. Leave it up." He turns on the bath and while it fills, he boosts me onto the countertop, helps me out of my shoes, and rubs my feet with firm thumbs.

"Sweet Jesus, you're good with your hands," I moan.

"Like that, do you?"

"Mm," I reply and sigh as his thumb pushes up my arch. "Just do this for about a year, and I'll be good to go."

"If the shoes hurt your feet so much, why do you wear them?"

"It's not the shoes' fault." When his hands still I open one eye to find him staring at me with disbelief. "They don't hurt my feet. You just have magical hands. You could rub me all day every day and I'd never get tired of it."

"Would it sound as sweet if I said that you could rub my cock all day every day and I'd never tire of it?" he wonders aloud, making me snort.

"No. It doesn't sound as nice. Sexy, but not nice." I grin up at him as he switches feet and administers the same attention to the other foot. "You looked so handsome tonight. Thank you for dressing up for me."

"My pleasure. I don't really mind wearing a suit." His hands glide up my calves to my thighs. "Mom used to make Josh and me wear suits to church on Sundays."

"I like your mom."

"She likes you."

He nibbles my lips as he lifts me off the counter and lowers me into the steamy water.

"Hot," I mutter and take a deep breath.

"Too hot?" he pauses.

"No, just need a second to get used to it." I grin and then sigh deeply as I feel my muscles loosen in the steam. "This tub is big enough for two."

"I was hoping you'd say that." He winks and climbs in behind me, pulls me against his chest, and kisses my head.

"Thank you for celebrating with me tonight."

"You're welcome. Congratulations, sugar." He kisses me again and pulls a washcloth off the ledge, wets and soaps it, and begins dragging it over my body. When he reaches my breasts, I suck in another breath as the soft cloth feels like it's going to peel my nipple right off.

"I'm sorry, baby. You're that sore?"

"Yeah. It's okay. Damn hormones."

He continues cleaning the rest of me, and when he's done, I take the cloth and return the favor, running it over his legs, hips, and stomach and then pay his dick special attention. He hardens in my grasp, but doesn't make any moves to make love to me again. Instead, once we're clean, he helps me out of the tub, dries me off, and leads me to the bed. I yawn widely.

"Tired?"

"It's been a long day," I reply.

He peels back the covers and tucks me next to him, covers us both, and wraps me in his arms. I glance up at him in surprise. He doesn't want to make love again?

"You'll most likely wake up with me inside you," he whispers and kisses my cheek, drags his nose to my jaw, and plants another kiss there. "But for to-night, I just want to hold you while you sleep."

I grin and sigh, luxuriating in his strong embrace, and let myself drift into blissful sleep.

# CHAPTER

## *Sixteen*

"Hi, Jill," Hannah says with a smile as she enters the small exam room. I'm naked under a worn blue hospital gown that's gaping open in the back, and there's a paper blanket over my lap.

"Hi, Dr. Malone," I reply with a grin.

"It's just Hannah," she says with a wave. "I'm not that formal."

"Oh, good," I reply.

"So, tell me what's going on." She sits on a black rolling stool and looks up at me expectantly.

"I might as well start at the beginning, so get comfy." I take a deep breath and start my story. "I have a diagnosis of unexplained infertility. My ex-husband and I tried for many years to get pregnant. We went through everything from artificial insemination to in vitro, and nothing worked."

"I did have a chance to read through your records from the other office," Hannah says and nods. "Sounds like it must have been a very frustrating time for you."

"That's an understatement," I reply softly. "Since the last treatments over a year ago, my cycles have been all screwy. I sometimes go several months between periods, and when that happens, I'd just get a medication to sort of jump-start my system again, then I'd be regular for a few more months."

"So, I take it you've been irregular again?" she asks while jotting down notes.

"Yeah. It just occurred to me the other day that I haven't had a period since about October."

"Are you having any sort of symptoms now?"

"Sore breasts, sleepy during the day, typical PMS for me, although my breasts are more tender than usual."

"Hmm, interesting. I see that you stopped by for a blood and urine sample yesterday and"—she taps some keys on her iPad—"it doesn't look like those results are in quite yet, so I'm going to leave you here for a moment and call the lab to see if they're ready."

"Thanks, Hannah. I appreciate it."

"No problem. Be back shortly."

When Hannah leaves the room, I grab my phone and see that I've missed a text from Zack.

Zack: **How was the dr?**

Me: **Still here. Waiting for blood results. What do u want for dinner?**

Zack: **Mexican?**

Me: **Yum. ;)**

The door opens and Hannah breezes back into the room, closes it behind her, and is examining her iPad closely.

"That was faster than I expected," I say jokingly. Hannah grins and finishes reading the report.

"The report just came through," she murmurs then looks up at me with bright eyes.

"So, do you need the name of my pharmacy?"

"Yes, but not for progesterone." Hannah sets her iPad down and faces me squarely. "Jill, I have a feeling this is going to shock the hell out of you, but you're pregnant."

I blink at her for several seconds and suddenly my stomach drops to my knees and a cold sweat breaks out all over my body.

"Excuse me?"

"You're pregnant, Jill."

I shake my head and fight to wrap my head around the words coming out of her mouth. "That's impossible."

"No, apparently it's not."

"I'm infertile."

"You have unexplained infertility. Many things can factor into that. It doesn't mean that you can *never* get pregnant, it means that your doctors could never understand *why* you weren't getting pregnant."

I bite my lip and keep my eyes trained on Hannah's face.

"I'm sorry. Did you just say that I'm fucking *pregnant*?"

"Yes." She smiles softly and waits for my mind to catch up. "I take it this isn't a good thing?"

"I don't know," I whisper. "I mean, of course it's good. It's a baby. Do you know how long and how hard I tried for this? What I put my body through for *years*?"

"Yes, Jill, I do. So, now we need to figure out how far along you are."

My heart stills and I feel my eyes go wide. "I haven't had a period in a while, but Zack and I first started sleeping together at the beginning of December. If I'm having symptoms already, that must be when I ovulated."

Hannah is nodding in agreement. "I agree. The symptoms you're having are typical for a pregnancy this early. No morning sickness yet?"

"No, just hungry. And really thirsty."

"That's normal too."

"Well, shit, those are also PMS symptoms."

"I know—why do you think women who are trying to get pregnant make themselves crazy, misreading symptoms?"

"This wasn't even in the realm of possibility for me," I whisper. "I think I'm in shock."

"That's perfectly normal too. I'm going to prescribe some prenatal vitamins for you. Get plenty of sleep, watch what you eat, and take care of yourself."

"No ultrasound?"

"It's way too early for that yet." Hannah smiles gently and squeezes my shoulder. "Congratulations. I'll want to see you again in four weeks."

"Thank you." I smile back at her and watch as she leaves the room. I move in what feels like slow motion, pulling my clothes on with shaking hands. I can't make the shaking stop.

Holy shit, I'm going to have a baby! Zack and I are going to have a baby. I smile widely and briefly wonder what Seth will think. Oh, I hope he's happy.

Shit, what if *Zack* isn't happy?

The thought stops me in my tracks, but then I shake it off. He just told me he *loves* me. We're in a monogamous, committed relationship, for crying out loud. Life happens and sometimes it throws you a curveball.

This curveball just happens to be in the form of a baby.

*A baby.*

I make my appointment for a month out, pick up my prescription, and walk on numb feet out to my car, where I sit in the driver's seat and stare at the building before me for long minutes. All that work. The long months—*years*—of medication and giving myself shots in the ass and hot flashes. The hundreds of ultrasounds and needle sticks and being told over and over again, *No*. No, it didn't work. No, you're not pregnant.

And now, after I'd given up all hope that it could ever happen, here I am in my hometown, finally truly in love with an incredible man, and pregnant.

I can't freaking wait to tell Zack.

And Cara. Should I call Cara? No, I should tell Zack first.

Shit, I don't know what to do.

I laugh at myself and start the car, wipe tears from my cheeks, and just before I pull away from the parking lot, I get another text.

Zack: **On my way to ur place. Just dropped Seth off.**

Me: **Perfect timing. Meet u there.**

I drive the short distance through town to my little house and pull into the driveway just before Zack, who pulls in behind me.

"Hey sugar," he says as he opens my door for me and gives me a big hug before following me to the door and inside the house. "You're a sight for sore eyes."

"Bad day?" I ask as we shed our coats and boots. Zack takes my hand in his and kisses my knuckles, sending happy zings up my arms and to my chest. *I'm dying to blurt it out!* Maybe we should have dinner first?

"Long day. Seth is moody, anxious to get to Josiah's house, and one of the ranch hands quit. We have less help in the winter anyway, so we need to find someone quickly to pick up the slack."

"I'm sorry," I murmur and step back into his arms,

holding him tightly around his waist and pressing my cheek to his chest. He rubs my back and presses a kiss to my head.

"It's okay. I'm feeling much better now." I hear the smile in his voice as I tip my head back. He leans in for a soft, thorough kiss that just about steals my breath away.

"I can cook you dinner, and you can hang out and relax for a while."

"That sounds great, but I'll help with dinner."

"I insist." I press my hand to his chest, rub it soothingly, loving the hard feel of his sternum and the muscles of his pecs, and frankly, I could just stand here all day and run my hands all over him. I want to tell him about the baby and watch his face light up with joy, but I also want to pick the perfect moment. I grin slyly and back away.

"What do you have up your sleeve?" His eyes narrow as he props his hands on his hips.

"I don't know what you're talking about." I shrug innocently and turn to walk to the kitchen. Rather than sitting down to relax, Zack follows me.

"Uh-huh," he says. "You're not a good liar."

"I'm not lying." I laugh and shake my head. *Not really. It's good news!* "If you insist on being in here, can you grab the chicken breasts out of the fridge?" I turn to the pantry and pull out ingredients to make chicken enchiladas. "The inspection on the Peterson house was this morning."

"That seems fast."

"It was. I pulled a few strings." I shrug and set a pan on the stove to brown the chicken in. "They're excited to move in, and I'd like for it to move as quickly as possible."

"Do they have kids?"

"Yes, three and a fourth on the way."

"Holy shit, that's a lot of kids."

I laugh as I turn the chicken. "The house is plenty big enough for all of them. That's one of the things they wanted, plenty of bedrooms and a nice yard. They've been renting a smaller place, so moving into this nice, new, big house is going to feel like heaven to them."

"I'm happy for them then," he replies and leans his hips against my kitchen counter as he watches me work. "You're a good cook."

"Thanks. I like to cook."

"This kitchen seems kind of small."

I nod and glance around the kitchen, then shrug. "It's just me here most of the time, so it's sufficient." *But it won't be just me for long!*

I smile softly and begin shredding the chicken.

"Remember how I mentioned that I want to re-model my kitchen?"

"I do. You're brave. Remodeling a kitchen is a pain in the ass."

"I know," he agrees with a chuckle. "I remember the last time Mom and Dad remodeled. But this time, I have Josh's place and Mom and Dad's new place nearby so we can go there for meals if need be."

"True. And you guys can come here too. That will help for sure."

"I want you to help with the remodel."

"I'm not great with a hammer and I know nothing about buzz saws," I reply as my heart picks up speed again.

"Funny." He swats my ass playfully as I wrap the enchiladas and lay them in a glass pan to slide into the oven. "You're a regular comedian."

"I know. Don't forget to tip your waitress."

"Ba dum bum."

Zack grins, just as his phone rings in his pocket. He frowns when he checks the display. "I'll be right back." He stomps through the kitchen and out the back door, his entire demeanor changed from just a few moments ago.

*I wonder who that was?*

I shrug and set the timer on the oven then set about cleaning up the small mess. Just as I toss the sponge into the sink, Zack comes back into the kitchen.

He's scowling and his body is tense.

"What's wrong?" I ask.

He shakes his head and takes a deep breath. "Nothing important."

I tilt my head and watch him as he scrubs his fingers through his hair. "Are you sure?"

"Yeah. It's nothing."

*Maybe the baby news will cheer him up!*

"So, um," I wring my hands and am suddenly so

damn nervous that cold sweat is back. "I have some news that might help your mood."

"More celebrating?" he asks.

"I think so." I nod and bite my lip, watching his face. He frowns and tilts his head.

"What's up?"

"I'm pregnant."

He blinks at me for a moment and his body stills. "Excuse me?"

"We're going to have a baby."

He swallows and I smile and continue quickly, not able to contain my excitement any longer. "I thought my cycles were just off again, so I made an appointment with Hannah, and it turns out that I'm freaking pregnant! I was so shocked! After all those years of trying so hard to have a baby and it not working, I assumed I was infertile, but well, apparently not."

His eyes are trained on the floor, and he hasn't hugged me yet. He must be in as much shock as I was in an hour ago.

"I thought this wasn't possible?" His voice is low. I step to him happily and wrap my arms around him.

"I know it's a shock. But isn't it great? I mean, *a baby*!"

He doesn't move. Doesn't hug me back.

"Oh my God! Lo and I will have babies around the same time. That's so cool!"

Suddenly his hands clench around my shoulders and he sets me away from him, then backs away, not touching me at all. When I look up into his face, he's gone completely pale and his eyes are just . . . *pissed.*

"So, let me get this straight." He rubs his fingers over his lips. His whole body is tight with anger.

*Oh no.*

"When you told me you couldn't have kids, that was a lie."

"No." I shake my head adamantly. "Zack, I tried for *years* to get pregnant and it didn't work. I was told that I had unexplained infertility."

"*Unexplained infertility,*" he repeats. His voice is hard and angry and deceptively calm.

"It means that they didn't know why I couldn't get pregnant, but I just couldn't."

He's shaking his head, and I can see that none of my words are sinking in at all.

"You lied. So, what? Your biological clock was ticking away so you thought you'd try your hand with me?" He laughs without humor and backs further away from me. "I'm an easy mark, right?"

"I'm twenty-nine! My biological clock isn't running out! I thought it was nonexistent!"

"I'm so fucking stupid," he mutters and scrubs his hands over his face. "I bought it. I believed you."

"Zack . . ." *What in the fuck is happening? Who is this man?*

"I fucking fell in love with you!" He rages and digs his fingers into his hair, paces around the kitchen, and then comes to a stop in front of me. I can't move. I feel tears fall down my cheeks, but I'm numb. "Oh, that's right. Turn on the tears." He looks like he's about to say more, but he shakes his head and exhales deeply, as if he's completely hurt and exhausted. "You know what? I didn't sign on for this."

He stomps through the kitchen to the living room and I follow him numbly.

"You're leaving? Without talking this through?"

I wrap my arms around myself and hold on tight. I blink the tears from my eyes and clear my face because I'll be fucking damned if I'll give him the satisfaction of seeing me cry.

He doesn't answer me or even look back at me as he shakes his head and leaves, slamming the door behind him, and I'm suddenly standing in my silent house alone.

What just happened?

I sink into the floor and look around with blind eyes. Did the man I love just reject me because I'm pregnant with his child?

The timer on the oven beeps, but I don't move. I can't get up off the floor. I hurt *everywhere.*

I don't know how long I stay here on the floor. I can smell dinner burning in the oven, and I know I need to get up and turn it off, but part of me just doesn't care. I'm not crying. I'm just . . . here.

Suddenly, my front door opens and Ty rushes in, chest heaving, eyes worried. Lo follows him, and while she makes a run for the kitchen, Ty kneels next to me and takes my face in his hands.

"Jilly? What's going on? Are you hurt?"

I just stare at him. I frown and look up at the ceiling.

"Why is there smoke?" I whisper.

"Your smoke alarms are going off, Jill. What the fuck is going on?"

Lauren is suddenly at his side. "There was something in the oven. It's off now, and I'm opening all the windows and doors to air it out."

"No, you stay here and I'll do that. Call for an ambulance."

"No," I say loudly. "I don't need an ambulance."

Ty and Lo exchange a worried glance just before he hurries through the house to open windows and doors, then comes back with two thick blankets.

"Here, sweetness, wrap up. It's about to get cold in here."

"Should we just take her home?" Lo asks and wraps the blanket around herself.

"Let's give it ten minutes to air out, and then yes, we'll take her with us."

"I'm right here," I whisper as Ty wraps me in the blanket. "I can hear you."

"You're on the fucking floor, catatonic, princess." He lifts me into his arms and sits on the couch with me in his lap. "The last time I found you like this . . ."

He can't finish the sentence, but I know exactly what he's talking about. I look up into his face and the tears finally come. "Oh my God, Ty."

I bury my face in his chest and cry. Not delicate, soft whimpers, but loud, keening cries. Desperate cries. Grief-stricken cries. I can't catch my breath, but I can't stop. Am I being dramatic? Maybe. I don't know. The way Zack looked at me when I told him I'm pregnant is not how a man in love with a woman looks at her. I should be pissed. I should flip him the bird and call it a day, but I'm just so damn sad.

Ty is stroking my back softly and I hear them murmuring back and forth between them. Finally, he stands, sets me on the couch, and leaves, but Lo wraps her arm around me and coos soothingly at me, yet I don't understand her words.

I just see Zack's cold eyes in my head, and feel the way he pushed me away.

I didn't do this on purpose! And I'm *happy* about the baby!

Why can't he be?

I'm lifted into Ty's arms again, placed in the backseat of my car, and I must doze off because the next thing I know, Ty has lifted me once more and he's carrying me up some stairs and laying me on a bed.

"I'll be back," Lo says as Ty covers me up and sits at my hip, brushing my hair away from my face.

"Talk to me, princess. What happened? Should I call Zack?"

"No," I whisper. "Zack isn't speaking to me."

His hand stills in my hair. "Why?"

I shake my head and clench my lips together, but the sob comes anyway. I can't talk about it yet. I want to sleep.

Suddenly, someone is wiping my face with a cool, wet washcloth. It feels heavenly, and makes me even sleepier.

"Sleepy," I whisper.

"Go to sleep, Jilly." Ty kisses my forehead. I can hear the concern, the frustration in his voice, and I want to open my eyes and tell him everything, but I can't.

All I can do is sleep.

❂ ❂ ❂

There's a cat lying on my back, purring, digging his claws into my shoulder in rhythmic little pushes. I roll to my side, pushing him off, and turn my head to open one eye, but it's swollen shut and crusty. Jesus Christ, did I get punched in the face?

"Here's a fresh washcloth." Lo's soft voice comes from beside me, and it all comes back again. The baby, Zack, Ty and Lo showing up at my place and bringing me home with them, and I feel the tears start again. "Oh, honey, don't cry."

She presses the washcloth against my forehead and brushes it over my eyes and cheeks. I take it from her and wipe my eyes clean, then struggle to open them. It's dark outside now. My head is pounding with the biggest headache of my life and my mouth is dry.

"Can I have some water?" I ask.

"There's a bottle right here, along with some Advil."

"I can't have Advil," I reply as I sit up and sip the water.

"Really?" She asks with knowing eyes, but I don't want to tell her. Not yet.

I shake my head and wince at the pain that comes with it. I lower myself back to the bed and take a long, deep breath.

"Where's Ty?"

"Downstairs making soup. He doesn't know what to do with himself, so he thought he'd make you some soup for when you wake up."

A few seconds later, Ty enters the room quietly, walks around to the other side of the bed, and sits on it cross-legged, watching me closely.

"Talk to me, princess."

"I'm pregnant." My voice is hollow.

"That's awesome!" Lo exclaims and takes my hand in hers.

Ty holds my gaze in his, his face sober, and I feel tears gather again.

"Why were you at my house?"

"We came by to say hi. Brought dessert. We could hear your smoke alarm from the driveway."

I nod and frown, glance down at my hands.

"He left me."

"What happened?"

I shrug one shoulder and wipe my eyes with the washcloth still in my hand. "I thought my cycles were off again." I hiccup and Lo offers me more water. "I dealt with infertility issues for a long time." I quickly fill Lo in on my history with my ex. "So I made an appointment with Hannah for today, thinking I just needed to get some meds and I'd be on track again."

My hands shake as I push them through my hair.

"But I'm pregnant." I start to laugh at the absurdity of it all, and once I start I can't stop. "Seriously? Pregnant."

It's hilarious to me all of a sudden.

"I took medication that made me throw up, get hot flashes, caused mood swings to rival those of an unmedicated schizophrenic, and I gave myself shots in my own ass for *years* to get pregnant. *Years!*" I laugh some more and wipe my eyes with the cloth. "And now that I'm happily divorced, and things are going well, and I finally came to grips with the fact that I'd never have kids, here I am. Pregnant."

"What happened next, Jill?" Ty pulls my hands from my face and pins me in his stare. "When we found you, your house was about to burn down and you were unresponsive on the floor."

"Zack came over for dinner," I whisper. "I knew he'd be surprised, and maybe a little apprehensive, but . . ." I shake my head and take a deep breath, feeling the tears gather again.

Fuck, my emotions are all over the damn place.

"But?"

"But he was angry. He thinks I did it on purpose."

"What the fuck?" Ty exclaims, but I grip his hand in mine and hold on tight.

"I need you to leave it be, Ty."

"Like hell! What the fuck is his problem?"

"He's scared," Lo says, and shakes her head. "It's scared him."

"He spent seven years in a war zone, Lo," I reply dryly. "Nothing scares him."

"That's not true," Ty replies. "She's right. You scared the shit out of him, Jilly."

I scowl at both of them.

"Well, that's ridiculous."

Ty's shaking his head as he thinks it over. "No, it's not. Given his past with Kensie, he's gotta be wrestling with some demons right now."

*Holy fuck.*

"I didn't even think about Kensie." I cover my face again and feel the tears fall down my cheeks. "I was so excited that I finally got pregnant, and that it's with Zack, that I didn't even think about that bitch and how they started together."

"Well, I can see that—" Lo begins but I interrupt her as anger shoots through me.

"But regardless, the things he said . . ." I shake my head, knowing in my heart I can't forgive him. "He was out of line. I can't be with someone who would speak to me like that. The way he looked at me . . ." I shake my head again. "No."

"What aren't you telling me?" Ty asks quietly.

"It doesn't matter. Don't go to him, please, unless you're going as a friend. I don't want you to beat him up or try to make it right. Leave it be, Ty. I can do this alone."

"Fuck that . . ."

"I mean it." I grip his hand in mine and hold his gaze. "For me."

"Zack will come around in a few days and he'll make it up to you, Jill." Lo's voice is strong and sure, but I just shake my head.

It's too late.

# CHAPTER

## Seventeen

### ZACK

"Maybe Jill can come over today and we can go snowmobiling again," Seth says with a smile. He was supposed to stay the whole night with Josiah, but there was a family emergency and I had to go pick him up at three in the morning.

Not that I was asleep anyway.

"Jill's not coming over today," I say gruffly, not meeting his eyes. How the fuck do I tell my kid that the woman we both fell in love with isn't coming back?

"Oh. Well, maybe she can come over tonight and we can make her dinner and watch a movie."

"Jill isn't going to be coming over anymore, Seth." My voice is hard and angry as the truth of the words hits me full force.

Seth's head snaps up and he's looking at me like I'm crazy.

"Jill and I aren't seeing each other anymore."

"What did you do?" he whispers.

"It's not that simple," I begin, but Seth's cheeks redden and he slams his spoon back into his cereal bowl, splashing milk on the table.

"WHAT DID YOU DO?" he yells. "Jill wouldn't leave us unless you did something to fuck it up!"

"Watch your mouth!" I yell back.

"No!" Tears form in his eyes, but he firms his chin, refusing to let me see how devastated he is, and I feel the same devastation all over again. I lay in bed all night, struggling with the knowledge that the woman I love deceived me.

"Seth." I take a deep breath and try to stay calm. "Sometimes things just don't work out."

There's no way in hell I'm going to tell him about the baby yet. He'll find out soon enough.

One step at a time.

"She loves us," he insists and wipes angrily at a tear that's escaped his eye. "She's the only one who's *ever* loved us! And you made her go away!"

"Seth . . ."

"No." He shakes his head and stands up from the table, glaring at me. "You need to fix this."

"There is no fixing it," I reply with frustration. "It is what it is, Seth. I'm sorry you're disappointed . . ."

"You better fix it!" He advances and pushes me, square in the chest, knocking me back a step.

"Whatever you did wrong, just say you're sorry. Jill will forgive you."

*But I don't know if I can forgive Jill.*

"I love her, Dad." He fists his hands at his sides. "She belongs here, with us. Why did you have to screw it up? Why do you have to make everything so damn *hard*?"

Before I can say anything else, he runs from the room, Thor running after him. He grabs his boots and coat and runs out back toward the barn.

Fuck.

Going after him won't do any good.

My head is pounding, and fuck me, my heart hurts. How could she play me like that? How the fuck did I fall for it *again*?

Yesterday, when Jill said she was pregnant, I heard Kensie's voice, saw her face, saying the same thing thirteen years ago, and watching my world fall apart around me. Kensie had smirked, pleased with herself for cornering me exactly where she wanted me. She'd told me she was on the pill, and I was a stupid eighteen-year-old kid who believed her.

Because I was thinking with my dick.

And if I'm honest, I was thinking with my dick with Jill too. Jesus, she's fucking beautiful. But she's more than that.

Would she have done this deliberately? Did she deserve all the shit I flung at her yesterday while it felt like I'd been sliced open and my guts poured all over the floor?

Probably not.

I glance around the kitchen and flinch.

I wanted to remodel the rest of this house *with her*. Give her anything she wanted. Make a life with her.

But on my own terms and in my own fucking time.

I punch the wall and curse a blue streak before grabbing my own coat and heading out to the barn.

❁  ❁  ❁

"Gonna talk about it?" Dad asks as he shovels fresh hay into the stall next to mine.

"About what?" I ask curtly.

"About why you and Seth are both moping around here today and acting like bears with burrs stuck up their asses," he replies and leans on the shovel, watching me closely.

"Nothin' to say."

"Bullshit." He narrows his eyes and shakes his head. "Must be about Jilly."

I shrug one shoulder with a jerk and keep my eyes trained on the hay on the floor.

"You fuck up?" he asks point-blank.

"No, she did."

I look up to find his eyebrows raised in surprise.

"She's pregnant."

"That's great," he replies soberly.

"No," I say calmly. "It isn't." I keep my eyes on my

dad, suddenly feeling confused and unsure about *everything.* "Is it?"

"Well, why wouldn't it be?"

"She told me *couldn't* get pregnant. I believed her. Just like I believed Kensie."

"Stop that bullshit right now. You're not a boy this time around, and Jill is *not* Kensie, son." He tosses the shovel aside and walks over to me, claps me on the shoulder. "A baby is always a blessing. Your mother and I waited twelve long years after we married to be blessed with you boys. Six miscarriages."

The door to the barn suddenly swings open violently and Ty, looking pissed as fuck, comes running straight for me.

"You son of a bitch." Suddenly, I'm pinned against the barn wall, and a fist makes contact with my left cheek, sending my head reeling back.

"What the fuck?"

"You fucking asshole," Ty growls. "I told you what I'd do if you hurt her."

I glance over at Dad, but he just has his arms crossed over his chest, watching us with interest.

"Look," I begin, but Ty takes another shot at my jaw this time, sending stars swirling over my head. "Let go of me."

"No," he snarls. "You weren't the one holding my sister all night while she cried, you piece of shit."

My eyes snap up to his and I swear under my

breath. "No, I was up all night dealing with the fact that the woman I fucking love lied to me!"

"She didn't fucking lie to you!"

He backs away, releasing my coat, and I rub my aching jaw. I can feel my left eye beginning to swell.

"Jesus, is pounding your fists on someone the only way you know to deal with shit?" I ask cruelly. "I can't imagine that goes over well in a courtroom."

"Fuck you," he spits. "You know"—he shakes his head and paces away, then turns around and glares at me—"I thought you'd come to your senses and at least call her, try to work things out, but when I finally dropped her off at her place this afternoon and you still hadn't tried to contact her, I decided you needed a come-to-Jesus talk. So here it is."

"I don't need your shit—" I begin but my dad shakes his head and points to the metal chair in the corner.

"Have a seat, son."

"I'll stand."

"Well, get comfortable, 'cause I'm about to tell you one hell of a story," Ty warns. "Did you know that Jill tried to get pregnant for five years?"

"She said she's infertile."

"Shut your mouth and *listen*, asshole. Jesus, you'd test the patience of a saint, and that's one thing I certainly am not."

Dad smirks but keeps quiet as he watches Ty pace.

"She went through hell. Meds. Surgeries. Procedures. And that's just the physical shit, man. Five years of shooting herself in the ass every day. And her asshole of an ex-husband was just ... *worthless.*"

He shakes his head in disgust and spits on the floor. "Long story short, it never worked. She didn't even miscarry, she just never got pregnant." He shrugs as if it's a mystery, and I just watch him quietly. I already know this part.

"And then one day she came home from work to find her husband fucking his secretary in their bed."

My jaw drops. Dad swears under his breath and paces away.

"What?"

"Oh, she didn't tell you that part, did she? She didn't tell anyone for a long time. It embarrassed her." He scrubs his hands through his hair. "Fucking *embarrassed her.* That's why she tossed him out on his ass. Not for ignoring her for the better part of their marriage, or the shitty things he'd say to her, or the way he'd belittle her in front of her coworkers. Things she should have left him for before the ink was dry on their marriage license. No, it took getting caught in bed with another woman for her to kick his ass to the curb. Then," he continues, on a roll, and all I can do is watch him, struck dumb, "the day before the Fourth of July, she finds out that the new wife—oh yeah, did I mention he married her two days after their divorce was final?—is pregnant."

I can't speak. I am consumed with so much anger and shame, I don't know what to do with myself.

"So she came home because she needed us. All of us. She moved on from that shitty time in her life. She'd dealt with the fact that she couldn't have kids, and she fell in love with you and *your* kid, and she was happier than I have ever seen her.

"Until Lo and I went to her house and found her in a tiny ball on the living room floor."

"What?" I roar. "Is she okay? What the fuck? Why didn't you call me?"

"She told me not to!" he yells back. "She was a mess *because of you!*"

"Ty, she told me she couldn't get pregnant."

"She didn't think she could!"

I lean against the barn wall and stare at the man I consider a brother, then glance over at my dad, spotting Josh leaning against the barn door as well. I have no idea how long he's been listening.

"Sounds like you have some apologizing to do," Josh mutters.

I hang my head with a long sigh, suddenly more exhausted than I've been in my life.

"It was like déjà vu," I mutter. "While Jill was telling me about her appointment at the doctor, I just saw Kensie in my head, thirteen years ago, and I reacted like a complete prick. I felt like she'd betrayed me, and I was being trapped all over again."

"That's not Jill," Ty replies. "She'll raise that baby by herself if she needs to. She wouldn't accept a proposal from you right now if you crawled across hot coals with the Hope Diamond."

"I fucked up."

"That's an understatement," Dad says and watches me with sober eyes. "You know, son, when you came home last summer, I worried about you. How you'd deal with Seth. How being at war for so long would affect you." He shakes his head and offers me a smile. "But you're the best father I've seen. I couldn't be prouder of the man you are, especially when you're with your boy. The effects of war seem to be lessening with time, although I know you'll always grieve for the boys you lost over there. But it seems to me, you have more PTSD from Kensie than you do from anything else."

"I . . ." *God, what have I done?*

"You were a boy then, like I said before. You're not now. Jill isn't Kensie. And she's been nothing but wonderful to both you and Seth. So, what are you going to do?"

"I'm going to grovel." I walk past Ty and pause, looking him in the eye. "I'm going to make it right."

"See that you do."

❀ ❀ ❀

I ring her doorbell for the third time and finally just bang on the door with my fist.

"Jill, I know you're in there!"

I listen for any sign of movement inside and when there still isn't any, I find her spare key under the ugly gnome on the porch and unlock the door.

"Jill?"

Nothing.

Her car is in the driveway. The lights in the living room and kitchen are off, but I can hear voices from her bedroom.

Who the hell is in her room with her? I march down the hall and fling open her bedroom door to find the television on, one of the New Year's Eve countdown shows on the screen, and Jill sitting up in bed with chips, ice cream, and cookies spread around her.

"What the fuck are you doing here?" she demands angrily.

"You didn't answer the door."

"I didn't hear it."

I glance back at the TV and smile. "Obviously."

She jerks up out of the bed, dressed only in an oversize T-shirt, and moves to walk past me. When I reach out to touch her, she jerks away, hands up as if in surrender.

"Don't fucking touch me."

*Punch to the gut.*

She glares at me and walks quickly out of her bedroom to the living room, flipping on lights along the way.

"I don't want you in my bedroom."

"Look, Jilly, I'm here to apologize."

"Good." She crosses her arms over her chest and watches me with an impassive face, but her cheeks are red and her eyes look glassy. "Who beat the shit out of you?"

"Ty," I reply. "He came out to see me today."

"I told him not to do that, but you deserve that black eye. I wish I'd been the one to give it to you."

"I'm sorry for the way I reacted yesterday, sugar. You didn't deserve that."

"I didn't lie to you."

"I know that now." I swallow hard and rub my hand over my mouth. "It was a shock and it knocked me on my ass."

"Good to know how you handle surprises. Remind me never to throw you a surprise party."

"I deserve that." I look at her longingly. Fuck, I want to pull her into my arms and hold her tight. "I love you, sugar."

"No." Her voice is loud and strong and her eyes are on fire. "You will not say that to me. You lost that right yesterday."

I frown and shove my hands in my pockets to keep from reaching for her.

"I don't need anyone who speaks to me the way you did yesterday."

"I was an idiot," I insist. "Jill, you need to know that it was a mirror image of what happened when Kensie got pregnant."

"No," she says again. "It's not. *I'm* not that woman. This baby"—she points to her flat stomach—"is not Seth."

"You have to understand—"

"And frankly, that's all bullshit anyway. No matter what happened in your past, it's *not okay* for you ever to speak to me or anyone else like that. You have an issue with your ex-wife? Take it up with her. *I'm* not your punching bag."

"You have to understand—" I try again.

"I understand," she interrupts. "I get it, Zack. I'm not a moron. After the initial shock wore off and I could think clearly, I understood your reaction."

I sigh in relief, but before I can say anything, she continues.

"But it doesn't excuse you. I understand you, but I can't trust you. I'll survive without you."

"Life is about so much more than surviving, sugar."

"Oh really?" She laughs humorlessly. "Those are your words of wisdom right now?"

"I fucking *love* you, Jill. Tell me what to do to make this right and I'll do it."

"There is no making it right. Love never really lasts, Zack. It's just one big fucking disappointment. I won't invite you back into my life, love you and your boy, and then wait for the day to come that I have to watch you decide to leave me like I'm nothing."

"That's not going to happen," I insist. I take a step toward her, but she holds her hands up again, stopping me. "God damn it, let me hold you!"

"No." She shakes her head and wipes a tear from her cheek.

"Jesus, Jilly," I begin but she shakes her head and walks away.

"Just leave, Zack."

"No. We can work this out."

"There's nothing to work out right now. I want you to go. I don't want to see you."

"Fine." I back toward the door. "I'll give you time, but Jill, you're mine. Baby or no baby."

She firms her lips and glares at me.

"Those are the words I needed *yesterday*, Zack."

"I'm giving them to you now, and by God, I'll prove it." I walk out of her house, shutting the door quietly behind me, and jog to my truck as the plan begins to form in my head. Twenty minutes later, when I pull up to my house, I rush inside.

"Seth?"

"In here," he calls from the family room, where the Christmas tree is still standing, playing his video game. He sets the controller aside as I walk into the room. "Well? Did you fix it?"

"*We're* going to fix it, but I need your help, buddy."

He eyes me for a long moment, then shrugs. "Okay."

# CHAPTER

## Eighteen

### JILLIAN

"How are you feeling?" Cara asks and joins me on her couch. I can't believe I'm at the ranch. But I refuse to tiptoe around, afraid of running into Zack.

"Fine. A little woozy now and then, but it's not too bad."

"Josh said Zack's been a mess this week."

I shrug and sip the decaffeinated tea Cara brewed for me. "It's been a helluva week."

"What's been going on? The last I heard from you, Zack showed up at your place New Year's Eve and you put him in his place and kicked his ass out."

"I'm sorry I haven't talked with you much," I murmur softly. "I'm still trying to wrap my head around everything. And I don't want to put you in the middle, since he's your brother-in-law."

"What's been happening?"

"Well, Zack wasn't lying when he said he'd prove to me that he's in it for the long haul. It started with flowers being delivered the next day."

"Such a man move," Cara says and rolls her eyes. "Of course, it's a man move because it works."

"They were pretty." I don't mention that I spent an hour crying and sniffing over them, missing Zack like crazy. "Then on Tuesday, he had lunch delivered to my office from the diner."

"That's your favorite place," she replies with a raised brow.

"I know, and he didn't just have it sent for me, but for the whole office. Then on Wednesday, Seth showed up after school to shovel my driveway."

"Aww," she replies and her face goes all gooey. "That's sweet."

"I know," I admit and sip my tea. "So of course I invited him inside for cookies and to chat. But you know, he never said anything about his dad, or getting back together with him. He just acted like everything was normal. And he came all week."

"We got a lot of snow last week," Cara says. "Who picked Seth up?"

"Zack. But he didn't come to the door, he just honked from the driveway."

"Why didn't he come inside?"

I bite my lip and look down at my mug. "Because I told him I didn't want to see him."

Cara nods thoughtfully. "Is that all that's happened?"

"No, yesterday I got a package in the mail."

"What was it?"

I grab my handbag and pull the heavy book out of it. "*What to Expect When You're Expecting*."

Cara giggles and takes it out of my hands to flip through. "This is kind of sweet."

"I know." I sigh and push my fingers through my hair. "He's softening me up a bit, but Cara, he was an asshole."

She nods and continues to flip through the book. "Ew. Don't look at page 328. It's scary."

"Thanks for the warning."

"So, you just fell out of love with him? Just like that?"

"Don't be stupid, Cara." I glare at my friend and then feel tears threaten when she raises her sober gaze to mine. "I miss him."

"He's right down the road there."

"I don't know if we can make it work. He said some pretty horrible things."

"Oh, please. Jill, people say mean things, especially when they're scared and worried and have the shock of a lifetime. He apologized, and is trying to prove to you that he loves you, respects you, and wants to work it out. What more do you want?"

"I want a guarantee that he'll never hurt me again."

"Well, you won't get that. In fact, I can pretty much guarantee that he *will*. Because he's a human being." She sets the book aside and takes my hand in hers. "But he's a good man, and he loves you like crazy."

"I'm still thinking."

"You're still a stubborn ass," Cara replies with a smile. "But it's cool. I think you're the bee's knees."

"You spend too much time around children," I reply dryly just as Josh comes through the front door. "Is Zack gone?"

"Yeah, he just pulled out. You have about an hour before he'll be back."

"Want me to go with you?" Cara asks with a frown.

"Nah, I'm fine. I'm just getting my stuff out of his place." I take my mug to the kitchen, rinse it out, and hug Cara close. "Thank you for everything."

"Don't give up on him," she replies. "Keep an open mind."

I nod and have to hold my breath to keep it together when Josh pulls me in for a big hug too. He's the same height and build as Zack, and being nestled in his arms is way too much like being held by the man I love.

I pull away and wave as I climb into my car and drive down to Zack's place. I park and when I reach the front door, Seth opens it wide.

"Dad's not here," he says, motioning for me to come in, "but you can wait for him if you want."

"No, it's okay, sweetie. I just wanted to grab a few things that I left here on my way home from my visit with Cara."

Seth's face falls and his shoulders sag. "Oh. Okay."

I pat his shoulder and climb the stairs quickly, trying my best to keep my tunnel vision in place. *Do not look at the family room where you had the best Christmas of your life. Do not look at his bed. Grab your clothes and stuff them in your bag. Do not think about how he made love to you in that shower. Grab your shampoo and your blow dryer. Do not look at the bed! Okay, down the stairs and you're almost home free.*

"Jill, can I ask you a question?" Seth asks as I come to the bottom of the stairs.

"Of course, buddy."

He frowns and seems uncertain, shoves his hands in his pockets, and looks so much like his dad right now, it almost breaks me.

"What is it, Seth?"

"You're not going to forgive him, are you?"

*And cue the tears.* I bite my lip, but can't stop the tears that come as I stare at this sweet boy. "I don't know."

"He won't tell me what happened." This surprises me. I didn't expect Zack to give Seth a blow-by-blow, but I thought for sure he'd have told him about the baby. "But I know he's sorry. We worked really hard last week to show you how sorry."

"You were both very nice to me last week," I assure him and, unable to hold back any longer, I pull Seth into my arms and hug him tightly. "I loved having you at my house after school and you're welcome to come by anytime you want. You don't even have to shovel or anything."

He wraps his arms around my middle and holds on with all of his strength. "I love you, Jill. You're the best mom I've ever had."

*Oh dear sweet Jesus, how am I going to live through this?*

"Seth, no matter what happens between me and your dad, I'm always going to be your friend. No matter what you need, you can count on me, do you hear me? No matter what."

He nods and sniffs and we stand like this for a long minute, crying and comforting each other.

As he pulls out of my arms, he glances outside and frowns. "What is she doing here?"

"Who?" I turn and follow his gaze and then feel my entire body burst into the flames of a thousand fires with the fury that races through my veins. "Stay here," I instruct Seth and step out on the porch and march down the steps to the driveway below.

"Well, Jillian Sullivan," Kensie sneers and approaches me. She looks . . . *old*. She's my age, but she looks at least ten years older. Tired. Her hair and nails are done perfectly, and her clothes are two sizes too small.

She looks cheap.

"What do you want, Kensie?"

"I want to see Seth. I haven't seen him in months."

"You're not going to see him today either."

"Oh?" She tilts her head to the side and narrows her eyes. "Who's going to stop me?"

"I am." I brace my hands on my hips and face her square on. She's a good five inches taller than me, and outweighs me by about twenty-five pounds, but I can take her easily if I need to.

"But I miss him so much." Tears miraculously form in her eyes and her lower lip wobbles, and I know it's a big, fat act.

"Wow, you're good at that."

"I don't know what you mean." She sniffs delicately and wipes an imaginary tear from her cheek. "It's been months and months since I've hugged my little pumpkin."

"Really? I heard the last time you saw him, you dumped him off right about where you're standing and drove away without a backward glance, so I'm going to make it very easy for you, Kensie. Get back in your car and drive away. Seth doesn't want to see you."

"I am his mother," she insists, still pretending to cry. "I have rights!"

"You gave up any rights you had when you abandoned him here."

She sobers and stares at me, realizing that she's not manipulating me the way she wants to.

"I'll see him," she says and takes a step closer to me. "And there's nothing you or anyone else can do about it."

"Oh, yes there is. You are such a pitiful excuse

for a mother. For a *woman*," I growl. "You let those motherfuckers you were fucking lay their hands on your child. They *hit* him!"

"He was fine," she scoffs. "He makes it sound way more dramatic than it was. What, are you fucking Zack now? Is he still as great of a lay as he used to be? That's the only thing he was ever good for." She smirks. "Don't tell me you're in love with him? Do you think you can take my place in *my* family?"

"Don't you touch her!" Seth yells from the top of the stairs, then clambers down them and shoves me behind him, protecting me. "Don't touch Jill."

"Hi, sweetie." Kensie sends him a fake smile. "Did you miss your mommy?"

"No. Go away."

"Now, that's no way to say hello to me. Come here, give me a hug."

"No." He shakes his head frantically and I take his shoulders in my hands and pull him against my side.

"Seth, you don't have to do anything you don't want to." I hear tires on the driveway, but my gaze doesn't leave the bitch before me.

Kensie snarls and reaches for Seth's arm, trying to pull him from my grasp. Seth cries out in pain and Kensie lets go, but laughs. "God, you're still a pussy."

I've had enough. I push Seth behind me, pull my fist back, and plant it right in her fucking smug mouth. She stumbles back and cries out, but I advance on her and punch her again, harder this time, knocking her flat on her ass.

"Jill!"

"I fucking hate you," I grind out between my teeth. "You'll never lay your hands on that boy ever again. Do you hear me? Never. Again."

Strong hands grip my arms but I shake them off and push my face in Kensie's. "If you ever even *think* his name again, I'll rip you apart."

Her lip is bleeding, she's panting, and her eyes are wide. "Zack! Are you going to let her treat me like this?" she shrieks.

"Absolutely," he replies softly. "Get the fuck out of here, Kensie."

"He's my son!" she yells and begins kicking and punching the snow like a four-year-old throwing a temper tantrum. "He's *mine*!"

"No," I yell and pull her up by her coat and shove her toward her car. "He's *mine*. Get the fuck off this property and don't come back. If you have a problem with that, call a fucking lawyer."

"Zack!"

"You heard her. Get the fuck off my property."

I spin around, searching for Seth, and see him standing next to the steps of the porch, his eyes wide and haunted. I run to him and pull him into my arms, kiss his head, and rock us both back and forth. "Are you okay?"

"She was going to hurt you," he sobs.

"No, she wasn't," I reply and cup his face in my hands, trapping his hazel gaze in my own. "She wasn't. And she won't hurt you ever again either."

He hugs me tight and then suddenly we're both in Zack's strong arms, being held and kissed, and for a brief moment I soak up his strength, and then the anger comes back full force.

"Seth, go inside now while I talk to your dad."

"No, I want to—"

"She's right. Go inside, buddy. Thor's crying for you."

It's then I notice that Thor is barking frantically at the window, scratching and trying to get out to us.

"Go comfort him," I say with an encouraging smile. Seth looks between the two of us and then nods once and trudges up the steps.

"Jilly, are you okay?" Zack asks after Seth shuts the door behind him. I spin on him, more pissed than I've ever been.

"Do you understand," I begin, trying my best to keep my voice low, "that you compared me to *that*?" I point in the direction that Kensie just drove in, toward town.

"No, I never—"

"Yes. You stood in my home and compared me to the woman who fucking abused your *child*." The enormity of it hits me full force and I can't stop the tears or the shaking that consumes my body. "I love you with every single molecule of my body, and you compared me to that piece of trash. Are you kidding me?"

"Jilly, that's not at all what I meant. You are nothing like Kensie. *Nothing*."

"You bet your ass I'm nothing like her. She doesn't give two shits about your son. You know that, right? Whatever she's here for is purely selfish and has nothing to do with wanting Seth." I shake my head and pace away from Zack toward my car. "And to think, I was ready to move on, to put last week behind us and give us a chance."

"Jill, we can still do that."

"No." I turn and watch him, watch his face fall and go pale. "No, we can't. When I told you the joyous news that I'm carrying your child, your first thought was that I was playing you the way *she* did." I purse my lips and shake my head, devastated all over again. "You will most likely be the only man I will ever love like this, but I'll be damned if I'll be put in that category ever again. You can come with me to doctor appointments, and you'll have full access to your child. I'll coparent with you. But that's all I'll give you."

I turn to leave, but am suddenly spun around and in Zack's arms. He's holding me flush against him, from chest to knees, my feet off the ground. He holds me to him, kissing me with a desperate fervor. Finally, after nibbling the corners of my lips, he rests his forehead against mine and whispers simply, "I love you so much."

He sets me on my feet, releases me, and backs away. With tears in his eyes, he says, "If that's what you want, I'll respect your decision."

I nod once and glance at the house to find Seth and Thor staring out the window. Seth is crying, swiping at the tears with the back of his hand.

I get in my car, and without a backward glance, drive away.

# CHAPTER

## *Nineteen*

"Jilly."

I roll over and pull the covers over my head. "Go away."

"Jill, you have to get out of bed," Ty replies with a smile in his voice, the sadist.

"No I don't. I don't have to go into the office today."

"It's after nine. It's time to get up, princess."

I roll to my back and peek one eye out of the covers, eyeing him suspiciously. "It hurts when someone you love says mean things. Like *it's time to wake up.*"

"Get out of bed. I brought coffee." Ty shakes his head and wanders out of my bedroom, leaving me to pull myself out of bed, yank on some yoga pants, and follow him.

"Why aren't you at work?" I yawn and sit on my couch, curling my legs up under me.

"Here, I got you decaf," he says and hands me a to-go cup from Drips and Sips.

"Wow. You really hate me. Waking me up this early and then shoving decaf in my face. What did I ever do to you?"

"You're a smart-ass. You know that, right?"

"I learned from the best." I sip the delicious white mocha and wait for my stomach to rebel. When it doesn't, I sigh in contentment and lean back against the cushions. "So, answer my question."

He braces his elbows on his knees. He's in his usual white dress shirt, sleeves rolled, and slacks. "I took a few hours of personal time."

"So go have sex with your fiancée. Which reminds me, I have to call her today. The wedding is less than a month away!"

"I'm aware, but thanks for the reminder."

"What's up, big brother?"

"I am staging an intervention, Jillian."

I blink at him for several moments, take a sip of my drink, and glance around the room. "Where is everyone else? You're an army of one, Ty."

"I'm all I need."

I tilt my head to the side and scowl at him in confusion. "What, exactly, are you intervening about?"

He stands and paces around my living room, the way he does in the courtroom, and I realize he's dead serious.

"I'm worried about you. It's been three weeks

since the incident with Kensie, and you've barely spoken to any of us. You don't join us for dinners or get-togethers. It's obvious you're avoiding Zack."

"I—"

"Just listen." He holds his hand up, stopping my retort, so I shut my mouth and frown at him. "You look like hell, Jill."

"I'm pregnant and I throw up more than I breathe, Ty."

"I get it, but you've let yourself go to hell."

"Fuck you." I set my coffee on the end table and stand. I'm not taking this sitting down.

"You look horrible. And I'm not just talking about the no makeup and not giving a shit about your hair—"

"Are you a girl? Talking about my makeup and hair?"

"You're sad." He stops and shoves his hands in his pockets, watching me closely. "You're so sad, princess."

"This is a *sadness intervention*?"

"It doesn't have to be like this, Jill."

"I'm not talking about this anymore. Between you and Cara, I've been over it a hundred times, Ty."

"But you don't fucking listen!" he explodes and I step back in surprise. Ty has never, ever raised his voice to me in anger, not even when we were kids. "You're so fucking stubborn—"

"I'm not stubborn! I'm hurt!" I scrub my hands over my face and turn away from him. "Zack may as well have told me that I am going to be the same kind of mother as *our* mom. He compared me to two of the most evil, despicable women I've ever known."

"Mom's not evil, Jill."

I glare at him and snarl, "Yes, she sure as fuck is."

"Look," he begins and raises his hands as if in defeat, "my point is, he *didn't* compare you to those women. That's not what he meant, and you know it. You're just too scared to admit it."

"What happens the next time I do something that *scares* him? Is he going to do this all over again, jumping to the wrong conclusions?"

"People learn, Jill. They grow. No, I don't think Zack would make this same mistake again. He's not stupid. He's human."

I shake my head and scrub my fingers against my oily scalp.

*Fuck, I really do need a shower.*

"From the beginning, you said that you both have a whole cargo hold full of baggage and that it would take a lot of work for anything good to come of a relationship between you two," Ty reminds me softly. "The baggage didn't disappear just because you fell in love."

"No, it just fell off the back of the truck and hit me square in the face." I cross my arms over my chest and watch my brother for a moment before saying, "What do you want from me?"

"I want you to be happy, and the path you're on right now isn't cutting it. I want you to have a talk with Zack and really listen to what he says. I want you to trust your own instincts and I want my sister and my best friend to love each other."

"You want a lot," I whisper. "I don't know, Ty. We're pretty broken."

"Sometimes," he replies and pulls me into his arms, hugging me tight, "two people have to fall apart before they can realize how much they need to fall back together. And now that you know better, you can do better."

"Thank you, Oprah," I mumble into his chest.

"I think Maya Angelou originally said that."

"Who are you?" I ask and pull away. "Since when are you all mushy and touchy-feely? It's weirding me out."

He laughs and shrugs. "I'm in touch with my touchy-feely side."

"Yuck." He laughs again and crosses his arms over his chest. I love him so much. "You know, Ty, you're my rock when everything else falls apart. I love you."

"I love you too."

"How is Zack?" I ask quietly.

"A fucking mess."

I nod and cringe, suddenly feeling guilty. "I'll think about what you said."

"Stop thinking everything to death and just fucking talk to the man." He shrugs into his coat and hugs me once more then tweaks the end of my nose. "Take a shower. Put on some makeup. And for God's sake, get out of those yoga pants."

"Yes, fashion guru."

He waves and leaves and I run for the bathroom, I have to pee so badly. When I finish and wipe, there is blood on the tissue and I immediately feel light-headed.

*Oh Christ Jesus, no.*

I mentally count the weeks in my head. I should be roughly six weeks pregnant. Many women miscarry around this time and never know they were pregnant. They just assume their period was late.

*No, no, no.*

I'm due to have my next appointment and ultrasound with Hannah in two days, but I definitely can't wait that long.

I wipe again, but there's no blood this time.

Oh God, what if I'm losing this baby?

I call the doctor's office and spill my story first to the receptionist, who transfers me to Hannah's nurse, and I tell it all over again, becoming more hysterical by the minute.

"Was it bright red or brown?" she asks.

"Brownish."

"Well, it could be normal . . ."

"But it could *not* be normal. Can I come in or not?" I sound like a complete bitch, but I can't help it. I'm panicking.

"Yes, Jill, come on in. Hannah will work you in."

"Thank you," I sob and end the call, then immediately call Cara.

"Hey, chickie," she answers with a grin in her voice.

"Cara," I cry and rush to my bedroom to find a bra. "I have to go to the doctor."

"What's happened? Jilly, are you okay?"

I can hear voices in the background but I don't know, or care, who it is. "No. I'm not okay. I'm spotting."

"Shit," she mutters. "Are you going to Hannah's office now?"

"Yes."

"You shouldn't drive yourself. You're too upset."

"I can't wait," I reply and shove my feet in boots. "But can you come meet me?"

"Of course I can. I'm on my way right now. Jill, drive *slow*, hear me?"

"I hear you. Oh God, Cara, I can't lose this baby." I clutch the phone tightly in my hand and lean against the front door. "I can't lose it."

"You're not gonna lose it, babe. Hannah will take care of it. Just get there in one piece. I'll be there in twenty minutes."

"Okay." I wipe my cheeks, grab my purse, and head out to my car. "Thank you."

I end the call, take a deep breath, then drive the short distance to Hannah's office.

"Hi, Jill. We're expecting you." The receptionist

smiles reassuringly. "Have a seat and someone will come get you in a moment."

"Thank you."

There's a woman sitting nearby reading her e-reader, snapping gum. She has to be at least a hundred months pregnant. Her belly is *huge*.

"Jill?" Hannah's nurse calls as she steps through the door that leads to the exam rooms.

"Hi." I stand and follow her back. "I'm sorry I was such a bitch on the phone. I'm just scared."

"Trust me, you're fine," she replies with a laugh. "I'm going to take some vitals and then Hannah will be in to talk with you. It might be a few minutes, she's on her way back here from the hospital. She just had a delivery."

"Oh, okay. Thank you."

She weighs me, takes my temperature and blood pressure, then has me change into the usual gown with paper blanket and I sit and wait.

And wait.

I check my phone every two minutes to look at the time. After ten minutes, there's commotion in the hallway, and I hear a man say, "Where is she! What room?"

*Zack!*

The door is flung open and Zack fills the doorway, his eyes wide with fear and chest heaving. When he sees me, he rushes in and pulls me into his arms.

"Did you come from the ranch?" I ask incredulously.

"Yes, I was there when you called Cara."

"I thought Cara was coming."

"If you think I'd let you be here, scared and bleeding, by yourself, you have another think coming."

"Zack, how fast did you drive?"

"Are we seriously talking about this right now?" he asks and leans back to look at me. I ease out of his grasp and his face falls, and my stomach clenches. Just when I'm about to reach for him again, Hannah knocks briskly and opens the door.

"Hi, Jill, thanks for waiting. Oh, hi, Zack." She shakes both of our hands and then begins making notes in her iPad. "Tell me what happened this morning."

"There was blood when I went to the bathroom."

Zack rubs his fingers over his mouth in agitation. God, I can't take my eyes off him. I haven't seen him in three weeks. He looks amazing. Tired. His eyes look sad and scared.

But he's the most gorgeous thing I've ever seen.

"How much blood?" Hannah asks. "Was it enough that you needed a pad in your underwear?"

"No, it was just on the toilet paper."

"What color?" I glance at Zack and feel my cheeks flush.

"Brown."

"And did you wipe again?"

"Yes, but there wasn't anything there."

She glances up at me and blinks, then back at her iPad.

"Well, this doesn't sound too daunting. Many women have minor spotting, especially in the early stages of pregnancy."

"Yes, but many women also miscarry at this stage and never even know they were pregnant. They just assume their period was late."

"That's true. We have you scheduled for your viability ultrasound on Friday, but since you're here, we'll go ahead and have a look. I think you're fine, but we'll do our best to put your mind at ease today."

"Thank you." I sigh in relief. Hannah rolls a machine that has a monitor and keyboard on it close to the table and instructs me to lie back, my feet in the stirrups.

"Dad, you can stand by Mom's head and watch with her," Hannah instructs Zack, who grins and stands next to me, still not touching me.

She unclips a long wand from the machine, covers it with a condom, and drips clear jelly over it.

"Um, that's not like any ultrasound thingy I've ever seen," I comment.

"This is a vaginal ultrasound. You're still too early for us to see anything externally."

"Oh, goodie," I reply dryly and curl my toes when she pushes my thighs wide.

"No signs of blood," she murmurs and grins up at me. "That's good."

I nod and then turn my gaze to the monitor as it comes to life. Hannah moves the wand back and forth, takes still photos of what looks like blobs to me.

"Hmm," she says and clicks the keys some more.

"Hmm what?" Zack asks impatiently.

Hannah grins. "Just a second."

I glance up at him. He's squinting, trying to make sense of the screen and what it is we're looking at.

"Well," Hannah says, "there's a heartbeat."

Sure enough, there is a little tiny flutter on the screen. Tears fill my eyes as I watch with awe as she points to the monitor.

"This is the amniotic sac, this is a baby, and the heartbeat." She moves the wand just a tiny bit and then chuckles as I see the heartbeat again.

"And there is baby B."

My head whips around to stare at Hannah in shock.

"Excuse me?"

"Baby B," Hannah repeats as I grab for Zack's hand. He holds it tightly in his and wraps his arm over my head, gently stroking my hair. "Looks like we have twins. There are two sacs, two babies."

My gaze finds Zack's as tears fall down my cheeks. "We're having two babies," I whisper.

"Yes, ma'am, we are," he replies and kisses my forehead.

*Holy Mary, mother of God, I'm having twins!*

# CHAPTER

## *Twenty*

**ZACK**

*Twins.*

The whooshing sounds of the heartbeats fill the air, along with Jill's soft sniffles as she watches the monitor with awe.

When Cara received the call from Jill that she was bleeding and on her way to the doctor, I thought I was going to have a heart attack. I had to get to her side to see for myself that she's okay.

And now we find out we're having twins.

I can't stop smiling.

I lean down and kiss Jilly's forehead again, breathing her in. God, I've missed her.

"Okay, guys, I'll print out copies of the photos for you to take with you and brag to everyone about." Hannah smiles and cleans up the ultrasound wand that looks like a torture device to me. Jill sits up and wipes her cheeks dry.

"Is everything okay?" she asks shakily.

"Yes, Jill. You're fine. I didn't see any signs of blood at all. Take it easy the rest of the day. No hanky-panky." She winks at us and backs toward the door. "Make an appointment for four weeks from now, but if you have any questions or concerns in the meantime, don't hesitate to call."

"Thanks, Hannah," I reply as she leaves the room. I give Jill space to pull her clothes on and grab her purse, and follow her out of the office to her car. "Jill . . ."

She turns abruptly and wraps her arms around me, holding on with all her might, and for the first time since that horrible night in her kitchen, I feel hope spread through me.

"Come home with me?" she asks softly.

"I'll be right behind you, sugar."

I feel her smile against me before she pulls away and gets in her car. When we step inside her house, I help her out of her coat and boots, slip out of my own, and am shocked when she says, "I'm going to take a shower. I need a minute to think." She bites her lip and looks at me uncertainly. "Do you mind waiting for me?"

"Take all the time you need, Jill. I'll be here. Have you eaten anything?"

"No."

"I'll make you some soup and a sandwich."

She nods and walks down to her room and I move into her kitchen to make the meal. Thirty minutes later, she comes into the kitchen, all scrubbed clean, her cheeks glowing and hair damp from the shower.

"You are so beautiful," I whisper, not even realizing I've spoken aloud.

"Thank you," she replies and turns her gaze down to her hands. "Thank you for feeding me."

"Three very important people need the fuel," I reply with a grin.

She smiles, and then her eyes fill with tears again.

"Aw, sugar, please don't cry. It kills me when you cry." I set her bowl of soup on the breakfast bar and then open my arms to her, and she walks willingly right inside them.

"I'm sorry," she says.

"Hey." I cup her face in my hands and kiss her gently, reveling in the touch of her lips on mine. "Eat first, then we'll talk."

"Okay." She nods and turns to the food set out for her. "Wow, this smells so good."

"It is good. I already ate some."

She smiles and eats her soup and sandwich with enthusiasm.

"I was hungry," she says. "I'm always hungry these days."

"That's a good sign," I reply. "You're eating for three."

"Good God, I'm going to be the size of this house!" she screeches.

"Probably not that big," I reply and laugh, the knots in my stomach finally loosening.

She drags the last bite of sandwich through the last of the soup and pops it in her mouth, and I take her bowl to the sink to rinse. When I turn back to her, she has her head resting in her hand and she's watching me quietly.

"Come on." I take her hand and lead her to the couch in the living room. She sits in the corner, and I sit right next to her, pulling her legs up over mine. "Talk to me, sugar."

"I don't know where to start," she whispers on a long sigh and closes her eyes.

"Well, I need to say this: I don't just want to be here for moments like today, Jill. I want to be here for *every* moment."

"I want that too," she says and opens her eyes to meet mine. She bites that plump lower lip of hers and takes my hand in her own, lacing our fingers. "What you said before, when I told you I was pregnant, hurt me a lot."

"I know. I don't know how much more I can apologize for that."

"You don't have to. I've already forgiven you for that. I probably forgave you for it the next night when you came here and apologized."

I frown down at her but wait for her to continue.

"But you also scared me. I mean, what if you're right, Zack?"

"What do you mean?"

"What if I *am* a shitty mom like Kensie? Like my own mom," she whispers.

"You are going to be an awesome mom, sugar."

"But I have that in me," she replies with wide blue eyes. "My mom is horrible. More than horrible. She's a monster. Ty doesn't even know about some of the things she said to me when I was a kid."

I reach down and pull her into my lap and she wraps her arms around my neck, buries her face in my neck, and continues her story.

"She didn't *encourage* me to hide in the closet from my dad. She put me there because I was in her way. She resented me and never let me forget it. You see, Seth and I have more in common than you'll ever know."

My arms tighten around her as anger flows through me. "Why didn't you tell Ty?"

"Because he couldn't do anything about it. Dad would have beat him until he should have been in the hospital."

"Oh, baby." I kiss her head and stroke my hands soothingly down her back. "How could you ever think that you could be that way with our babies? With Seth? Look at how fiercely you protected him against Kensie. You would die for my boy, Jilly."

Just remembering the sight of her pushing Seth behind her while she attacked Kensie both humbles and infuriates me. She should never have been in that position in the first place.

"I love him," she says and swallows hard. "I love you both."

"Do you still love me?" I whisper and push her back so I can look in her eyes.

"So much," she replies. "I've missed you."

I cup her face gently and kiss her softly, barely grazing my lips over hers, then nibbling the side of her mouth, the way I do that always makes her grin. I kiss her cheek and pull my nose down her jaw, taking in a deep breath of her fresh scent.

"God, I missed you too, sugar," I growl. "Last night was the last night we'll ever spend apart. Understand?"

"Moving in with me?" she asks sassily and brushes happy tears off her cheeks.

"No, you're moving in with me. You have a kitchen remodel to oversee, and my kid misses you."

"He likes me." She shrugs and grins. "What else?"

"What else?" I pretend that I don't know what she's talking about.

"Yes. What else?"

"Well . . ." I tilt my head from side to side, as though I'm thinking about her question very seriously. "We can live in sin for the next sixty years."

She smacks my arm and laughs. "I'm not talking about marriage."

"I am."

She sobers and blinks, surprised.

"My life has been so much better since the day I found you," I begin and swallow hard as I think of the words I want to say. "I've met many people in my life. I've watched some of them die. Lost touch with others. There are few people in my life that I feel permanently connected to, who fit into the puzzle that is my life. My son. My parents. Josh, Ty, and Cara.

"Now these two new babies." I rub her belly gently and smile up into her eyes. "And you. I want the parts of you that you refuse to give anyone else, Jill. I can't imagine anything better in this life than sharing it with you. Choosing you, every day."

I brush a tear off her cheek with my fingertip, then cradle her face in my hand, rubbing my thumb over the apple of her cheek.

"You're mine. You belong on the ranch with Seth and me, and I'm never letting you go ever again. I'll screw up." I cringe and shake my head. "I will make mistakes, but you have to know that of every person that drifts in and out of your life, no one will ever love you the way I do."

"Did you just ask me to marry you?" she whispers.

"If the answer is yes, then yes, I did."

She smiles and pulls her fingertips down my cheek.

"My answer is yes. As long as we can do it before I'm too big to fit into a dress."

"I'll marry you tomorrow, my love."

# Epilogue

— OCTOBER —

**JILLIAN**

"Are you ready for visitors?" Hannah asks as she finishes checking me and assuring me that I am good to go. "You have quite a lineup out there."

"You can send them in," I reply with a smile. "They're all family."

"Big family," she replies and smiles at Zack. "Congratulations again. They're beautiful."

"Can I hold one, please?" I ask and hold my arms out. My handsome husband is holding both of our newborn babies, one in the crook of each arm. "Wait, I need a picture of that."

I grab my phone and snap the photo.

"Can I come in?" Seth asks from the doorway.

"Good timing, buddy. Come stand by your dad so I can take your picture."

"She's going to take pictures all the time, isn't she?" he asks Zack as he joins him at my bedside.

"Yes, I am," I reply and feel my heart expand at the picture before me. Two handsome guys grin at me over the heads of our babies. After I snap the photo, Seth gently takes our daughter from his dad's arms, already a pro, and sits in the rocking chair in the corner, gazing down at her with awe.

"I guess that leaves me with my little guy," I say and sigh with happiness as Zack lays our son in my arms. Zack kisses my forehead and gently pulls the tip of his finger down our son's cheek. "They're so small," I whisper.

"They'll grow."

"Where are my grandbabies?" Nancy demands as she stalks into the room with a wide smile and tears in her eyes. "Oh, look how precious they are. Hello, sweet girl." She kisses both of my cheeks and then my son's head and looks at me with a hopeful smile.

"Here, you take him," I offer. Nancy cradles him close and then walks over to sit next to Seth, cooing over both babies.

"They're gorgeous, just like their mama," Jeff says with a wink.

"Is this where the party is?" Josh asks from the doorway and saunters in with Cara, Ty, and Lo in tow.

Ty is carrying his daughter, Layla, in his arms.

"Hey, princess." He kisses my cheek and smiles warmly. "You good?"

"I'm sleepy and happy and sore. And very, very good."

"They are precious!" Cara exclaims, leaning over the babies before she rushes to me for hugs. Zack is pulled around the room in a flurry of hugs and claps on the back.

"Can I at least hold my niece?" I ask and hold my hands out for the sweet, tiny baby girl. Ty gives her to me, and I grin at the sweet pink flower pinned to her jet-black hair. I can't wait to dress my daughter up.

"What have you named them?" Lo asks and settles into my brother's side.

"Well, Mama King is holding Miles Jeffrey King," I reply with a wide smile at Jeff, who immediately tears up and hugs Zack close.

"And your daughter?" Nancy asks with a rough voice.

"That one has been harder," Zack replies and shares a glance with me. *Harder, right.* He just doesn't know a good girl name when it smacks him in the ass.

"We can't agree on one," I reply dryly and nod at Cara when she asks if she can take Layla.

"I've always liked the name Sarah," Seth says as he gazes down at his sister. He hasn't been able to take his eyes off her. "Mom, can we call her Sarah?"

My heart stops as it always does when Seth calls me *Mom.* I don't know if I'll ever get used to it.

I certainly hope not.

"I like Sarah," I murmur to Zack, who is gazing at me with such fierce love it steals the breath from me.

"Me too."

"I think it should be Sarah Hope," Seth continues, "because of how it all started."

"What do you mean, buddy?" Nancy asks and runs her hand over his hair.

"I hoped for a real family for a long time. That's really what I wanted for Christmas." He blushes and shrugs, but doesn't look away from his baby sister. "Her middle name should be Hope."

"I think Seth just named his sister," I reply softly. "Sarah Hope King. Has a nice ring to it."

Seth smiles proudly. "She's pretty."

"Oh! Speaking of pretty, here," Cara says and hands me her phone. "Look at our wedding photos."

"Ugh," I mutter and page through the photos on her phone. It was a beautiful day for a wedding on the Lazy K Ranch. Josh and Cara chose to exchange vows by the big old tree that has all of our initials carved in the side. It's where he proposed, and it's their special place. "I look like a cow. At least Lo moved her wedding up so I wasn't the size of a house in my dress. And I was kind enough to pay her the same respect." I frown over at my friend as she smiles widely and leans on her husband. "You're mean."

"You looked beautiful that day, and every day. You were carrying precious cargo, sugar," Zack says and kisses my head as he looks at the photos over my shoulder. He leans in and whispers in my ear, "And I can't wait to see you round with my baby again."

"Jesus, how many kids do you plan on me pop-ping out?"

"A few more." He winks.

"Let's enjoy the two I just popped out this morn-ing for a while before we talk about more."

Josh hops on the bed next to mine that's currently empty. "What do you say, baby, wanna take advan-tage of this semiprivate room? I'll pull the curtain and everything."

He wiggles his eyebrows at Cara and we all laugh, but Cara suddenly hands Layla off to Zack and makes a run for the en suite bathroom. We can hear her hurling her guts out and Lo and I share a look of surprise.

"Good God, man. Is this your version of foreplay?" Ty asks with disgust. "You're lucky she didn't leave you at the altar."

Josh shields his hand from Seth's line of vision and flips Ty off, but Seth laughs and says, "It's okay, Uncle Josh. I flip people the bird all the time."

"Seth King," I say sternly. "You do not."

"I'm thirteen," he says with a shrug, as if that ex-plains everything.

"I don't care if you're *thirty*, you will not flip people the bird."

"Right." He rolls his eyes, but catches the look on my face and sobers immediately. "I mean, yes ma'am."

I can't help but smile over at him. He's such a smart aleck, and he looks so sweet with Sarah nes-tled in his arms.

Cara comes stumbling out of the bathroom and looks . . . *green*.

"You okay?" I ask. "*Mom?*"

She bites her lip and glances at her husband, who is grinning smugly. "We didn't want to hijack your special day, but yeah. I'm fine. And very pregnant."

"More grandbabies, Jeff!" Nancy cries and laughs as he kisses her cheek. "Our babies are giving us more babies."

"I love you, sugar," Zack whispers in my ear as I gaze lovingly around the room at our big, beautiful family, that continues to grow at an alarming rate.

"I love you too," I reply before kissing him softly. I search the room for my babies and hold my hands out. "Someone hand me one of my babies, please."

"You're so greedy," Cara says with a frown and passes Miles over. My son nestles in close and sighs deeply, unaware of all of the love surrounding him.

"Yeah, I am," I agree and smile at her. "But I have everything I ever wanted right here in this room."

Keep reading to see how
it all began for Cara and Josh in
*New York Times* bestselling author
Kristen Proby's first book in her
Love Under the Big Sky series,

# Loving Cara

On sale now!

# CHAPTER

*One*

— EARLY SUMMER —

## CARA

"Cara, do you have a minute?" My boss, Kyle Reardon, pokes his head in my open classroom door and offers me a warm smile.

"Sure, what's up?"

He saunters in and takes a long look around my empty classroom. The breeze from the open windows ruffles his hair, and he runs his hand through it as he leans against my desk. "Looks like you're ready to get out of here for a few months." He gazes down at me warmly. "Remember last week when you mentioned that you'd be up for a tutoring job this summer?" I roll back in my chair and look up at him. He's handsome, with short copper hair and blue eyes, a nice build.

He's also married with four children.

"I do," I confirm.

"Well, I have one for you."

"Who?"

"You know the King family, right? They run that big ranch just outside of town."

"Of course, I grew up here, Kyle," I reply dryly. In a town the size of Cunningham Falls, Montana, we pretty much all know each other, especially those of us who grew up here, just as our parents did, and their parents before them.

"Zack's boy, Seth, needs a tutor this summer."

"Zack's back in town?" I ask, my eyebrows raised in surprise.

"I don't think so." Kyle shakes his head and shrugs. "I can't tell you their business, small town or not. Seth is staying with Jeff and Nancy, and Josh is helping too."

"Oh," I mutter, surprised. "So for whom would I be working, exactly?"

"So proper," Kyle teases me, and grins. "You'll be working for Josh. You can go straight to his place on Monday morning. They'd like you to come Monday through Friday, about nine until noon."

"Geez, he must need a lot of tutoring."

The laughter leaves Kyle's eyes and he sighs. "He's a really smart kid, but he's stubborn and has a bit of an attitude. I'm warning you, he's not an easy kid to work with. He's only been here for three months. He refuses to do the work or hand it in."

"Does he start trouble?" I steeple my fingers in front of me, thinking.

"No, he just keeps to himself. Doesn't say much to anyone."

I'll have to work with Josh King, which won't be difficult. He was always nice to me in high school, smiles at me in passing when I see him around town. He and his brother are nice guys.

Rumor has it he's a womanizer, but nice nonetheless.

And I'd be lying if I said I hadn't had a crush on him for as long as I can remember.

But I can be professional and teach Josh's nephew. I didn't really want to paint my entire house this summer, anyway.

"Okay, I'll give it a go."

"Great, thanks, Cara." Kyle stands and turns to leave my classroom. "Have a good summer!"

"You too!" I call after him as he goes whistling down the dark, deserted hallway.

Cool, I have a summer job.

I love my town. Like, wholeheartedly, never want to move away, love it. I don't understand how Jillian, my best friend since kindergarten, can stand living so far away in California. Our town is small, only about six thousand full-time residents, but the population doubles in the peak of summer and the heart of winter with tourists here for skiing, hiking, swimming, and all the other fun outdoor activities that the brochures brag about.

We sit in a valley surrounded by tall mountains, and when it's sunny, the sky is so big and blue it almost hurts the eyes.

I pull into the long gravel driveway off the highway just outside town and follow it past the large, white main house to the back of the property where Josh's house sits. It's not as big as the main house, but it's still large, bigger than my house in town, and is surrounded by tall evergreen trees and long lines of white wooden fences.

I do not envy the poor sap who has to paint the fences every few years.

The butterflies I've kept at bay come back with a vengeance, fluttering in my belly as I come to a stop in front of his house. Josh and his brother are twins, and until Zack broke his nose in football their senior year, it was almost impossible to tell them apart. They're both big guys, tall and broad shouldered. Zack always had a more intense look in his face, while Josh is more laid-back, quick to smile or tease—especially me, it seemed. In high school I was invisible to most people, having been a little too round, a lot too plain, but Josh noticed me.

He used to pull on my horrible curls as he'd walk past me at school, and of course because he was two years ahead of me, and a football star, I was crazy about him. My hair naturally falls in tight ringlets, but I've since straightened it, thank God.

I haven't seen much of Josh over the years. Each of us went away to college, and since we've both returned, I may catch a glimpse of him at the grocery store or in a restaurant, but never long enough to talk to him. I wonder if the rumors of his womanizing are true.

They were in high school.

I just hope he hasn't turned into one of those cowboys who wear tight Wrangler jeans and straw cowboy hats.

My lips twitch at the thought as I pull myself out of my compact Toyota. The front door swings open, and there he is, all six foot three of him. Only with great effort does my jaw not drop.

Jesus, we breed hot men in Montana.

Josh's hair is dark, dark brown and he has chocolate-colored eyes to match. His olive skin has acquired a deep tan, and when he smiles, he has a dimple in his left cheek that can melt panties at twenty paces.

Dark stubble is on his chin this morning, and he flashes

that cocky smile as he steps onto the porch. His jeans—Levi's, not Wranglers—ride low on his hips, and a plain white T-shirt hugs his muscular chest and arms. I can't help but wonder what he smells like.

*Down, girl.*

Following directly behind Josh is a tall, blond woman I don't recognize, laughing at something he must have said just before he sauntered through the door. They stop on the covered front porch long enough for him to smile sweetly down at her. He pulls his large hand down her arm and murmurs, "Have a good day, and good luck."

"Thanks, Josh," she responds, and bounces down the steps of the front porch, nods at me, and hops into her Jeep.

"Carolina Donovan," Josh murmurs, and stuffs his hands in his pockets.

"You know I hate it when you call me Carolina." I roll my eyes. "My parents should have been brought up on child-abuse charges for that name."

Josh laughs and shakes his head. "It's a beautiful name." He frowns and rocks back on his heels. "You look great, Cara."

"Uh, you've seen me around town over the years, Josh," I remind him with a half smile. "I hope I didn't interrupt anything?" I grimace inside, regretting the question immediately. *Mom always said, never ask a question you don't want the answer to.*

He shrugs one shoulder and offers me that cocky grin. God, he's such a charmer. "Nah, we were finished."

I frown at him. *What does that mean?*

"So, where is Seth?" I ask, changing the subject.

Josh frowns in turn and looks toward the big house. "He should be on his way in a few minutes. I have to warn you, Cara, working with Seth may not be a day at the beach. He's a good kid, but he's having a rough time of it." Josh rubs his hand over his face and sighs.

"Why is he here and not with his mom?"

"Because the bitch dropped him off here so she can be footloose and fancy-free. She's filed for divorce. Good riddance. I wish she'd brought him to us years ago."

"Oh." I don't know what else to say. I never liked Kensie King. She was a bitch in high school, but she was pretty and popular, and I'm quite sure Zack never planned on knocking her up.

But none of that is Seth's fault.

"What areas does he need help in?" I ask, and pull my tote bag out of the passenger seat. When I turn around, Josh's eyes are on my ass and he's chewing on his lower lip. I frown and stand up straight, self-conscious of my round behind.

"Josh?"

"I'm sorry, what?" He shakes his head and narrows his eyes on my face.

"What areas does Seth need the most help in?"

"All of them. He failed every class this spring."

"*Every* class?" I ask incredulously.

"Yeah. He's a smart kid, I don't know what his problem is."

"I don't need a tutor!" a young male voice calls out. I turn to see Seth riding a BMX bike from the big house down the driveway.

"Seth, don't start." Josh's eyes narrow and he folds his arms over his chest. "Ms. Donovan is here to help. You will be nice."

Seth rolls his eyes and hops off the bike, laying it on its side, and mirrors his uncle's stance, arms crossed over his chest.

God, he looks just like his dad and his uncle. He could

be their younger brother. He's going to inherit their height and has the same dark hair, but his eyes are hazel.

He's going to be a knockout someday.

And right now he's scowling at me.

"Hi, Seth. I'm Cara."

"What is it, Cara or Ms. Donovan?" he asks defiantly.

"Seth!" Josh begins, but I interrupt him. Seth isn't the first difficult child I've come across.

"Since it's summer, and I'm in your home, it's Cara. But if you see me at school, it's Ms. Donovan. Sound fair?"

Seth shrugs his slim shoulders and twists his lips as if he wants to say something smart but doesn't dare in his uncle's company.

Smart kid.

"Where do you want us?" I ask Josh, who is still glaring at Seth. They're clearly frustrated with each other.

"You can sit at the kitchen table. The house is empty during the day since I'm out working, so you shouldn't be interrupted." Josh motions for us to go in ahead of him, and as I walk past, he reaches out to pull my hair. "What happened to your curls?"

"I voted them off the island," I reply dryly, then almost trip as he laughs, sending shivers down my spine.

He leans in and whispers, "I liked them."

I shrug and follow Seth to the kitchen. "I didn't."

Josh's home is spacious; the floor plan is open from the living area right inside the front door through to the eat-in kitchen with its maple cabinets the color of honey and smooth, light granite countertops. The windows are wide and I can see all over the property from inside the main room.

I immediately feel at home here, despite the obvious bachelor-pad feel to it. Large, brown leather couches face a floor-to-ceiling river-rock fireplace with a flat-screen TV mounted above it. Fishing, hunting, and men's-health magazines are scattered on the coffee table, along with an empty coffee mug. Not a throw pillow or knickknack to be found anywhere.

Typical guy.

Seth pulls a chair away from the table and plops down in it, resting his head on his folded arms.

"Seth, sit up." Josh is exasperated and Seth just sinks deeper into his slouch.

"I think we're good to go." I grin at Josh but he scowls.

"Are you sure?"

"Yep, we're good. You get to work and leave us be so we can too."

I turn my back on him, dismissing him, and begin pulling worksheets, pens, and a book out of my bag.

"I'll be working nearby today, so just call my cell if you need me."

"Fine." I wave him off, not looking over at him. I sense him still standing behind me. Finally I turn and raise an eyebrow. "You're still here."

He's watching me carefully, leaning against the countertop, his rough hands tucked in his pockets. My eyes are drawn to his biceps, straining against the sleeves of his tee. "You got really pushy."

"I'm a teacher. It's either be pushy or die a long, slow death. Now go. We have work to do today."

"You'll have lunch with us before you go." Josh pushes himself away from the counter and saunters to the front door, grabs an old, faded-green baseball cap, and settles it backward on his head. "I'm pushy too."

He grins and that dimple winks at me before he leaves the house, shutting the door behind him.

Good God, I will not be able to focus if he doesn't leave us be while I'm here.

"You ready to get to work?" I ask Seth, thumbing through my writing worksheets until I find the one I want.

"This is a waste of time," he grumbles.

"Why do you say that?"

He shrugs again and buries his face in his arms.

"Well, I don't consider it a waste of time. What's your favorite subject?"

No answer.

"Least favorite?"

No answer.

"I personally like math, but I always sucked at it."

Seth shifts his head slightly and one eye peeks at me.

"Are you good at math?" I ask him.

"It's easy."

"Not for me." I sigh.

"But you're a teacher." Seth finally sits up and frowns at me.

"That doesn't mean I'm good at everything. Teachers aren't superhuman or anything."

"I can do math."

"Okay, let's start there."

Seth eyes me for a minute and then shrugs. It seems shrugging is his favorite form of communication.

"Are you really going to stay and have lunch?"

"Does that make you uncomfortable?" I pass him the math worksheet.

"No, I don't care." He picks up a pencil and starts marking the sheet, digging right in, and I grin.

"Does the food suck?"

"No, Gram packs us a lunch every day."

"Well then, I'll stay."

His lips twitch, but he doesn't smile—yet somehow I think I just won a big battle.

"So, looks like fried chicken and potato salad, home-made rolls, and fruit." Josh pulls the last of the food out of the ice chest and passes Seth a Coke.

"Your mom goes all out."

"She's been making lunch for ranch hands for almost forty years. It's habit."

We're sitting on Josh's back patio. It's partially covered, with a hanging swing on one side and a picnic table on the other and looks out over a large meadow where cattle are grazing.

"Do you get a lot of deer back here?" I ask.

He nods and swallows. "Usually in the evening and very early mornings. A moose walked through last week."

"That was cool," Seth murmurs, and Josh looks up in surprise.

*Does Seth never talk to him?*

"Yeah, it was," Josh agrees softly.

"Do you fish?" Seth asks me as he takes a big bite out of a chicken breast, sending golden pieces of fried batter down the front of his shirt. His dark hair is a bit too long and falls over one eye. I grin at him. He's adorable.

"No. I hate fishing."

"How can you hate to fish?!" Seth exclaims, as if I'd just admitted to hating ice cream.

"It's dirty." I wrinkle my nose and Josh bursts out laughing.

"Everything here is dirty, sweetheart." Josh shakes his head and nudges me lightly with his elbow.

*He's such a flirt!*

"But you live in Montana!" Seth exclaims, examining me as if I were a science project, his chicken momentarily forgotten.

"I live in town, Seth. Always have. My dad loves to fish. I just never really got into it." I shrug and take a bite of delicious homemade potato salad.

"But you like horses, right?" He shovels a heaping forkful of potato salad into his mouth.

"I've never ridden one." I chuckle and shake my head as I watch him eat. "Are they starving you here, Seth? The way you're eating, you'd think you haven't seen food in days."

Seth just blinks at me. He slowly smiles, but I cut him off before he can voice the idea I can see forming in that sharp brain of his.

"I'm not getting on a horse."

"Why not?" Josh asks with a broad smile.

"Well . . ." I look back and forth between the two guys and then sigh when I can't come up with a good reason not to. "I'm not dressed for riding."

Josh's gaze falls to my red sundress before his brown eyes find mine again. "Wear jeans tomorrow."

"I'm not here to learn how to ride a horse, I'm here to teach Seth."

"No reason that you can't do both," Josh replies with a grin, and winks at me, his dimple creasing his cheek, waking those butterflies in my stomach.

"Am I keeping you from work?" I change the subject and pop a piece of watermelon in my mouth, doing my best not to squirm in my chair.

"I have to go paint the fence," Seth mutters, and swigs down the last of his Coke, making me laugh.

"What?" he asks.

"When I drove up to the house and saw the white

fence, I thought to myself, 'I don't envy the person who has to paint this every couple of years.'"

"It was either paint the fence or shovel the horse shit," Seth replies matter-of-factly.

"Mouth!" Josh scowls, pinning Seth with a look, and Seth rolls his eyes.

"Horse crap."

"I think I'd take the fence too," I agree, but Seth just shrugs his thin shoulders and frowns. "You look so much like your dad." I shake my head and reach for another piece of watermelon before I realize that both Seth and Josh have gone still.

"I do not," Seth whispers.

"Well, you look just like your uncle Josh, and Josh and Zack are twins, so . . ." I tilt my head to one side and watch Seth's face tighten.

"I'm nothing like my dad," he insists.

"Okay, I'm sorry."

Seth pins me with a scowl, then grabs his trash and lets himself into the house to dump it, stalks through the house, and slams the front door behind him.

"I'm sorry," I whisper again.

"It's okay. He's pissed at my brother. Won't talk about it, just won't have anything at all to do with him." Josh purses his lips and sighs, still watching the path Seth took through the house. My eyes are glued to his lips and I'm mortified to realize that I want him to kiss me.

And not just a sweet thank-you-for-teaching-my-nephew kiss, but a long, slow kiss that lasts forever and makes me forget how to breathe. I want to sink my fingers into his thick, dark hair and feel his large, callused hands glide down my back as he pulls me against him.

I want him to touch me.

Josh begins to pack up the remains of our lunch and I take a deep breath and join him.

"When he smiled at you earlier? That's the first time I've seen him smile since he's been here."

"Josh, I'm so sorry. He's a great kid, and he's really smart. I think we'll have him back on track with his grades without a problem."

"Thank you." Josh replaces the lid on the fruit and throws it in the cooler. "You know, Kyle didn't tell me who he was sending out here. I was surprised when I saw it was you."

"Why?"

"I don't know, but I'm glad you're here. I wasn't kidding before—you look fantastic."

I blush and concentrate on rewrapping the chicken and placing it in the cooler.

"I'm not a hermit, Josh. Like I said before, you've seen me around."

"In passing. Not like this. I like it."

I stand up and cross my arms over my chest, then frown when he stands too and is more than a foot taller than me.

I've always been so damn short.

"Are you flirting with me?" I ask.

"Maybe." He pushes the lid down on the ice chest, then moves around the table to stand right next to me, and I have to tilt my head way back to see his eyes. "You always were a little thing."

"Little?! Oh my God." I giggle and throw a hand over my mouth. "I'm just short. Hell, in high school I was f—"

"If you say *fat*, I will take you over my knee, Carolina. You were not fat then, you're not fat now, and next to me, you *are* tiny." He sets his mouth in a disapproving line and pulls on a lock of my hair. "Your pretty blond hair is soft."

"Don't f-flirt with me," I stutter halfheartedly. Instead of moving away, I sway toward him, my heart racing.

"Why not?" He grins and continues to gently pull my hair between his thumb and forefinger, watching the strands as they fall out of his grasp.

"Because I'm your employee for the summer, and I like my job. It's not like there are dozens of middle schools here in town that I can work at if I get fired." I step away, pulling myself together, doing my best to remind myself of the blonde I saw leaving his house this morning and how I do *not* want to be another notch in Josh King's bedpost. I open his sliding screen door and gather my tote bag and purse and turn to find him standing right behind me again. "I have to go."

He sighs, props his hands on his hips, and looks as if he wants to say more, so I turn on my heel and walk briskly to the door.

"I'll walk you out," he mutters, and walks quickly to keep up with me. He holds his front door open for me, and I feel his hand on my lower back as he guides me to my little blue car.

He opens the door for me and settles my bags into the passenger seat.

"You're very chivalrous," I inform him dryly.

As I move to sit in the driver's seat, he runs his hand down my bare arm, very much as he did with Blondie this morning, and smiles.

"Thanks for doing this, Cara. Don't forget to wear jeans tomorrow." With that he winks and shuts my door, stepping back to watch me drive away.

*Looks like I'll be wearing shorts tomorrow.*

It's Lauren's turn for
Love Under the Big Sky!

Keep reading for a peek at
*New York Times* bestselling author
Kristen Proby's second installment in
the Love Under the Big Sky series,

# Seducing Lauren

On sale now!

# CHAPTER

## LAUREN

"Hey, Lauren."

"Hi, Jacob, what can I do for you?" I ask with a smile, and open my front door wider for the friendly county sheriff's deputy.

"Well, I'm serving you." He offers me an embarrassed smile and hands me a large envelope, then backs away. "Have a good day."

I move back inside, shut the door, and stare down at the envelope in surprise.

*Served?*

I rip open the envelope and see bright, flaming inferno red as I read the court document. And read it again.

"The fucker is *suing me*?" I exclaim to an empty room, and read the letter clutched in my now trembling hands for the third time. "Hell no!"

I grab my handbag and slide my feet into flip-flops, barely managing not to fall down the porch steps as I tear out of my house to my Mercedes and pull out of the circular driveway.

I live at the edge of Cunningham Falls, Montana. The small town was named after my great-grandfather Albert Cunningham. Ours is a tourist town that boasts a five-star ski resort and a plethora of outdoor activities for any season. Thankfully, summer tourist season is over, and ski season is still a few months away, so traffic into town is light.

I zoom past the post office and into the heart of downtown, where my lawyer's office is. Without paying any attention to the yellow curb, I park quickly and march into the old building.

The receptionist's head jerks up in surprise as I approach her and slam the letter still clutched in my hand on her desk.

"*This,*" I say between clenched teeth, "isn't going to happen."

"Ms. Cunningham, do you have an appointment?"

"No, I don't have an appointment, but someone had better have time to see me." I am seething; my breath is coming in harsh pants.

"Lauren." My head whips up at the sound of my name and I find Ty Sullivan frowning at me from his office doorway. "I can see you. Come in."

I turn my narrowed eyes on Ty and follow him into his office, too agitated to sit while I wait for him to shut the door and walk behind his desk.

"What's going on?"

"I need a new lawyer."

"What's going on?" he asks again, and calmly leans against the windowsill behind his desk. He crosses his arms over his chest. The sleeves of his white button-down are rolled, giving me a great view of the colorful tattoo on his right arm.

"*This* is what's going on!" I thrust the letter at him. "Jack is trying to sue me for half of a trust fund that he has no right to."

Ty's handsome face frowns as he skims the letter. "You came into the trust while you were still married?"

"Yes," I confirm warily.

"And you didn't tell him about it?" he asks with raised brows.

"I didn't even know the damn thing existed until after my parents died, Ty. Until *after* I kicked Jack out." I turn and pace away, breathing deeply, trying to calm down. "He doesn't deserve a dime of my inheritance. This isn't about money, it's about principle."

"I agree." Ty shrugs. "Have you talked with Cary?"

"I was just served with the letter," I mumble, and sink into a leather chair in defeat. "Cary's a nice guy, but I just don't think he's the right lawyer for this job." I glance up at Ty and my heart skips a beat as I take him in now that I'm calming down. He's tall, much taller than me—which is saying something, given that I stand higher than five foot eight. He has broad shoulders and lean hips, and holy hell, the things this man does to a suit should be illegal in all fifty states.

But more than that, he's kind and funny and has a bit of a bad-boy side to him too, hence the tattoos.

He's been front and center in many of my fantasies for most of my life.

I bite my lips and glance down as his eyes narrow on my face.

"Why do you say that?" he asks calmly.

"It took two freaking years for the divorce to be final, Ty. I don't want Cary to drag this out too."

"It wasn't necessarily Cary's fault that the divorce took so long, Lauren. Jack had a good lawyer and your divorce was a mess."

*That's the fucking understatement of the year.* "Will you take my case?"

"No," he replies quickly.

"What?" My dazed eyes return to his. "Why?"

He shakes his head and sighs as he takes a seat behind his desk. "I have a full load as it is, Lo."

"You're more aggressive than Cary," I begin, but halt when he scowls.

"I really don't think I can help you."

I sit back and stare at him, stunned. "You mean you won't." I hate the hurt I hear in my voice, but I can't hide it. I know Ty and I aren't super close, but I've considered him a friend. I can't believe he's shooting me down.

He folds the letter and hands it back to me, his mouth set in a firm line and blue-gray eyes sober. "No, I won't. Make an appointment with Cary and talk it over with him."

My hand automatically reaches out and takes the letter from Ty, and I'm just deeply embarrassed.

"Of course," I whisper, and rise quickly, ready to escape this office. "I'm sorry for intruding."

"Lo . . ."

"No, you're right. It was unprofessional for me to just show up like this. I apologize." I clear my throat and offer him a bright, fake smile, then beeline it for the door. "Thanks anyway."

"Did you want to make an appointment, Lauren?" Sylvia, the receptionist, asks as I hurry past her desk.

"No, I'll call. Thanks."

I can't get to my car fast enough. Why did I think Ty would help me? *No one will help me.*

All the connections I have in this town, all the money I have, and that asshole is still making my life a living hell.

I drive home in a daze, and when I pull up behind a shiny black Jaguar, my heart sinks further.

*Today fucking sucks.*

I pull my cell phone out of my bag, prepared to call for help if need be, and climb out of my car. I walk briskly past him and up the steps to the front door.

"Hey, gorgeous."

"I told you not to come here, Jack. I don't want to see you." *How can he still make me so damn nervous?*

"Aww, don't be like that, baby. You're making this so much harder than it needs to be."

I round on him, shocked and pissed all over again. "I'm the one making this hard?" I shake my head and laugh at the lunacy of this situation. "I don't want you here. The divorce has been final for weeks now, and you have no business being here. And now you're going to fucking *sue me*?"

He loses his smug smile and his mouth tightens as his brown eyes narrow. "No, I'll tell you what will make it easy, Lauren. You paying me what's rightfully mine is what will make it easy. You hid that money from me, and I'm entitled to half."

"I'll never pay you off, you son of a bitch." I'm panting and glaring, so fucking angry.

"Oh, honey, I think you will." He moves in close and drags his knuckles down my cheek. I jerk my head away, but he grabs my chin in his hand, squeezing until there's just a bit of pain. "Or maybe I'll just come back here and claim what's mine. You are still mine, you know."

My stomach rolls as he runs his nose up my neck, sniffing deeply. Every part of me stills. *What the fuck is this?*

"A man has the right to fuck his wife whenever he pleases."

"I'm not your wife," I grind out, glaring at him as he pulls back and stares me in the face.

He flashes an evil grin and presses harder against me. "You'll always be mine. No piece of paper can change that."

I don't answer, but instead just continue to glare at him in hatred.

"Maybe you should just go ahead and write that check."

He pushes away from me and backs down the stairs toward his flashy car, a car he bought with my parents' money, and snickers as he looks me up and down. "You've kept that hot body of yours in shape, Lo. It's mighty tempting."

*I swear I'm going to throw up.*

I can't answer him. I can only stand here and glower, shaking in rage and fear, as he winks again and hops in his Jag and drives away.

Jesus Christ, he just threatened to rape me. I might not be able to prove it, but I knew what his words meant.

I let myself into the house and reset the alarm with shaking fingers. I take off in a sprint to the back of the house and heave into the toilet, over and over until there's nothing left and my body shivers and convulses in revulsion.

How can someone who once claimed to love me be so damn evil?

When the vomiting has passed, I rinse my mouth and head to the indoor pool that my parents had built when I was on the swim team in high school. I strip out of my clothes, but before I pull my swim cap on, I dial a familiar number on my phone and wait for an answer.

"Hull." Brad is a police detective in town, and someone I trust implicitly.

"It's Lauren."

"Hey, sugar, what's up?"

"Jack just left."

"What did that son of a bitch want?" Brad's voice is steel.

"He threatened me." My voice is shaky and I hate myself for sounding so vulnerable. "I want it documented that he was here."

"Did you record it, Lo?"

"No. I wasn't expecting it. He's been an asshole in the past, but this is the first time he's come out and threatened me since he . . ." I pace beside the pool, unable to finish the sentence.

"That's because I put the fear of God and jail time in him." Brad is quiet for a moment. "Is there anything you need?"

I laugh humorlessly and shake my head. "Yeah, I need my asshole ex to go away. But for now I'll settle for a swim."

"Keep your alarm on. Call me if you need me."

"I will. Thanks, Brad."

"Anytime, sugar."

We ring off. I tuck my long, auburn hair into my swim cap and then dive into the Olympic-size lap pool. The warm water glides over my naked skin, and I begin the first of countless laps, back and forth, across the pool. Swimming is one of two things in this world I do well, and it clears my head.

I do some of my best thinking in the pool.

*Is all of this worth it?* I ask myself. When I married

Jack almost five years ago, I was convinced that he was in love with me and that we'd be together forever. He'd been on my swim team in college. He was handsome and charming.

And unbeknownst to me, he'd been after my money all along.

My parents were still alive then, and even they had fallen for his charms. My father had been a brilliant businessman and had done all he could to convince me to have Jack sign a prenuptial agreement so in the event of a divorce, Jack couldn't stake any claim to my sizable trust fund.

But I stood my ground, blind with love and promises of forever, insistent that a prenup was unnecessary.

My dad would lose his mind if he knew what was happening now. If only I'd listened to him!

I tuck and roll, then push off the wall, turning into a backstroke.

The small amount of money that Jack is trying to lay claim to is nothing compared to the money I have that Jack knows nothing about. Since our legal separation, I've become very successful in my career, but I wasn't lying when I told Ty that it's not about the money.

This is my heritage. My family worked hard for this land, for the wealth they amassed, and Jack doesn't deserve another fucking dime of it. That's why the divorce took so long. I fought him with everything in me to assure that he didn't get his greedy hands on my family's money.

In the end he won a sizable settlement that all of the lawyers talked me into.

Jack wasn't happy. He wanted more.

I push off the edge of the pool and glide underwater until I reach the surface and then move into a front crawl.

After my parents died in a winter car accident just over two years ago, Jack made it clear that he didn't love me, had been sleeping around since we were dating, but expected me to keep him in his comfortable lifestyle.

When I threw a fit and kicked him out, he slammed me against the wall and landed a punch to my stomach, certain to avoid bruising me, before he left.

Thanks to threats from Brad, and Jack's knowing how well-known I am in this town, he's not bothered me since. Until now.

And now he's threatening me.

It's not worth it. Living in constant fear of seeing Jack around town, of finding myself in the middle of another humiliating scene. Seeing the pity in the eyes of people I've known my whole life.

And now, coming home to an ambush because he's feeling desperate?

I'm done.

I pull myself out of the water, exhausted and panting, and resigned to see Cary in the morning to agree to a settlement.

It's time to move on.

It's early when I leave the house and drive to the lawyer's office. I don't have an appointment, and I don't even know for sure if anyone is there yet, but I couldn't sleep last night. I couldn't lose myself in work.

I need to get this over with.

When I stride to the front door, I'm surprised to find

it unlocked. Sylvia isn't in yet, but I hear voices back in Cary's office.

I step through his door like I belong there, and both Cary's and Ty's faces register surprise when they see me in the doorway.

"You know, Lo, we have these things called phones, where you call and make what's called an appointment." Ty's gray eyes are narrowed, but his lips are quirked in a smile. He's in a power suit today, making my mouth immediately water. His shoulders look even broader in the black jacket, and the blue tie makes his eyes shine.

"Ha ha." I sit heavily in the seat before Cary's desk. "I'm sick of this shit."

"Ty told me you came by yesterday." Cary leans back in his chair.

"I was fucking served papers," I mutter, and push my hands though my hair. "But I think I want to settle."

Ty's eyebrows climb into his hairline. "I'll leave you two alone."

"You can stay," I mutter. "I could use both of your opinions. I'll pay double for the hour."

"That's not necessary." Ty's voice is clipped and he frowns as he gazes at me. "Why the change of heart?"

I lean back in the chair and tilt my head back, looking at the tin tiles on the ceiling. "Because Jack's an asshole. Because now he's decided to threaten me." I shake my head and look Cary in the eye. "But no payments. It's going to be in one lump sum and he needs to sign a contract stating that he'll never ask for another dime."

"Wait, back up." Ty pushes away from the desk and glowers down at me. "What do you mean he threatened you?"

"It doesn't matter."

"Lauren," Cary interrupts, "it does matter. What the hell happened?"

"When I returned home, Jack was at the house."

"Does he still have a key?" Ty asks.

"No." I shake my head adamantly. "I changed all the locks and installed a new alarm system the day he left."

"So he was waiting outside," Cary clarifies.

"Yes. I told him to leave, that I didn't want to see him and he isn't welcome at the house. He said I was making things harder than they need to be." I laugh humorlessly as Cary's eyebrows climb toward his blond hairline. "I reminded him that there's nothing difficult about this at all. We're divorced. It's over, and he can just go away." I shrug and look away, not wanting to continue.

"What did he threaten you with?" Ty asks softly.

I raise my eyes to his and suddenly my stomach rolls. "I'm going to be sick."

I bolt from the room and run to the restroom in the hallway, barely making it in time to lose the half gallon of coffee I consumed this morning. When the dry-heaving stops, I rinse my mouth and open the door, finding Ty on the other side.

"Are you okay?" he asks quietly.

I nod, embarrassed.

He reaches up and gently tucks a stray piece of my hair behind my ear. "What did he threaten you with?" He leads me back to Cary's office.

I swallow and cross my arms over my chest. I don't want to say it aloud. "He just threatened to be a dick."

"Bullshit," Cary responds, leaning forward in his chair. "Lo, the man wasn't afraid to put his hands on you when you told him to leave—"

"What?" Ty exclaims.

"—so you need to tell me what he threatened to do to you if you don't give him what he wants."

I shake my head and close my eyes, remembering the feel of Jack's nose pressed to my neck and the crazy look in his eyes when he wasn't getting what he wanted.

"Excuse us for a minute, Cary." Ty takes my hand in his and leads me toward the door.

"Uh, my client, Ty, remember?"

"We'll be right back," Ty assures him, and leads me into his office and shuts the door behind us.

"What did the asshole threaten to do to you, Lauren?"

"You said no yesterday, Ty. This isn't your case."

He shrugs, as if what I just said is of no consequence. "Answer me."

I simply shake my head. "It doesn't matter. Cary and I will figure it out. You don't have to stay in there with us."

I try to walk past him but he catches my hand in his, keeping me in place.

"Lauren . . ."

"Stop, Ty. You don't want me, I get it."

"Are you fucking kidding me?" His voice is deceptively calm. "Do you know why I turned you down yesterday, Lauren?"

I shake my head, my eyes wide and pinned to his.

"Because it would be a conflict of interest. I can't be your lawyer because I'm your friend, and I want to be a whole lot more than that."

If I thought I was stunned before, it's nothing compared to this. My jaw drops as he closes the gap between us. He doesn't touch me, but his face is mere inches from mine. His eyes are on my lips as I bite them and watch him, completely thrown by this turn of events.

"You have the most beautiful lips, Lo."

"What?" I whisper.

He takes a deep breath as he lays his thumb gently on my lower lip and pulls it from my teeth. I can't tear my gaze away from his mouth and I take a deep breath, inhaling the musky scent of him.

I've forgotten Jack and his threats, the lawsuit.

Everything.

Ty clears his throat and backs away, watching me carefully. "Cary will remain your lawyer, but I want to know what the hell is going on, Lo. I can help."

I blink and continue to stare at him, completely dumbstruck. *He wants me?*

"And another thing, Lauren. You're not settling. Fuck Jack and his lawyer."

Get email updates on

# KRISTEN PROBY,

exclusive offers,

and other great book recommendations

from Simon & Schuster.

---

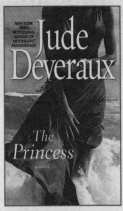
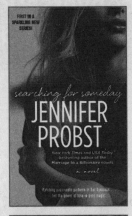

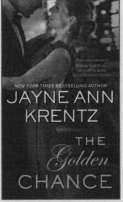